# CHRISTMAS ONCE AGAIN

JINA BACARR

Boldwood

First published in Great Britain in 2019 by Boldwood Books Ltd.

Copyright © Jina Bacarr, 2019

Cover Design by Becky Glibbery

The moral right of Jina Bacarr to be identified as the author of this work has been asserted in accordance with the Copyright, Designs and Patents Act 1988.

All rights reserved. No part of this book may be reproduced in any form or by any electronic or mechanical means, including information storage and retrieval systems, without written permission from the author, except for the use of brief quotations in a book review.

This book is a work of fiction and, except in the case of historical fact, any resemblance to actual persons, living or dead, is purely coincidental.

Every effort has been made to obtain the necessary permissions with reference to copyright material, both illustrative and quoted. We apologise for any omissions in this respect and will be pleased to make the appropriate acknowledgements in any future edition.

A CIP catalogue record for this book is available from the British Library.

Paperback ISBN 978-1-83889-366-8

Ebook ISBN 978-1-83889-364-4

Kindle ISBN 978-1-83889-365-1

Audio CD ISBN 978-1-83889-367-5

MP3 CD ISBN 978-1-83889-412-2

Digital audio download ISBN 978-1-83889-369-9

Boldwood Books Ltd
23 Bowerdean Street
London SW6 3TN
www.boldwoodbooks.com

*For Mom*

Who says you can't go home again?

# 1

DECEMBER 12, 1943

'I bet you my last pair of stockings, little sister, I'll be saying *I do* before Christmas.'

I whirl around in a circle, pretending the most wonderful man in the world is holding me in his arms, my heart soaring. A pot of Ma's meat gravy simmers on the burner, the smell tickling my fancy to have my own kitchen soon. So many wonderful memories here. Planked floors, big white stove humming with good cooking, Ma's rocker and her rosewood sewing box. Wallpaper dotted with daisies, their yellow petals turned golden over the years – and four ceramic angels lined up on top of the spice rack. A tradition we do every year along with listening to the holiday radio shows, but this Christmas is even more special to me. It's crazy I feel so confident, even though he hasn't actually asked me yet. But I know he will.

Eyes popping, Lucy swallows the spoonful of jam she shoved into her mouth. '*You*, Kate? Married?' Slender and graceful like a young doe, she's not as tall as me, though at sixteen she's already filling out her sweaters. Dark brown hair rich with honeyed highlights frames her oval face and an army of freckles deepen in color on her cheeks as she laughs. 'I hear Santa's taken.'

I ignore her sarcasm and scoop Ma's holiday cherry jam onto crackers. 'It's a secret, so don't tell anyone.' I wink at her, not letting up with my tease. I can't. I'm too excited. Lucy adores secrets. Her face beams with excitement, like she got away with something without Ma finding out. Like using a pillow case for a laundry bag since bedding is hard to come by, or borrowing my two dollar face powder when she thinks I'm not looking.

Despite my affection for her, I pray she keeps my news under her hat. She loves to talk as much as she loves flirting with the soldiers down at the canteen, but I have to tell somebody the news or I'll burst. What are sisters for if you can't tease them? Besides, when Jeff *does* ask me, I'll need her help fitting my bridal suit to get the hem straight. A gray suit with a frog clasp I made from extra silk Ma had left over from before the war. I'm lucky to have it. I want to look pretty for him. I never thought of myself as the pinup type, but Jeff makes me feel special and loved. He says I stand up taller when he catches my eye and that brings me closer to kissing him. Ma also noticed how much more confident I am. She was curious about why I saved up for two months to buy a blue silk hat with a wispy veil to go with my red coat with the fake fur collar when I have a perfectly good black hat.

I just smiled.

'What's there to tell?' Lucy points to my bare finger smeared with jam. 'You're not wearing a ring, so you can't be engaged.'

I smile. 'You don't know everything about me.'

'I know you're sweet on some guy.'

I raise a brow. 'Snooping again?'

'Me?' She bats her eyelashes. 'I don't have to. Not the way you go around singing to yourself when you come home from your job at the mill. How you stop and sigh when we walk past Wrightwood House on our way to town.'

A winsome smile makes my lips curl. I love working at the paper mill. I started out in the typing pool after I graduated from high school. I worked my way up to private secretary to Mr Clayborn in the billing and acquisitions department. He needed a girl who could think and not just type, he said. Nothing top secret about what I do, but I've been told not to ask questions. Anyway, I have other things on my mind. Even when I'm dead tired from typing a pile of my shorthand notes, I get warm all over when I think about the man I want to marry.

A light comes on in Lucy's swimming green eyes. 'So my big sister has stars in her eyes for Jeffrey Rushbrooke.'

'Don't get your garter belt in a twist.' I grab another cherry jam filled cracker. 'You don't know anything of the sort.'

Surprisingly, Lucy goes quiet, like she's mulling over her reply before saying something that might upset me. She gossips more than Mrs Widget the neighbor, but she's a good egg. Bouncy and full of cheer, especially this time of year. She loves Christmas as much as I do and helped me pile Ma's holiday cherry jam into glass jars.

For me, the Christmas season begins when Ma takes us kids cherry picking in the woods. Lucy, Frank Junior, and me. When the days are long, the nights are hot, and the cherries are big and sweet and perfect to pick for jam. Before the war, Ma made the sweetest jam in the county with cinnamon and lemon zest, but since rationing started, we've had food shortages. We cheered when the government doubled the sugar rations so we could make jam for the boys passing through our small town. The trains stop here every day and Lucy makes it a high priority to meet the train and flirt with the soldiers. She talks about nothing else.

'He'll never marry you, Kate,' she says, her sad puppy eyes showing real concern. I've never seen her look so serious. 'You know what Ma says about them rich people.'

'*Those* rich people.'

She wriggles her nose. 'It doesn't matter how good you talk, we're not his kind.'

I shrug. 'The bet's still on.'

'You're a fool, Kate Arden.' She sighs. 'Falling for a guy who doesn't know you're alive.'

Lucy never went up to Wrightwood House with Ma and me when we were kids, never knew Jeff and I were pals.

I grin. 'He knows.'

She stares at me straight on. 'Then why don't you bring him around the house to meet Ma and Pop?'

'You know I can't.' The hoarseness in my voice reveals how much that hurts me.

Because my romance is a secret. Is Lucy right? Am I a fool?

'I thought so,' she says smugly. 'No wonder you sneak out after supper when Ma isn't looking. Wearing that dark red lipstick smeared all over your mouth – I see it's gone when you creep back in, carrying your shoes behind your back.' She ties back her long hair with a baby blue ribbon. 'I'm not a child. I know what you're up to.'

'Then why are you acting like one?' I'm miffed. 'Can't a girl get some fresh air after dinner?'

'During a blackout drill?' Lucy rolls her eyes.

'You're spying on me.'

'I'm not spying. Mr Horner, my teacher, says we have to keep our eyes open. That you can't be too careful these days.'

I tingle. How can I explain I'll do anything to be with Jeff? I never tire of looking at him and feeling his lips brushing mine. The way he stands taller than any man at the mill, his dark hair falling across his brow because he hates slicking it back, his dark eyes always alert. He's as tough as you expect from a boy who grew up working on the factory floor. His father was grooming him to take over someday, but wielding a heavy hand.

But I know another side of him. The artist.

The young man who reads stories to me in French and kisses me every time I reach to muss up his hair. I don't care if he is the boss's son. We love each other, pledged we'd be together when we were kids, and that's enough for me. I fell for him the first time I saw him up at Wrightwood House. I was eleven. He was fourteen. I glanced up at him after gumming up the errand Ma sent me on and caught the glint in his dark eyes, a flash that seized my imagination, that told me that I wasn't a nobody, that I was somebody. I never forgot it.

'I've already said enough, Lucy,' I say with assurance. 'Case closed.'

'You're no fun, Kate.' Lucy puts her hands on her hips and stares at me. 'What are you hiding from me?'

'Nothing. Besides, you're too young to know anything more.'

'I'm sixteen.' She gives me a curvy smile. 'I know more than you think I do.'

I frown. That's what worries me. With the war on, girls like Lucy are growing up faster than they should. She's still in high school, for Pete's sake. As sisters go, we're close, though since I turned nineteen, I feel more like a woman than a screaming bobby-soxer. A teen swooning over her favorite movie star. Lucy knows what she wants. A soldier and a family. If anyone is born to be a homemaker, it's my kid sister.

I want a home, too, but I don't want to wait till the war is over. My need to marry this man burns within me.

I can't stand it anymore and I squeeze my legs together to quell the ache low in my belly. I turn away so she doesn't see my cheeks tint. I'm always in awe of his broad shoulders filling the doorway of his office. Standing there and watching me when I walk by. Smiling. He smiles at all the ladies on the factory floor, but the smile he gives me is different. Flirty with a smirk, like we share a secret. We do, and that knowing look we give each other reflects our love. Two hearts entwined in a communion we both hold sacred. Everything around us stops except for the hum of the machinery on the factory floor. I can barely keep walking, knowing he's watching me. I ache for him touching me. I can't wait for the day when we're married. Him lying next to me on our wedding night, his rich, masculine smell filling me up when I close my eyes.

I wipe the sweat forming above my lip, not caring if I smear jam on my face. I *have* to be married before Christmas. No telling when he'll be called up. Surely Uncle Sam will put on his Santa cap and not ask the boys to leave home during the holidays. Why, I'd do anything to be with him, even elope so we can be together. Then when we're married, I won't have to sneak out anymore. He'll come home on a furlough and we'll have our own apartment near the paper mill. I already have the kitchen curtains made. Cheery and bright. Like I want my home to be. A place where I can make him forget how much he hates the life his father mapped out for him, and how the old man treats him.

'Mrs Jeffrey Rushbrooke...' I sigh. My man won't let me down. Not after what he said to me down by the big ole cherry tree last night below stars in the sky on a night so clear. Words that he said to me when we were kids and he told me someday he'd marry me. I believed him then and I believe him now.

Lucy doesn't know I've been meeting him nearly every day since last summer when he came home from college and saw me working down at the mill. Imagine my surprise when he asked me to have a chocolate malted milk at the dairy with him.

He drove me to the dairy farm over in the next town in his cute blue roadster and we sat in a back booth and talked for hours. How I grew up and how pretty I turned out. His words, not mine, and I keep them close to my heart.

'He may be the best-looking guy in Posey Creek, but he comes from money,' Lucy says, regarding me with concern. 'His mother is so uppity she'll never accept you in her inner circle.'

'Jeff respects his parents, but he's his own man,' I assure her. 'He could spend the war here in Posey Creek overseeing production at the mill, but he enlisted in the Army Air Force so he can fly bombers.'

'I'm not saying the handsome young Mr Rushbrooke isn't as wonderful as you say he is, Kate, but there are some things this war won't change. Like how his folks look down on us because we're not rich.'

'We *are* rich, Lucy.' I hug her tight and a familiar scent fills my nostrils. She smells like my favorite perfume, *Paris Rose*. I don't hold it against her. 'We have each other, and Ma and

Pop and Frank Junior, and that's more important than anything.'

Is that a sniffle I hear coming from my little sister? Not that she'll admit family is as important as breathing. At sixteen, I didn't either.

'Oh, Kate, I'll die if that awful woman does anything to make you unhappy. You're the best sister ever and I'd hate to see you get hurt.'

My heart pings. I'm touched by her words. 'I won't. You don't know Jeff like I do.'

'You know what Ma says. The cherry doesn't fall far from the tree.'

'You mean apple,' I say, smiling.

'Whatever, if Ma says it, it's true.' She recovers from her sentimental moment as quickly as it came and sticks her finger into the cherry jam and licks it clean. 'You're on, Kate, I'll take that bet.' Then she raises up her skirt and makes a face when her white socks slide down her calves. 'I can hardly wait to be the only girl at school with a new pair of nylons.'

'I'd sharpen your eyebrow pencil if I were you, sister dear,' I say, filled with the confidence only a girl in love can have. 'The only way you'll be wearing seams this holiday is to draw them.'

## 2

POSEY CREEK TRAIN STATION

Racing toward the station platform, my overnight case bumping against my hip, I refuse to give in to the dread seeping through me. I'm late. I've never been so scared. I don't see Jeff anywhere. The train station is packed with servicemen and civilians scrambling not to miss their train. There are fewer holiday travelers this year with gifts. Their faces reflect the uncertainty of what lies ahead.

The fear of the unknown.

A sagging garland of pine hangs over the ticket window, its lovely Christmassy smell depleted by the strong scent of an army on the move.

I keep going. Gray silk peeks from under my red coat with the six shiny gold buttons, my pumps with the worn heels tapping out a quick rhythm. Of course he won't leave without me. We're eloping. He can't leave without his bride.

I'd simply die. Breathing hard, I keep going in spite of my fears. My heart tugs when I glance at a railway worker handling the big sacks of Christmas rush mail. Letters filled with love and hope for a happy homecoming when the frost melts. I'll be sending Jeff letters like that after we're married.

I couldn't believe it when he asked me after the Saturday night Christmas dance. We braved the cold night, leaving the dreamy music behind to make music of our own. I rushed into his arms like water cascading into a dam, twirled around and told him a million times, yes, yes! I wondered how long our bliss would last before he was called up, how soon I'd be sewing insignia patches on his uniform when he came home on furlough, then how crushed my heart would be when he left for overseas. But not in that moment. Nothing could take away my joy when he pulled me close to him, crushing me against his broad chest.

'You've made me so happy, Jelly Girl.' His pet name for me since we were kids. Then he nuzzled his face in my hair like he was afraid I'd say no, which was when I realized that although Jeff is a hero in my eyes, that he's perfect and good and kind, he's still a man made from flesh and blood... and he was scared. Scared he wouldn't come back. To his home. To me.

I grew up then. I had to be strong for both of us.

I held onto his hand as we walked down the festive lane with red bows and fake candy canes tied onto the bushes and even if I couldn't see his face in the dark, I knew he felt reassured I'd love him forever.

'Nothing can separate us, Jeff, not even this war.' I squeezed his hand. 'I promise you that with my whole heart.'

'I believe you, Kate. Somehow I know nothing can take you from me.'

'You do?'

'I do.' He laughed, then laid out his plans for us to go to Washington DC on the 7.10 a.m. train and get hitched, then call my family with the news He grinned so widely, I felt thoroughly convinced we were set on a course not even fate could alter. I've never felt such confidence race through my veins, such exhilaration that no matter what I'd be there for him when he came home from the war.

We floated in that lovely dream for what seemed like forever, talking about our hopes for the future and then, with cover of a blackout to hide us, we spoke in hushed whispers of our secret desires to love each other as man and wife.

I'll never ~~get~~ forget the warmth of his body pressed against mine, his deep voice setting off a slow burn in me that made me snuggle up closer to him – and yes, I admit it, I didn't hold back the tears of joy that wet my cheeks. Tears fresh with the promise of a wonderful future together, where we could live out our years in perfect harmony.

Like Ma and Pop. I get all warm inside when I see them together, more so now that I understand what's behind that secret look they give each other. The love they share. It shines on their faces and I want that for Jeff and me more than anything, to keep the pledge we made to each other when we were kids. We both know that we have something special, like you see in the pictures. That spark in his eye, the way my stomach drops down to my knees, the feeling no one else is in the room but us. No one can break that deep bond. Not even a war can separate us. When he's overseas, our memories will never fade. I tingle every time I think about the richness of his voice, the mischief in his eyes that turns them into a chocolaty deep amber when he leans down and sneaks a kiss from me. I *have* to find him. The train whistle blows and my heart stops.

My breath catches.

The impatient train whistle warns me to hurry, but I don't

know where Jeff is. I twist my head around, looking everywhere for him. A deep chill cuts through me, sending me into
a panic. In spite of my fake fur collar, my teeth chatter as I try
to cope with the cold. What railcar did he say? I dig my hand
into my coat pocket for my ticket and feel only the folded-up
drawing he made of me on an October autumn day. A loving
memento I keep close to me. No, he has our train tickets,
surely he's looking for me. He was supposed to pick me up
down the road from my house, but something must have
happened. I fret, and play with my gloves. I can't give up, I'll
find him. I wouldn't have been so late if the minister's wife,
Mildred, hadn't had a flat tire while giving me a lift. She is an
angel in my eyes, a woman who finds strength in helping
others and she knew how important it was for me to get to
the train station this morning.

I ran the rest of the way. I breathe out hard. Jeff won't
leave without me. He loves me.

I break into a run dramatically like they do in the
pictures, my hair blowing wild in the wind, tears running
down my cheeks. I jam through the turnstile at the train
station, looking down for only a moment when the bottom
gold button on my coat rips off. I don't stop.

I race up and down the platform, but I don't see Jeff
anywhere. Breathless, I look right then left. *Where is he?*

'Miss Kate Arden,' calls out a crotchety voice behind me.
'*Miss Arden!*'

I wave at the stationmaster. 'I'm Kate Arden.'

'For you, miss.'

My legs crumble beneath me when he hands me a letter
and I rip it open. My hand goes to my mouth when I read the
hastily scribbled words.

My darling Kate,

I don't have much time to explain, but I've been called up to report for duty in Washington without delay. Please understand, it happened so fast. But it's urgent that I leave this morning. A change of plans. I wish I could say more, but I'm under orders and can't tell you the details except I have no choice but to report earlier for pilot training school.

My heart aches to tell you this, Jelly Girl, but we have to wait to get married till I come home on furlough—

A sudden spasm makes me hunch my shoulders, a pain that radiates to my heart which is beating so fast, too fast. I crumple up the letter without finishing reading it. No doubt Jeff didn't want to upset Ma and Pop by showing up at the house, so he gave the letter to the stationmaster. Still, I can't stop shaking. No, this isn't happening. It can't be. There's got to be a way.

Breathing hard, I scan every face I see, looking for Jeff. I *have* to find him. The 7.10 train to Washington hasn't left yet. *Our* train.

I fly through the train station, a cold winter air rushing between my legs, the hissing steam of the big locomotive filling my ears.

I shoot a glance at several young men boarding the third railcar. All going to camp, I imagine. Then I see him. Brows crossed, running his hand through his dark hair, eyes shooting a painful look as he boards the *next* car but suddenly he turns around, as if looking for me. That moment of pure longing on his face is forever seared into my mind. Of course he knew I'd search for him, but if we missed each other, he didn't want me to think he didn't love me so he wrote the letter.

'Jeff, Jeff!' I yell as I race madly toward him and he jumps off the three rail steps with ease and jams toward me.

Tall and strong, his long overcoat whipping against his muscular legs, no hat as usual, eyes blazing hot with so much love for me, my legs buckle. I want to grab him, kiss him, but I control the urge because I'm still reeling over the painful words in his letter. It's a mistake, it *has* to be. We'll be celebrating Christmas together this year and for years to come.

'Kate, how did you find me?' His laugh is anxious, but still I hear mirth in his voice like he's happy to see me.

'It's our wedding day, Jeff.' I snuggle up to his broad chest, once again feeling safe and protected. 'I wouldn't miss it for the world.'

'Didn't you read my letter?' His joy turns to something dark in his eyes I can't read, a raw fear I've never seen there before. Even the tiny jagged scar above his right brow deepens. As if he's unsure how to explain the awful words he wrote with a shaky hand.

'Yes, but it doesn't mean we can't get married anyway,' I plead, looking at him, my lashes wet with tears I refuse to let fall.

'Oh, Kate... Jelly Girl, my orders came through and I have to go alone. That's why I couldn't pick you up,' he says, shaking his head. 'I gave the stationmaster directions to deliver the letter to you at the mill if he didn't find you.' Then, before I can speak, he cups my face in his hand. 'Just know that whatever happens in this war, I love you and always will.'

'Then show me, Jeff,' I whisper with so much need for him, and we both forget we're in a train station filled with soldiers and civilians, porters. Smoky and loud, but not for us. As if time stands still. I'll never forget his hand sliding around my waist and, before I can rise up on my toes to kiss him, he presses me close to him.

'I have to go, Jelly Girl.' He blurts out the words in a hot whisper in my ear and panic overwhelms me.

'You can't get on that train without me, Jeff, *you can't!*'

I pout, curl my lower lip, and stomp my foot. Yes, I'm acting like a silly schoolgirl, but I have a right. I'm supposed to get married today.

I look around at the civilians seeing off soldiers, the anguish on their faces. A child's trembling hand brushing the sleeve of an Army uniform, the mumbled words of a man telling his wife not to worry with a cracking voice, the sniffling sounds of a mother who can't look into her son's eyes because she doesn't want him to see her crying.

Oh, what a selfish girl you are, Kate Arden. There's a war going on and all you think about is yourself. Let him go. Do his part, while you do yours here on the home front.

I glance back at Jeff, the sun spilling down from the heavens through the glass ceiling, his jaw set with a purpose so true I accept what I know now is my job in this war. To be the strong woman I purport to be. To keep him in my heart, but let him go.

The train whistle drags me out of my stupor with a sharp blast. The piercing look in his eyes makes me tremble. It tells me he doesn't want to leave me like this, hurting so.

'It's not goodbye, Jeff,' I begin, that holy voice that keeps whispering inside me louder, clearer than ever. 'What is it you always tell me in French?'

'Au revoir.' He nuzzles his cheek against mine. 'Till we meet again.'

I repeat the words with what I'm certain is a horrible accent, but he smiles. Slow and heartfelt. His face bears the smoothness of youth, but his expression is that of a man who knows he's facing the brutality of war, something I can't grasp no matter how many newsreels I see. But I see it on his face and it scares me.

Taking a breath to fuel my courage, I pull up something deep inside me that's been brewing for a while. I knew this day would come when Jeff went away to camp, I just didn't expect it so soon. So, like the supportive officer's wife I want to be, I let him go. Without any more drama, without breaking down, I remain strong.

But not before I give him my most precious possession.

His drawing of me.

'So you don't forget me, Jeff.' I press the folded-up drawing into his hand and he flinches. 'This way I'll be with you wherever they send you.'

There's a longing in his dark eyes that tells me everything I want to know, a deep pain he struggles to keep under control that transforms his handsome features into sharp edges. His lips are tight as he says. 'You don't know how difficult this is for me, Kate.'

His words reverberate with a longing so deep that just hearing him say them triggers a crazy set of emotions that make me want to plead for him to take me with him. Ride on that train as far as I can go, holding him, loving him with every clickety-clack of the wheels.

When he wraps his arms around my shoulders, pulling me so close I can't breathe, my blood heats up and some unforeseen spark in my brain reminds me he's just as scared of the future as I am. It's up to me to allay his fears.

With our hearts beating in unison, hands clasped together, foreheads touching, we speak in low whispers to each other. Reaffirming our love, making our peace with the winds of war that tear us apart because we know there is no other choice if the world is ever to be free.

'I love you, Jelly Girl.' His low, gravelly voice chills me, his words vibrating in me even as he lifts my hat veil and kisses me warmly. I hug every last moment with him to my heart and button it up to keep his words safe from the fraying embers of time.

'I love you, too, Jeff. For always.'

With a sudden blast of steam, the great locomotive comes to life, wheels turning, gray smoke pouring out of its belly, and even I can feel the urgency in the air pushing us forward. Jeff gives me one more kiss that stings because I know it's the last kiss I'll have from him until he returns.

Then he's gone.

And my soul goes with him.

I stand there as the train pulls out of the station, watching and waving, until my arm is so tired it turns numb. Long, lonely months without his arms around me, his lips on mine. I tune out everything around me as passengers gather on the platform, waiting for the next train. The choked sobs, passionate farewells, the hurried whispers of soldiers' promises to their mothers and sweethearts, promises they pray they can keep. The heaviness hanging in the air. In spite of the well-meaning holiday Santa posters and posts entwined with red and green and silver ribbons, nobody says Merry Christmas. It hurts too much, wondering if it will be the last time they say it to their soldier or sailor.

It's then I realize I have a job to do in this war, too. At the paper mill. Typing government requisitions, checking on the factory production of ration cartons and ammo boxes. Doing whatever I can to bring Jeff and all our boys home. I bite my lip, determined not to cry. He'll be back. I know he will.

And I'll be waiting for him.

## 3

I never saw Jeff again.

It was Christmas twelve years ago, and it still hurts. A throb of pain that acts up around this time every year. I ignore the rest of the world and go into my shell. For years I questioned why I didn't get on that train, ride as far as I could go until I had to get off.

Now I go through every detail like it's a typed word upon the page that never fades with time. Then I go about the rest of my day until next year when I go through the same ritual all over again. Because I can't let him go.

I still love him.

The memory of that morning is more painful this time of year when my usual, busy routine is interrupted with dodging the mistletoe hanging in the doorway of the break-room. Every sprig of holly is like a thorn pricking my heart.

This obsession of mine hasn't done wonders for my personal life, which is why I'm a single thirty-one year old woman who prefers to think of herself as a career girl and not an old maid sifting through her memories like they're tear-stained dance cards. Not easy to do in this couples' society when everyone is striving for that cookie-cutter life. I haven't embraced it nor do I intend to.

I'm successful. I worked my way up at Holtford Company to food editor. It's an established publishing company that's been around for over a hundred years.

I came to New York in 1947 after realizing life in Posey Creek was a dead-end for me. I had no desire to be pitied because I didn't marry right after the war like most girls. I'd lost Jeff and no one could replace him in my heart. So I took the money I saved and headed to the city to pursue a career. I was more determined than ever to make something of myself. I worked as a proofreader for a while then I jumped at the opportunity when there was an opening in the fashion section, attending trunk shows and writing about poor little rich girls' weddings. From the small towns to the big cities, brides-to-be wanted to copy their swanky designer gowns. According to the columns, every girl of marriageable age is tying the knot as fast as she can in this postwar world and moving to suburbia. Except me. I haven't moved on from my wartime romance.

I tried. I was engaged to a Wall Street guy for longer than I want to admit. We always found an excuse not to tie the knot. His job, my job. The market was up, then down. It never felt 'right'. As if I was cheating on Jeff. So I threw myself into my work. Finally, we went our separate ways. That was a year ago.

I check the time, looking down at my tiny, gold-plated wristwatch. Thirty minutes to go.

I'm lucky to be sitting at this desk in a tall building on Park Avenue. My break came when I started submitting stories to the food column about the ins and outs of modern home cooking. Fate and a kindly food editor stepped in and opened up a new world to me. When I was growing up, Ma was so dedicated to her cooking, we kids swore she slept with her apron on over her nightgown.

*Sweet angel of the frying pan*, I called her. She passed her love of baking and cooking on to me.

I savor the last drop of coffee in my cup, letting it linger on my tongue, but the sugar is long gone. It tastes bitter. I set my cup down and it rattles on the saucer. The last time I saw Jeff is a day I'll never forget. Yet I relive it with a temerity that gets stronger every year, as if by wishing things had turned out differently I can make it happen. Turn the past upside down like a snow globe and make everything come out better. That I jump on that train with him and somehow we get married. If only. Two little words.

In spite of my efforts, nothing changes. Everything is the same. Well, not really. Ma devoted herself to taking care of Pop after he had a stroke. He passed in 1951, his heart broken. He got hit real hard when we got the news about Frank Junior getting wounded in Korea during the winter offensive in late 1950. When my brother came home from the war, he was never the same. It killed Pop more than if he'd died in action. I wish I'd spent more time trying to understand the gangly boy who wanted to be a baseball player, not a mill worker. Pop started drinking heavy when his boy left town to cure his mental scars from the war on his own. It did him in. He was a good man and worked hard at the mill. I wasn't close to my father, but I respected him. He didn't know how to show his feelings, which was common in men of that generation.

When I lost Ma a year later in 1952, I cried for days. I adored my mother. She was apple pie and pink yarn and smelled like rainwater. Ma carried on the best she could after

God took her boys with Frankie making his way across the country to handle his problems in his own way. It hurt her bad, not knowing how her son was doing pained her more than she let on. I saw her crying on my last visit, her shoulders hunched as she hung up the laundry outside, thinking no one heard her. In the end, she died from pneumonia, like she was just exhausted from living.

Then there's Lucy. My spinning top. Never sitting still. My scatterbrained sister never let up teasing me about Jeff, but she never left my side when I heard the heartbreaking news. *MIA,* came the whispers at the mill, then months later we heard Jeff was killed when his plane was hit by flak and went down over Germany. No one in the crew of ten survived. The next day I saw a Gold Star pennant hanging in the window at Wrightwood House. My whole world ended. My little sister cried with me.

She was there for me when Jeff's mother ignored me at the memorial. Mrs Rushbrooke had seen me enough times at the house when Jeff was around to know I wasn't just another girl from the mill stuck on her son. I always wondered if she suspected we were dating later on, but as long as it didn't upset her world, she didn't make a ruckus. Until Jeff didn't come back. As if it was my fault. She ordered me to never, *ever* cross her doorstep again. Then she smashed the jar of cherry jam I brought for her against the wall. I never understood why, if she was just grieving or she really knew about us. I told no one. Not even Ma. I never told her about my secret plans to marry Jeff, though she had a notion I was seeing him. She hoped I'd get over him, find somebody else and get married. How could I? I loved him so much, I couldn't let him go. It was a deep romantic love left unfulfilled. No man could ever compete with that. I didn't want anyone but him.

Lucy kept my secret. I lived my life through her after Jeff left. I was more excited than she was at her wedding after she found her soldier, Jimmie, and corralled him with her freckled smile. She wrote to a lot of soldiers during the war, but this boy won her heart with his dimples and big strong hands. Now she's got three kids and a loving husband and lives in the big old house where we grew up. Built over a hundred years ago and nestled among oak and cherry trees, the house has belonged to Ma's family since her grandpa won it in a poker game.

Which brings me to part two of my yearly scenario. Lucy's annual phone call, when she begs me to come home for the holidays. I can't. Ma understood the memories were too painful and welcomed me home whenever I could make the trip, though I haven't been back since she's been gone. The pain of losing Jeff at Christmas is too raw. I keep my memory of him hidden in the deepest pocket of my heart. With a button on it. I never look inside except this time of year and then only for a little while. Because it hurts so much, I want to avoid going home for Christmas this year. Again. Besides, I have plans. A quiet holiday in Vermont. Lounging before a roaring fireplace. The notes for that book I'm writing spread out on a bearskin rug.

I glance down again at my watch. Fifteen minutes to go. Which means it's time for my sister to ring me. Her youngest, Billie, is probably napping and the twins, Maureen and Melinda, are ensconced in front of the television set with their coloring books. No doubt Jimmie, her hunky husband, is out somewhere banging nails on a new house for a lucky family. He's a builder and recently became a partner in a construction business. She couldn't have gotten a better man. Hardworking, a strong father, and he loves her to pieces.

I squirm in my swivel chair as I skim through the assortment of bills from suppliers, fan mail for our writers, and handwritten recipes from housewives eager to see their name in the magazine until one letter catches my eye.

The envelope is engraved on the left with *On to Victory for Liberty!* I see a big red V and the Statue of Liberty, an eagle, and flying aircraft. No stamp. It says *Free* in the upper right-hand corner and is addressed to 'Miss Kate Arden' at my old address in Posey Creek. It was never postmarked. Somehow they tracked me down here to the publishing company.

A knowing sensation sends chills down my back. I haven't seen stationery like this since the war. I turn it over. The envelope is wrinkled, but sealed up tight. Like it was stuffed in the bottom of a drawer for a long time. No return address.

I tap my nails on the envelope, a tingling on my scalp giving me a funny feeling. Like opening the letter will bring back the past. You'd think I'd embrace it. Hurry to read it. I can't. I'm afraid to go there. I know what happened and there's a certain comfort in that. Whoever sent this letter is opening up a new wound when the old one is still healing.

'Where did this old letter come from, Bette?' I call out to my assistant.

'Oh, *that* one,' she says, popping her head in. 'It came in a large brown envelope for you marked *Special Delivery*.'

I smile, almost in relief. 'Another fruitcake recipe from an overzealous ladies auxiliary club, I imagine. I wonder where they got the war stationery.' Funny, how we cling to our ration book ways. Every time I pull on a pair of hosiery and try to get the seams straight, I take extra care not to snag them with my nails. I can't help but think about that bet with my sister. Lucy won the stockings fair and square, but I was never prouder of her than when she donated them to the war effort. She wanted to do her part, she said, since nylons were important for making war materials like parachutes and rope and netting. She did it for me.

That doesn't mean I'll give in and spend Christmas in Posey Creek.

Still, I'm intrigued by this strange letter. I grab my pearl-handled opener just as the phone rings.

I pick up the phone and cradle the receiver to my ear. The words *'I'm not coming home for Christmas, I'm working on a book,'* are out of my mouth before she can speak.

'I know how important your work is to you, Kate,' Lucy says, her words catching in her throat, 'but you've *got* to come home this year.' I hear her suck in a sharp breath. That isn't like her. 'With Ma gone, the girls need you.'

'The girls don't even know I exist,' I say, laughing. I adore her twins, but the eight year olds are more interested in their paper dolls than me.

She sighs. Another cleansing breath, then in that winsome voice I know so well when she's hurting, she says. 'I need you, big sister.'

I freeze. A strange longing hits me, seizes my brain like a merry-go-round suddenly coming to a grinding stop. And Lucy is waving madly at me, her face crushed with worry, her whole body shaking. The roof caving in couldn't have hit me any harder.

'Kate...' I hear my sister's voice coming from the receiver.

'I'm here, Lucy,' I warble into the phone like a wounded wren when I hear the ache in my sister's voice. Cold water splashed into my face couldn't make it any clearer. I acted like a selfish prig. Something hits me then. This bird is through flying away. Time to grow up. 'Talk to me, what's wrong?'

'I know you have plans... and I understand why it's hard

for you to come home for the holidays, but I'm all alone with the kids—'

'Where's Jimmie?'

'We had a fight.'

'About what?' I can't keep the surprise out of my voice. They never fight over anything except where to hang the Christmas wreath.

'I'll tell you when you get here... if you can make it.'

'I'll be there, Lucy. Don't you worry about anything, you hear?' I take a moment to compose myself and say what's on my mind. 'It's time I came home.'

*Time I move on*, I add silently.

'Oh, Kate... thank you.' I hear her sob a sigh of relief. There's more going on than her wanting me to come home. I'll find out soon enough. I have a lot to do in two days. Cancel my reservations at the inn. That bearskin rug will have to wait. Pack a tote bag filled with Christmas presents instead of sending them by overnight post. Make a train reservation. I can take the *Mistletoe Flyer* on Thursday, a special Christmas train that runs only during the holidays with a twenty-minute layover in Philadelphia before heading west, making stops along the way in rural towns, including Posey Creek.

I feel lighter, noting my hour of self-pity is up. It's been replaced with something I've avoided for a long time. I'm ashamed of how stubborn I've been. I never meant to hurt my sister by hiding my own pain. I made it home for Easter and chocolate bunnies, summer cherry harvesting, even Halloween before Ma passed. Christmas? Never. It's time to face my fears and my heartache. Jeff is gone and no amount of longing for him every Christmas is going to change that.

It isn't until I hang up that I remember the strange letter.

Somehow it doesn't seem important anymore. My sister needs me. Or is there another reason? One that makes my knees weak: the suspicion there's something in that letter I don't want to know. I stuff it into my handbag unopened. Whatever it is, it can wait.

I'm going home for Christmas.

## 4

---

I stare out the window as the train leaves the station in New York and fidget with my gloves. A nervous habit I can't break. I looked up at the big clock under the glass dome before I boarded and thought about how fragile time is, knowing I've wasted it with my meanderings over the years, but also knowing I'll never get it back. I couldn't ignore the Christmas tree brightening up the station lobby with its multi-colored lights, as if welcoming me home before I even got on the train. New Yorkers say the only time the railroad station is cheery is during the holidays, which makes me smile. Earlier I got into the holiday spirit by looking at the gorgeous window displays in the department stores and became mesmerized by a homey scene: a small town with picket fences, kids on sleds, skaters twirling around in a circle on a frozen pond, and a train *choo-chooing* its way around them. Like Posey Creek. A tug at my heartstrings I can't ignore.

I'm on a mission to help my little sister. I won't let her lose the wonderful life she's built for herself because of a silly spat with the man who adores her. I'll talk with Jimmie myself if I have to, though I'm no marriage expert. Still, I love my sister and pray I won't break down and sob on *her* shoulder. I'm not going home to unload on her, but to help her. The only way I can do that is to take a walk through the past and face it once and for all. A cleansing renewal. Find my way back home.

As the city whirls by me in a blur outside the window, I'm determined to bring myself under control. Pulling up old memories that haven't healed won't be easy, my ears burning every time I hear someone mention Jeff, my stomach clenching, pulse racing. I press my hand over my heart to slow it down.

When the conductor enters the car and calls out, 'Two hours to Philadelphia,' as the train speeds along the tracks, I let my mind wander and my heart remember the warm summer day I first met Jeff. A smile curves over my lips as I pull back the memory of how our friendship started with a bannister at Wrightwood House and a bowl of jelly.

It was 1935. I was eleven.

The country was in the middle of the Great Depression and Ma reminded us often how lucky we were Pop had a job. Most of the town worked in the paper mill turning out fancy goods and every Christmas each family got a chicken and extra coal.

Life was good in Posey Creek. The air was filled with the fragrance of sweet fruit. Colorful butterflies landed on my shoulder as I carried the basket of the ripest cherries up to Wrightwood House. My mother often took me along with her on her weekly trips to the big house on the hill and I peeked into the private lives of the Rushbrookes. I found out they had as many problems as the rest of us. Why that surprised me, I don't know. This was a time when going to the picture show on Saturday afternoon was the only peek we had into the lives of rich folks who lived in big houses. We ogled their automobiles with long running boards and giggled at the ladies who wore silk dresses and smoked cigarettes and flirted with gentlemen with slicked back hair.

I went with Ma that day to help the cook who was ailing. She finished setting up the cherry jelly on the saucer and asked me to take it outside to let it cool. No sooner did I sneak through the front part of the house instead of going out the back like I should, when this teenage boy came sliding down the long, winding bannister toward me like an electric pony at Steele Pier. He knocked me down, spilling jelly all over my pinafore.

'You okay, Jelly Girl?' he asked me, helping me up. He shot me a concerned look, the tone in his voice telling me he meant it. And that big smile when he called me 'Jelly Girl.' Wow. Like we shared a secret that only heightened our curiosity about each other.

I could barely nod. I felt wonderfully special. Not awkward or silly like most boys made me feel. I didn't want to let go of his hand, big and strong even then, his warmth taking me to a new place I never wanted to leave.

'I'm in the groove.' I lifted my chin and tried to act all grown up.

He laughed, then squeezed my hand. 'Me, too, Jelly Girl, now that we've met.'

There. He said it again. Called me his Jelly Girl. I wanted to melt into a puddle of jam right in the middle of Mrs Rush-brooke's hallway.

'I'm sorry I spilled the jelly, but I took a shortcut through here and then, well, you...' I lowered my eyes, knowing this wasn't going to sit well with Ma. She'd probably make me clean floors for a month of Sundays.

He grinned. 'I'm not.'

My eyes widened. 'You're not?'

He shook his head and chuckled. 'Nope. If you didn't take that shortcut, I never would have met you.'

'Oh,' was all I could say. He let go of my hand and I felt a sudden lightheadedness, disoriented. He was so good-looking. Taller than any boy I knew with a shock of dark hair that never look combed and the darkest eyes the color of shiny licorice fringed with long, dark lashes and that smile. Crooked but beautiful. A cute scar above his right eyebrow made him even more appealing, like he was a dashing pirate. I knew who he was. I heard the cook telling Ma to make sure Mr Jeffrey ate his spinach so he didn't get into any more trouble, seeing how he got tossed out of military school for not obeying the rules. That made him a hero in my eyes. I didn't like rules either, like how girls couldn't go on adventures or write stories.

Jeff was around fourteen then and already he had the good looks that would stay with him as he matured into a cocky teenager and then the handsomest man I ever saw.

And me? I was thoroughly convinced I'd never wash my hand again.

When his father saw me scrambling to clean up the spilled jelly, he raised a hand toward Jeff that set a fire in me. I had the feeling this wasn't the first time he struck him. I couldn't let him hurt my prince. Before he could stop me, I stepped forward and took the blame. Saying I wasn't supposed to be going through here and I slipped.

*Mr Jeffrey had nothing to do with the unfortunate turn of events that led me to slide like a turtle across the elegant foyer.*

I remember how I impressed Jeff with my explanation. I had a way with words, Ma said, which she attributed to my

Irish grandfather, *who could spin a yarn faster than he could turn a card or down a pint.* I didn't mind the 500-word essay I had to write, apologizing to Mrs Rushbrooke for messing up her hardwood floor. All that mattered was that I saved my prince from the horrible dragon.

'You're not so dumb, for a girl,' Jeff said later when no one could hear us. He smiled at me with that toothy grin I grew to love so much as he studied me, his mood playful.

'You're not so bad... for a boy,' I snickered, returning the stare. I realize now I never outgrew my infatuation with him, the years never dimming this day when our worlds collided over a bowl of spilled jelly.

He grinned. 'Someday I'm going to marry you, Jelly Girl.'

I couldn't speak. My heart pounded, my head spun, and I didn't dare speak and say something stupid. My hero, the boy I decided then and there I would adore forever, said he wanted to marry me. Me? The girl who lived on the other side of town. Who didn't have fancy eyelet batiste dresses with velvet bows like rich girls wore. Who never smeared lipstick on her mouth like other girls, though I wanted to. I floated on a cloud filled with cherry jelly. Then he tweaked my nose and he was off. We saw each other at odd times after that. I snooped around when I went with Ma to Wrightwood House, hoping to catch a glimpse of him. Sometimes I did when he was home from school (he got kicked out of more than one military school) and we'd sneak off to the kitchen and talk about our favorite movies and books. Every time, he winked at me like we had a secret.

I never forgot what he said, that someday he'd marry me.

As I crossed the threshold from girlhood into becoming a teenager, I thought of no one but him. I kept the memory of him close to my heart, ignoring other boys' interest in me,

which made Ma breathe easier when I developed a woman's
body. I was tall and slender, but I saw how she tried to fit my
bodices so tight they flattened me out. She didn't like me
wearing lipstick, but I told her all the girls did. When the war
came, we wore dark red lipstick to boost our morale and the
soldiers', too, and began to crochet and knit more since
clothing was rationed. Skirts got shorter and Ma would be
happier if I got a job on the mill floor and wore trousers like
the other female workers. I was fast becoming a woman. I
saw her scowl when I found some shimmery blue yarn in the
sewing bin and knitted myself a sweater. I was wearing that
sweater when Jeff noticed me that summer we bumped into
each other at the factory. We hadn't seen each other since he
went back to boarding school at seventeen and I started high
school at fourteen.

Sparks flew.

*We're not kids anymore*, his eyes said, taking in my curves
and nodding his head in approval. I didn't dare hope it would
go further than that, but something sparked between us just
like it did when we were kids. Searching and accepting,
touching fingertips, then grabbing hands like we did that first
time and easing into each other and the years melted away. I
was his Jelly Girl again. Then letting our hearts open up
without the fear of getting hurt because we just *knew* we were
meant to be with each other.

We began to see each other. A lot. He was my whole
world. The way he laughed, listened to my wild tales, and
then tousled my hair when we lay on the grass under the big
ole cherry tree. Our spot. Then he took out his sketchpad and
drew me. Wispy, light, airy fragments of summer days. Or the
crisp chill of autumn. He wanted to build things, he said,
showing me his sketches. Modern structures with clean lines.

He had three years under his belt at the nearby university studying business, but he also took classes in architecture, even if his pa was dead set against it. Jeff didn't come home during college breaks, rather than get an earful from his father about how following his dream wasn't going to keep the family business going.

Now he wished he had, he said, his loving gaze making me warm all over, lowering than slowly crawling up to meet my eyes, promising me something I wanted so badly.

I didn't know what, if anything, would come of us, but I hoped with all my heart. Jeff had no choice but to leave college when the family mill started making paper for the US Army. He came home to run the mill. Bad blood existed between his father and him and I often wondered what would have happened if Jeff finished his studies after the war. His younger brother, Timothy, squandered the profits the mill made during the war years and it closed down. It didn't matter to Mr Rushbrooke. He never recovered. He spent his final days far away in a facility where he didn't have to be reminded he was a fool and lost everything.

When winter came in 1943, the cherry tree stood as a reminder we were at war, the bleakness of winter emptying its branches. But I lived for the summer days, embracing the ache in my belly to meet Jeff whenever I could. Sometimes we sneaked into the old stone cottage nearby used by trappers and spent the whole day exploring the abandoned structure filled with arrowheads, leather scraps, and pottery. It was warm and snug and filled with straw. We talked about what we wanted to do after the war. Make a home, have children. Grow old together.

What makes my heart pound even now, is how heated our breath became when we touched each other. How hard his body was against mine, his strong arms lifting me up and carrying me to the bed of straw. Laying me down... and then lifting up my sparkly blue sweater.

Oh. I let out a deep sigh. As the train speeds along the tracks taking me home, I can't help but wonder what might have been.

# 5

I undo the frog clasp on my suit jacket and the top two pearl buttons on my blouse. I'm sweating, imbibing in my indulgent trip to the past and forgot where I am. On a train. *The Mistletoe Flyer*. Staring out the window, paying little attention to the numerous train stops. Passengers getting on and off.

Passing barren fields and deep woods. White clapboard farmhouses and red barns. A homespun embroidery stitched together with tradition and changing little over time, making the past harder to escape.

I look at the schedule clutched in my hand. We're due to arrive at 4.40 p.m. It's two thirty now. I panic. I need more time. What if I break down when I see the train station decorated for the holidays? What if I lose my nerve? It's a soul-wrenching trip, especially when I know it will make my loneliness even more unbearable.

I glance down at my handbag and a small hatbox, my red coat with the fake fur collar slung over my seat. Ah, yes, that red coat. In a moment of pure whimsy, I grabbed my old coat instead of my smart black one with the braided collar. The red coat is a classic. Slim fit, classy gold buttons. If I'm going home, I want to feel young again. Not like a stuffy career woman. After the war, I found myself pushed into rigid, boxy designs made to put women back into the kitchen. I rebelled against it as I rebelled against society's rules back in 1943. Ripping the plastic cover off my red coat was liberating. The bottom button is still missing, but who will notice except me? I smile. To let something go, you have to embrace it first. That's what this trip is about. Letting go. So I donned the same outfit I wore on the day Jeff left though my grey suit is a bit snugger and I couldn't forget my blue silk hat with the wispy veil. I chuckle. I'm an old softie when it comes to family heirlooms. Like Ma's famous Christmas apron with the bright red cherry print that faded more every year. Pop's pipe fashioned from briarwood and handed down to him from his father-in-law. The older man won it in a poker game. Frank Junior's baseball autographed by the 1949 Phillies. I take a moment, remembering the last we heard from Frankie. He's out in California where it's warm, picking up odd jobs. He doesn't want to come home. Without Ma and Pop, he says, there isn't any reason to. He met a girl and he's thinking of marrying her. We were thrilled at the news. I pray Lucy can convince him to come home for Christmas. If she can get me packing my bag, why won't it work on Frankie, too?

Pushing aside my offbeat philosophical leanings, I look around me. The train is packed, the holiday travelers excited to be aboard. It's three days until Christmas and I'm lucky to find a seat in the back where it isn't full. The conductor tips his cap to me and checks my ticket. He has a sprig of pine pinned to his lapel. The scent is divine. Puts me in the holiday spirit.

I poke around in my purse for my mirror when my fingers

wrap around the strange letter and my breath catches. I wish it was from Jeff and lost all these years, but I know it isn't. Who would go to all that trouble to find me? The sudden curiosity to know what's in that letter makes my pulse throb.

I open the envelope and begin to read, the clickety-clack of the train wheels taking me back in time when I see the date. *October 1948.* A sharp memory stabs my brain. I recognize the Signal Corps US Army insignia engraved on the paper. A sepia rendering of a soldier talking on a portable radio. The same stationery Jeff used to write me.

I received two letters from him, then nothing. He wrote me about fifteen mile hikes, chowtime, and then school at night. How much he missed me and loved me. I cherish those letters, keep them hidden in a book of French literature he gave me.

I nearly choke now when I scan the bright, blue-inked words written by a soldier who served with Jeff. A radio operator named Herbie, a farm boy from Iowa. He was part of a three man team on a secret mission overseas with Jeff along with a British operative.

I sit very still, stunned. His words hit me hard in the chest and I swear I stop breathing. Is this a cruel joke? Or in God's name, can it be true? Jeff never hinted at any secret mission. All he talked about was flying bombers. I should toss the letter back into my purse, but a nagging itch crawling up my spine makes me read further, as if tempting me with a fierce kind of hope that it *is* true. That there's something here about the man I loved that will soothe my soul after all these years.

It was very hush hush, the soldier wrote, but the three men learned to trust each other and shared stories from home. Jeff talked about me all the time and he had every intention of coming home and marrying me, but their mission was compromised because of a traitor among the rural fighters they teamed up with and Jeff died trying to save others.

The sergeant never spoke of it after the war, but he was plagued with nightmares about a promise he made that wouldn't let him go.

To assuage his conscience, he wrote the letter on stationery he commandeered from a buddy in the hospital before he was shipped back to the States after the war. Then he left instructions with his wife to send the letter to me upon his death.

Now the letter is in my hands.

I couldn't talk about the mission during the war, Miss Arden. Even now, I can't give you all the details. Maybe someday our stories and what we did for the Office of Strategic Services can be told, but not when we're facing an unknown future.

What I can tell you is this: Jeff and I never received the intelligence that would have changed everything. We were set up on that moonless night by a traitor. A French collaborator who loved his wine more than his country. He sold us out. A two-timing son of a gun we called 'Leftie' because he was constantly reminding us to eat with our forks in our left hands.

He had a mean streak like you never seen. Like someone cut out his heart. I remember the time he kicked and beat a starving stray dog with the butt of his rifle. Jeff got so mad, they nearly came to blows. We should have known then he wasn't to be trusted. If we hadn't listened to him, we never would have walked into a trap. The Nazis had us surrounded before we could fire off a shot.

Jeff smelled the enemy before we did and brought down them Nazis with his pistol, but he couldn't save the Résistance fighters working with us. Or the Brit. The man went down fast. A bullet to the heart. But he rigged the explosives so we could set off the blast and derail the supply train and clog up the railway route. A key line of communications.

What we did that night stopped the Nazi flow of men, arms, and tanks into Southern France for months. Helped the Allies with the invasion yet to come. Jeff forged so deep into the underground, cavorting with the Vichy, I forgot he wasn't French. He became one of them so he could get the information we needed. Without him, it never would have happened.

Afterward, I escaped into the woods but I was later captured and spent the last two years of the war in a POW camp. I never saw Jeff again. If he wasn't killed in the blast, the Gestapo got him. God knows what they did to him. No one in the Army would tell me anything officially except he died somewhere in Europe.

The reason I'm telling you this, Jelly Girl (I told you he couldn't stop talking about you), is I made Jeff a promise I'd tell you the truth. I owed him that much, seeing how he saved me from a Nazi bullet when we parachuted into France.

By the time you read this, I shall be gone, off to that place in the sky where old soldiers go to tell their stories to anybody up there who will listen. It can't hurt for you to know this now and that your man loved you more than life itself. That he never stopped kicking himself in the pants for leaving you at the train station on that December morning instead of eloping with you, and how he couldn't wait to get home and marry you on his first furlough. That he couldn't live without you.

Yours in God,

1st Sergeant Herbert 'Herbie' Drew Peterson.

My hand shaking, I put down the letter. My heart is pumping wildly, outrageous denial of what I read firing up my blood, my whole body tingling. I glance over my shoulder to see if anyone is watching me, scan the passengers reading newspapers or gazing out the window. Everyone is going about their business. Calmly. With no interest in me.

I want to jump up and tell them my whole life changed in an instant. That while I'm reliving every precious second I spent with Jeff, this soldier's letter has dropped a bomb into my lap and I don't know what to do next. It's like an air raid drill during the war when you least expect it. You know it can happen, but you don't know how you'll react until it does. Only this is no drill. This is real.

I hold the letter to my chest to catch my breath. I can't believe it. Something I suspected for a long time, but never put into words. Until now.

Jeff was a spy.

# 6

I can't stop shaking. There's a sudden shifting in my bones and blood rushes to my face, as if the earth has tilted and I'm sliding off the edge of the world. I believe everything the soldier wrote.

Holding the letter in my hand, I'm aware of a sensation like I'm hanging suspended between now and the past. I get the strangest feeling I'm seeing into another world and Jeff is giving the sergeant the okay to tell me what happened that night.

I feel increasingly vindicated as the train takes me closer to home, a sense of relief hitting me. That my curiosity isn't misguided. I never talk about it, but I had the feeling Jeff didn't die somewhere over Germany. He wasn't supposed to be called up for another month even though his father tried to get him deferred from service to run the factory. Jeff hated his father interfering. Said he wanted to fight the Nazis in a way only he could. He wanted me to think he meant by air as a pilot. I know differently now.

I first suspected the Rushbrookes had close ties with

Washington when I was in high school. After I helped Ma deliver the jams and jellies, I often wandered around the big house, imagining what it was like to live there. One day I sneaked into the library and plopped down in the corner with a book where no one could see me. His father, the gruff Mr Ambrose Rushbrooke, rushed in and picked up the ringing phone. 'Yes, Mr President, I understand. I'll leave for the continent immediately.' He paused and I didn't dare breathe. I was dumbfounded. 'Yes, I'll bring my boy with me.' Pause. 'That's correct. Jeffrey speaks fluent French. He was reared by a nanny from Paris from the day he was born until he went away to military school. I'm pleased you believe he could be useful.'

Then he hung up. I never forgot it.

Jeff left for a trip to the French Riviera and then Paris soon after, according to the cook when Ma and I came back the next week. It wasn't the only trip he and his father made together to Europe over the next two years. He often teased me about these excursions, saying he'd teach me French so we could go together someday. I thought it wildly exciting, but I couldn't imagine why Mr Rushbrooke had a conversation with the President about their trip. I never told anyone what I heard. Not even Jeff. I was afraid he'd think I was a snoop.

I found out after the war that several high profile figures like Mr Rushbrooke often went on low key missions to Europe and Asia to assess what was happening abroad before we entered the conflict in late 1941. I had no idea back then that meant Jeff and his father were spying for the US government, but I often wondered if there was more to those trips than he let on. The letter from the sergeant proved what I suspected, but was never sure of. No wonder he was eager to get into the fight and do it 'his way'.

Nothing has changed in the railcar since I started reading the letter. The passengers jostle about, the smell of pine from the fresh wreaths placed at each end of the car putting everyone in a holiday mood. The landscape blurs outside the passenger windows. The train whistle blasts its shrill sound.

But I've changed. I feel his loss more than ever. He loved me so much, he'd have married me no matter what. Jeff bent the rules when it came to us, defying his family by wanting to elope with me. He drew me into his seductive world of art and French literature with wild enthusiasm and wit and humor. He showed me that love in so many ways. Not with fancy gifts, but gifts from the heart. He protected me like a knight for his lady whenever we were together – will I ever forget him carrying me over a big rain puddle in his strong arms? – but also let me fly on my own so I'd be strong, independent. He inspired me to make something out of myself even after he was gone. How many times have I sat in my New York office, mulling over a piece for my column, or jumping out of my seat with excitement when I read a heartfelt *thank-you* from a reader for lifting her up on a dreary day with my story. I get a heaviness in my chest because he's not there to say, *'I'm so proud of you, Jelly Girl.'* It's then I get teary-eyed. I've kept myself under control until now, but this new revelation about Jeff jolts me. I debate whether or not to tell Lucy about the sergeant's letter, but she has her own problems. Best to wait until I help her sort them out. The sad thing is, I have no one to share this news with. I need a strong cup of coffee to fuel my spirit. I get up to go to the observation car when—

A dizzy feeling comes over me.

I put my hand on the back of the seat to steady myself. I must appear strange to the other passengers, taking deep breaths, then I begin pacing back and forth in the aisle.

The conductor comes by, tips his cap. He's the grandfatherly type. Curious, but nice. 'Everything okay, miss?'

'Yes. I'm going home for Christmas for the first time in years.' I wipe away the mist around my eyes and put my red coat on, then tuck the letter into the deep side pocket as I sit down. I'll put it back into my purse later. 'Getting sentimental, I guess.' I pull my veil down so he can't see the wetness on my cheeks. I'm embarrassed by my weepiness so I ask him if we're on schedule.

'We should reach the Posey Creek station within the hour,' he says, 'though we have two more stops first.'

'I've never ridden on a Christmas train before,' I say, trying to change the subject.

'There's something magical about it that gets to my old bones,' says the conductor, his eyes twinkling behind his wire-rimmed glasses. 'Who knows? St Nick himself might show up.'

'I saw the jolly old man during the war.' I don't wipe away the tear traveling down my cheek. 'Pop dressed up like Santa back in 1943 when the troop trains came through on Christmas Eve.'

'I remember that Christmas Eve, miss.' The conductor takes off his glasses and breathes on them before wiping them clean with his handkerchief. 'I was on duty that day and we had the most passengers ever in the history of the railroad.' He takes a moment. 'We had soldiers hanging out the windows and falling over each other in the aisles. It was a sight to remember.'

I laugh. 'So was my pop dressed up as St Nick.'

How can I have forgotten that? Pop with his pillow-stuffed, red flannel Santa suit Ma whipped up from old blankets. The beard she made from scraps of sheep's wool. Meanwhile, I sulked at home feeling sorry for myself. Jeff was off to training camp and I was so filled with despair at not marrying him. What a complete, utter fool I was. I tried so hard to be strong, brave. But I was young and at times I thought more of my own romantic wants and desires. I tried hard to remember that we were in this fight together and we on the home front were soldiers in our own way, but that day I lost control and cried my eyes out.

I'm embarrassed even now. I let my family down. I wish I could go back to that Christmastime and see Pop handing out the bags of Ma's homemade cherry and nut candy and cookies to the soldiers eager for a piece of home. Ma bringing hot coffee to the boys. Frank Junior tossing a baseball back and forth with the servicemen, many of them boys themselves. Lucy twirling the bright holiday ribbon in her hair around her finger while she flirted with every soldier who caught her eye. I wish I hadn't been so filled with my own problems, pining over Jeff leaving. I wish I'd been there with them…

But I can't go back.

Then for some reason I can't explain, goose bumps rise on my arms as I keep rubbing the buttons on my coat, ignoring the empty buttonhole, a strange energy crackling through my fingers. As if I'm wishing on a magic lamp. I'd give anything to go back and relive that day when Jeff left and the buttons on my coat shone golden. All six of them. I teeter back and forth in my mind, knowing what I'm asking for is impossible, but wishing it with all my heart. I'm caught in the collision of my past with what I deem isn't a fair shake. I'd give anything for Jeff to have a fighting chance to survive. To warn him about the traitor. He was a good man, a valiant soldier. Doesn't he deserve that?

I stand up. The compulsion to see Jeff is so strong, I can't stop myself. My mind wanders off track and I stand there in defiance of the past. The more fired up I get, the more my pulse pounds. The unfairness of war, the slender difference between life and death. The fragility of freedom and how easily it can be taken away because of another man's greed.

A deep grieving pain revisits me and I go numb.

When the train speeds through a deep, dark tunnel at a fast clip, jarring me, I refuse to back down.

I hear a terrible, loud noise. Grinding, piercing, making my ears hurt. A screech so hair-raising, my skin prickles. I don't move when the whistle shrills and the sudden grinding of emergency air brakes sends numerous pairs of anxious eyes including mine in that direction.

My heart stops. My God, we nearly clipped the train stalled on the next tracks.

Then the lights flicker on and off and everyone gasps when they go out completely. In the next few seconds, a myriad of emotions run through me. Anger. *A traitor killed my love.* Dismay. *I believed a lie all these years.* Self-pity. *I'll never love again.*

Terror. *I'm more alone than ever.*

A sudden determination rises in me to confront the past head on, do something to make my heart whole again and go on with my life. The rising up of such strength from deep within my soul fuels my wish. There's no mistaking I break through a barrier.

That moment changes everything.

That stark realization is electric. Clashing with the past as

I stand suspended between the two and a force springs to life and pulls me along on its flowing tide. An indignant chill permeates throughout every pore in my body, seeping into every bone, every muscle. I feel a tingling sensation from head to toe, as if the blood drains from my being, but something inside me urges me on. My knees buckle and a second jolt rocks me when the whistle blows and the train lunges forward.

This time, it knocks me off my feet.

*Jeff, Jeff… where are you? You didn't have to die… if only…*

Caught off balance, I reach out for something to hold onto as I stumble forward but there's nothing there. I'm thrust forward, whirling through the air like a discarded ragdoll tossed into a toy chest and reeking of lost dreams.

I scream and go headfirst into the darkness.

## 7

I have no recollection of the train pulling into the Posey Creek station but when my head clears, we've stopped. I hear the engine snorting as it sits idle on the tracks. The air is hot and still. A foggy haze surrounds me, blurring my vision. The last thing I remember is being thrown off balance in the dark tunnel when the train slammed to a stop. I hit the floor hard – did I bang my head?

Even more strange, I'm sitting back in my seat. I lean back, the rough fabric scraping against my neck. The red holiday velvet coverlet on the headrest is replaced by a white one. No scent of pine. Instead, the raw, musky smell of men on the move stings my nostrils.

Yes, men. Soldiers.

I swivel my head around, my jaw dropping. So many soldiers, I can't count them. Racing to the windows, picking up their dice and cards, scrambling to get off. I know then what the foggy haze is. Cigarette smoke.

'Conductor!' I call out when I see a friendly railroad man making his way down the aisle. He tips his hat.

'Yes, miss?'

'What happened?'

'The boys got rambunctious and started jumping off the train before we stopped. Them young fellows can smell hot coffee a mile away.' He looks at me strangely. 'I don't recollect seeing you before. When did you come aboard?'

I don't answer his question. Instead, I take a second look at the conductor. I swear it's the same railway man I spoke to earlier, but he looks different. No pine sprig in his lapel. No wire-rimmed glasses. Younger looking. I must be imagining things.

'Why are the soldiers jumping off the train?' I stand up, look around.

'The trackside canteen, miss.'

'Canteen?' My voice is a low whisper, as if I'm afraid to say it any louder lest I actually believe the insanity rolling around in my brain.

Surely, I didn't hear him right. I didn't.

'Some of these boys have been on this train for days and can't afford to eat in the dining car.' He regards me with a critical eye, as if I should know that.

'Days?' I say, trying to process. I can't. 'Where are they going?'

'They're heading home on furlough or they've got a delay en-route to visit their folks before being shipped overseas. Like that sailor helping the good sister.' He points to a wiry seaman bouncing a little boy on his knee. 'These boys will remember times like this when they're in the middle of the fighting.'

'Fighting?' I mutter, frustrated. 'The conflict in Korea ended two years ago.'

'You okay, miss?' He looks at me as if I'm crazy.

'Yes, I mean, no. How did I get here?'

'I wouldn't know, miss. I was in the next car when we stopped. We don't get many civilian passengers these days, especially pretty ladies like you.' He shoots his eyes downward, realizing he stepped over the line. 'Begging your pardon, miss, but you're quite a hit with the soldiers.'

I don't realize till then the hard stares in my direction. Whispers. Deep sighs. Giving me looks that make me feel like I'm the living, breathing version of the wrinkled, dog-eared photo of a sweetheart in every man's wallet. Men gawk at me like I appeared in a puff of smoke.

Maybe I did.

I allow myself that moment of humor because either this whole scenario is going to disappear as quickly as it came, or I'm in trouble, *deep* trouble. I smooth down my red coat, my gray silk suit underneath wrinkled like I was sitting for hours. I must look a mess.

I need to freshen up. I look around my seat. Then under it. Nothing but empty space. Where is my purse and my hatbox? My God, what if someone stole them? Then what? No, there's got to be another explanation. Did I wander into another train car in the darkness? That doesn't seem plausible. Then what *did* happen to me?

I shiver. It's cold in here, what with the soldiers raising up every window and a blast of winter surging in. I stand there, trying to focus. Then I notice a poster tacked up in the back of the railcar. *Is your trip necessary?* it reads. I haven't seen anything like that since the war.

I blink. I can't be more surprised at the crazy thoughts swirling around in my brain than if I landed on a different planet. Fingers trembling, I start buttoning up my coat when—

I stop. *Don't count the buttons. You're not ready.*

I survey the area. The conductor is right. There are no civilian passengers except for two businessmen gathering up their briefcases, the taller man wearing the topcoat hastily making his way off the train. I look away and catch the other civilian passenger studying me as if he knows me. The gentleman with silver hair and a moustache checks his watch, then looks at me and smiles. He starts to say something. When I don't acknowledge him, he shrugs and gets off the train. That sets off a tingle down my spine like I've walked through this scenario before. I rub my forehead, pushing aside that silly notion, wishing I had two aspirin, when I overhear the nun asking the sailor to assist her getting the children off the train.

'Be glad to help.' He stands at attention, ready.

'God bless you, young man, and keep you safe.' She lays a hand on his sleeve and smiles at him. I swear he blushes.

'Where to, Sister?' He picks up her big black satchel.

'The Reverend Mother will be waiting for us on the platform, then it's off to St Mary Cecilia's, the children's new home.'

St Mary Cecilia's? Can't be. The orphanage run by the nuns closed after the war. In God's name, where am I?

'Kate, there you are!'

I spin around and see a young girl bouncing down the aisle. The soldiers are whistling and cheering, making way for her like she's a princess walking the red carpet.

'Lucy?' I gasp. It *is* my little sister, isn't it? She looks so young and not so innocent in her slim tweed skirt and fuzzy white sweater, bobby sox, and loafers. She has Ma's long, black overcoat slung over her shoulders. Strutting and flirting, she doesn't look a bit cold. I see a familiar holiday ribbon tied in her hair in a bow as red as her lipstick. Or is it *my* lipstick she's wearing? What makes me think that?

'How'd you get on the train before me?' Lucy says, laughing and looking over her shoulder at a cute corporal with broad shoulders. I'm not surprised when he winks at her and she winks back.

'I – I don't know,' I utter with a stupid smile on my face.

'It don't – doesn't matter. See, I'm learning?' She laughs. 'What's important is you gave out the cherry jam and cracker sandwiches we made yesterday.'

'Yesterday?' I barely get the words out.

'Yes.' She cups her mouth with her hand. 'Don't forget our bet. The next train we meet, I'll be wearing nylons and not these ugly bobby sox.' She grins. 'Right, big sister?'

*Oh no.* Crackers and cherry jam. Nylons and that silly bet. All that happened the week before Jeff and I were going to elope and get married. Now here I am. On the train. With a whole world of things in my mind no one else knows. Frightening things. Like how the war drags on until 1945 and so many of these boys will never make it home.

The ladies and girls of Posey Creek met every train that stopped here during the war. A chance to give the servicemen and women a few moments of home. Not only our jam cracker sandwiches, but pies and cookies. Cakes and coffee served in white ceramic cups. Bottles of milk. Reading material, writing paper, even razors.

Many soldiers were tired and homesick. They reveled in getting off the train and stretching their legs. Posey Creek was a water stop where the trains rolled in and remained here for ten to fifteen minutes, long enough for us to give these men whatever we could. We weren't a big town, but we did our part to assure the soldiers we were behind them. Was it enough? I wonder now.

I was so wrapped up in doing my part to help these soldiers, I didn't see how scared many of them were. How could we? We were young and innocent ourselves and had no idea the horrors of war facing these men. The women, too, especially the nurses who served on the battlefield. What these servicemen and women experienced after they pulled out of the train station in our little town and went overseas stayed with them long after they came home to their wives, husbands, and sweethearts.

Like how the war affected our local pastor, Reverend Summers, when he returned to Posey Creek after serving in the South Pacific. The chaplain was a shadow of himself after the war, but his faith kept him strong. He counseled released prisoners of war with mental scars so horrible, he told his wife, Mildred, he questioned how God could allow it.

What sticks in my mind is when he came to see me after he heard about Jeff. Even a reverend isn't immune to pillow talk. Mildred, a stalwart ally in my plan to marry Jeff, was worried about me.

He tried to help me, speaking with me about the Jeff we both knew, the rambunctious kid who got into one scrape after another because he was so curious about everything. The talented boy who never heard a word of his Sunday school lesson because he was drawing in his prayer book.

Then Reverend Summers told me the family didn't receive a letter about Jeff's last mission from the Army chaplain assigned to his unit. That it was his job to help the family through their grieving process by providing as many details as possible about their loved one's final days.

I was in too much pain to dig deeper into why Jeff didn't

come back. I had my suspicions, but I kept them to myself. Back then, I had no choice but to accept the explanation the Army handed down, that Jeff died returning from a bombing mission over Germany.

Now I do. Jeff never flew with that crew.

A new sparkle of hope ripples through me, giving me confidence. That letter is more real to me than ever. It's the reason I'm here. My hand goes to my coat pocket and the paper crackles between my fingers. *Yes*, it's there. Even more fantastic is the tingling sensation I get in my gloved fingers as I count the buttons on my coat. One... two... I keep going... three, four... until I get to the bottom...

Five... *six*. I suck in my breath, disbelieving. All there.

That means everything swirling around in my mind is true. Somehow, somewhere, I found a portal to a moment in time so important to me that when I had the chance to walk through it, I didn't hesitate. Could my red coat be the conduit? I'm wearing the same clothes. I try to understand what happened to me and, after putting aside anything remotely practical, I settle on the whimsical. It's what I want, isn't it?

*Yes. My darling Jeff. I'm here to save you.*

I pat my coat pocket. Nothing will stop me from warning him. *Nothing*. In spite of the chaos and turmoil roiling through my brain, an unbelievable and impossible scenario is rewriting itself, like pages flipping backwards. Stopping at a place in a book written twelve years ago. The signs are there. The train filled with soldiers. My kid sister sixteen again. The poster. The different interior of the train. Lastly, the sixth button on my coat. As shiny and new as it was then.

I'm home for Christmas. *Really* home. My heart sings.

Ma is in the kitchen fixing supper and Pop will head

home later from the mill with his dented, old lunch pail. Frank Junior is out on the baseball field throwing pitches.

My heart sings loudest of all when I think about Jeff. The only man I ever loved. He's at the mill, but he'll be waiting for me tonight down at the big ole cherry tree. I accept what I know is impossible. I want it so bad, I don't care. I link arms with my sister and get off the train.

In 1943.

# 8

DECEMBER 13, 1943

'Did you hear the news, Kate?' Lucy smiles as pretty as a paper doll as we walk up and down the train platform, giving out donuts to soldiers hanging out the train windows.

'You mean the reduced ration points for pork, or the coal shortage?' I ask, trying to read the headlines on the newspaper in a soldier's hand while he gulps down a bottle of milk. *The Posey Creek Courier*. My heart skips a beat when I read about Yank planes bombing Germany and the Japanese fortifying the Marshall Islands.

The date on the newspaper confirms I'm back home a week before Jeff gets called up and leaves for training. A week before we're going to elope and get married. Whether it was fate or a bump on the head that brought me here, I'm not leaving.

Lucy has no idea what turmoil burns within me. She grins like an innocent kitten playing tag with a ball of yarn. 'Who needs coal?' she says, flirting with another soldier. 'I've got plenty of company to keep me warm.'

'Lucy Arden, explain yourself and no more flirting.' I'm fired up. I feel so powerless to help these boys.

'You're too darn serious, Kate,' she says, 'especially at Christmas.'

'You're right, little sister. These soldiers need smiles, not pouts.'

'To get everybody into the holiday spirit,' she says, 'Mrs Summers will carry on the Christmas tree lighting ceremony before the dance on Saturday night.'

I blink. Christmas lights during the war?

'Are you sure, Lucy?' I squeeze my eyes shut. Is my dream over before it starts? Is this a cruel joke? A retelling of history in my time I don't know about?

Then I remember why the memory escapes me. I didn't go to the ceremony. I thought only of myself and getting ready for the dance. Another childish moment I'm not proud of.

'It's only for an hour and starts at five-thirty. We're going to sing Christmas carols and light candles. Mrs Summers said she's hoping we'll have a big tall tree with shiny tinsel and ornaments the children made at Sunday school. She hinted she's working on special stars everyone will love.' Lucy lowers her voice. 'I heard most people tossed their glass ornaments made *you know where*.'

Not surprising some folks covered the Made in Germany or Made in Japan labels with war stamps to hide it. Our boys are fighting and dying over there so it's understandable we'll do anything to assuage our pain.

I exhale, trying to get my bearings. The train station is as I remember it, but filled with servicemen and canteen ladies. I'm tense, nervous. I fidget with the buttons on my coat. Lucy notices I'm not myself so she hits me with, 'Ma says I can wear your green corduroy jumper since you don't wear it anymore.'

'It's yours, Lucy.' I give her a squeeze.

'It'll look so pretty with your white lace blouse.' She glances sideways to gauge my reaction.

'Yes, it will, won't it?' I say, not protesting. How can I refuse her anything?

She blinks. 'Your charm bracelet, too.'

'Anything you want, Lucy, it's yours.' I smile at her.

'Are you feeling okay, Kate? You *never* let me wear your charm bracelet.'

A sterling silver bracelet I got for my sixteenth birthday. Ma sold extra jam to get it for me and that makes it special. Tiny charms including a Victorian heart, flowers, a tiny teddy bear, and a cute puppy with big eyes. When war was declared, we added charms for neighbors who went off to war. A medical insignia charm for Annie Bolton. We went to school together and she joined the WACs, Women's Army Corps, as a nurse. Sailor cap charms for the Pedesky brothers, both serving on the same ship in the Navy. A tank charm for Wally Smith, all grown up and a tank commander. Others followed and it became a family piece over the duration of the war. I gave it to my sister for her graduation as a way of passing it down.

'Why not?' I say without missing a beat. 'It will be yours someday, so why wait? I want you to enjoy it now.'

'Now I *know* something's wrong.' She pulls me along as if she doesn't know what I'll say next and heads toward the first-aid booth. 'I'm taking you to the Red Cross lady and have her take your temperature.'

'I'm fine,' I say, laughing.

'If you're sure you're okay, Kate,' she insists, anxious to leave.

'I'm sure.'

She exhales with relief and then fluffs her hair. 'There's this Marine waiting for me over by the coffee urn.' She lowers her eyes. 'He's so dreamy.'

'What about the corporal I saw you winking at?' I tease her. A warmth spreads through me. It feels good to spar with her again. We often traded flippant comments in good fun and fought over silly things like who got the last of the root beer since the government put restrictions on production. But we were always there for each other if one of us was hurting.

'Don't worry, big sister, there's enough of me to go around.'

'That's what I'm worried about, Lucy. These are nice boys, but they're still men.'

'*Men-in-training*, Helen calls them.' She sucks in a sharp breath. 'I love training them.'

I roll my eyes. Oh, God, help me, did my little sister have to grow up so fast? I'll keep an eye on her while I'm here. So many young girls – some younger than Lucy – ended up as Victory Girls, often following servicemen to camp or entertaining them at home when their parents were at work or asleep. They wanted so much to grab a piece of what they saw as the excitement of war, they lost their innocence for a movie and a bag of peanuts.

I make a mental note to have a talk with Helen. Helen Linder has been my best friend since she and her mom moved here when I was in the eighth grade. They came here from Indiana to start again in a new town after her father died. Her mother opened a small dress shop in town, specializing in designing hats. She's a lovely woman with graceful hands and a long neck made more elegant by the elaborate chignon she wears piled up high on her head.

Helen, on the other hand, has the kind of figure men ogle. She never lost her new girl-in-town status and is considered 'fast'. She's a charmer. Smart and funny. She's an only child and spoiled rotten, but you can't help but like her. She has a quirky way of looking at the world that makes you think twice. I admired that about her and wished I could be the same. She inspired me to leave Posey Creek after the war and in a strange way I have her to thank for giving me the gumption to go after a job in New York. Helen has to be here somewhere. She always met the trains. No doubt I'll find her surrounded by soldiers. But first, I have to set Lucy straight.

'Men have, you know, feelings that can get out of control.'

'I can take care of myself, Kate,' Lucy says, and then whispers in my ear. 'It's you I'm worried about.'

'What do you mean?' I ask warily.

'You've been walking with me for ten minutes up and down the train platform with every soldier and sailor giving you the eye and you ignore them. And you haven't once mentioned your beau. Your *secret* beau,' she emphasizes, her eyes darting everywhere.

'You don't believe me about Jeff marrying me, do you?' I can't suppress a cold shudder running through me as I utter those words. Knowing it didn't happen and doing my best not to give myself away.

'Nope. See you around, Kate.'

Then she's off, waving to a smiling Marine munching on a sandwich and a donut at the same time. I can't see his face clearly with his cap pulled down low, but I have no doubt he's handsome. I see him pointing at me and asking questions. My little sister looks peeved. I'm worried about her. If there's one thing I don't want to change, it's her meeting Jimmie and marrying him. Whatever they fought about is real enough in Lucy's eyes to ask me to come home, but I have no doubt they're meant for each other no matter what.

A thought occurs to me. What if I don't get back to my own time? What will happen to Lucy? I must admit it's overwhelming, trying to live both in the past and the future. How will I get back after I save Jeff? Or is that part of the deal? That I stay here?

It's too much for me. I can't take it in all at once. All I know is I have to find Jeff and live every moment I can with him. Because it will have to last me the rest of my life if I can't change the future.

I wander up and down the train platform, planning my next move. I love every minute of what I see. Ladies and girls waving handkerchiefs and carrying baskets of food for the soldiers piling off the train or hanging out the windows for the ten-minute stop. I see the porters loading luggage, the mail clerks heaving great sacks into the freight car. Letters from men in the middle of the fighting, letters from wives and mothers and sweethearts sending them a snapshot photo. It's the most thrilling thing I've witnessed. A country at war. Showing strength and support for our boys.

I let the tears well up. I can't help it. I don't know if I'm crying for the boys shipping out or because I'm home. Both, I guess. Two very different emotions pulling at me so hard, I don't know which end is up. There's so much I want to do, see, and oh, God, I want to grab Ma by her apron strings and take refuge in her arms. Tell her I love her. Get Pop to open up more with me. Hug my brother, Frank Junior, already taller than me and tell him to keep his head down in the future. Do I dare believe I can save him, too?

I look at every face, hoping somehow Jeff is here at the station, helping out the volunteers with lifting the big pots of coffee and checking the schedule with the railroad workers.

He used to like chatting with the soldiers. Hearing their stories, giving them encouragement, telling them his mill was ready to supply them with the writing paper they needed to send their letters home to their sweethearts and their families when they were overseas. He was aching to get into uniform, but he couldn't immediately. Not while the mill was running at full steam twenty-four hours a day, every day except Sunday, turning out war materials for the fight. Running the family business wasn't his calling, he told me more than once. Serving his country was. But for now, in 1943, I remember he'd resigned himself to his role at the mill. He stepped up production by utilizing the manufacturing methods he learned while he was away at college. I typed up the letters and the memorandums authorizing the changes.

A funny smile lights me up inside and I bite down on my lip. I'll never forget the time he slipped a personal memo between my shorthand notes. A drawing he did of me on an October day when the sun hung lazily in the sky like an orange pumpkin, when a light breeze kicked up and blew my hair around my shoulders. He caught the moment in a pencil sketch as I leaned up against the cherry tree and looked out over the fields plump with the harvest. He added a colonial stone house standing in the distance as a nice backdrop. An elegant two story home we passed by a few times in his roadster when we took the dirt road by the river. When I asked him why, he said the house held happy memories for him. He didn't explain further and I never asked.

I was too intrigued by his drawing of me.

'Is that me?' I said, not believing the soft, elegant profile was mine. Wispy ash blonde hair curling at the ends. My lips full, my nose straight. I looked like I belonged in another time when ladies flirted with handsome highwaymen who sought to steal a kiss. I held the paper by the edges, careful not to touch the soft, gray-black etches depicting a young girl in love. Strong yet tender strokes. As if the artist was intimate with her and madly in love. My cheeks tinted pink when I saw the words scrawled across the top.

J.G. Ma chérie pour toujours.

My darling forever. *J.G.* for Jelly Girl.

I stared at him, not knowing what to say.

'You're even more beautiful when you look at me like that,' he said as I wrapped my arms around his neck and he picked me up and twirled me around. I was so young and he was so strong. If what I believed happened to me is real, that was only weeks ago here.

When I was nineteen.

A sudden grab to my insides makes me come to a stop. Not move another step in this sea of humanity everywhere around me. Soldiers, girls, and ladies. Neighbors waving at me, asking me to grab a basket and hand out sandwiches. As if nothing about me is different. As if I *am* nineteen. That's impossible, isn't it?

I look around me. Every soldier smiling at me, every local girl handing out coffee, is exactly as they should be. Not me. I'm older. Twelve years older. Okay, maybe I haven't changed that much. My curves are more womanly, but I still cut a slim figure in pumps and a fitted suit. My hair is shorter and blonder, my brows finely arched, cheeks rouged. I wear pancake makeup and red, red lipstick. Some things never change, but I can't possibly look the same as I did at nineteen in a tight pink sweater and pencil-thin skirt. I'm afraid to go into the powder room. Afraid to look into a mirror. Afraid of what I'll see.

But I do it anyway.

## 9

One tiny mirror hangs by a crooked wire over the sink.

The two faucets with their ornate, decorative handles are tarnished as if nothing erases the fingerprints of time. The white tiled walls with the blue pinpoint flowers look exactly as I remember. The powder room is clean and smells of a sharp antiseptic. No doubt the stationmaster's wife doesn't want the servicewomen who pass through Posey Creek to linger too long primping at the mirror and miss their train pulling out.

A precocious teenage girl is doing her best to draw a bow mouth in the mirror. She goes over her lips numerous times. It's anything but a perfect bow.

I stand behind her, fussing with my hat, waiting for my big moment to look into the glass, trying to get a peek. I can't see myself clearly. The mirror hangs at an odd angle and is warped around the edges, like a funhouse mirror. I'm wearing the same suit and shoes from my own time along with the red coat.

The key to my coming here.

'Mind if I show you a lipstick trick?' I'm anxious to get my turn at the mirror.

'I... guess so.' Her brow furrows as she wipes her lips clean with her handkerchief.

'You'll be pretty as a picture when I'm done.' I take the tube of color and make the bow in the middle of her lips and then start at the corners of her mouth and apply the color inward. Then do her lower lip.

She looks at herself in the mirror and squeals. 'That's perfect.'

I smile. 'I learned that trick from a salesgirl at the makeup counter at—' I stop before I say the name of an exclusive department store in New York. I'd never traveled any farther than the Jersey shore when I was nineteen. I don't need any slipups.

'You're Lucy's sister, aren't you?' the girl says, warming to me.

'Yes.' I stand where the light from the high open window shines down on me. I can't look too different if she recognizes me.

The teenage girl looks down at my legs. 'I see Lucy didn't win the bet.'

'What?' I ask, not liking where this is going.

'You're wearing the stockings.'

'I am?'

*Oh, God, how does she know?*

'I ran my last pair a month ago. My mother says we can't afford leg makeup, so I have to use gravy to color my legs.' She snickers. 'Except my ma's gravy is too greasy.'

'It's important to save grease for the war effort,' I say like a schoolteacher before I can stop myself. I smile, remembering how Ma salvaged drippings along with tin cans.

'I'm doing my part feeding the soldiers.' She winks. 'Thanks to your help with my lipstick.' Then she's off before I can stop her.

'Hey, wait!' I call after her. I follow her outside. 'Did Lucy say why we made the bet?'

She's gone, lost in the crowd scurrying to make sure all the service personnel have food and newspapers before the train leaves. I can barely contain myself. Wait until I get my hands on my mouthy little sister. She's exactly the type the government preaches to with their campaign about not gossiping. If she told anybody about Jeff and me, I'll wring her neck. I forget about looking into the mirror – or is it because I don't want to? – and go after Lucy. I find her grabbing a magazine and a newspaper.

'Why did you tell your friends about our bet?' I ask, upset.

'I... I don't know.' She avoids my gaze. 'I guess because everybody was talking about what they're getting for Christmas and I wanted to show them up.' She smirks. 'Especially that prissy Gloria Allen. She was bragging about getting a silk nightgown and French perfume.'

'Forget Gloria.'

'I didn't tell anyone about you and Jeff, I swear.' She stands up straighter, lifts her chin. Her eyes take on the color of a warm green sea, begging me to believe her. I have no choice. I carry around the guilt of knowing what will happen to her a few Christmases from now. She's such an innocent. That doesn't let her completely off the hook. I let Lucy be my mirror before I take another step in this world.

'Do I look different, Lucy?'

'No.' She wriggles her nose. 'Except that's a fancy suit for work.'

It's supposed to be my wedding suit. I never got the

chance back in this time to ask her to help me with the hem, but I couldn't resist wearing it for my trip home, as if it has a special magic and it has. I'm here. Am I crazy or does it feel a bit looser?

'You're wearing your favorite red coat,' she continues. 'I've never seen that blue silk hat before.'

I hid it in my closet, waiting for the day Jeff and I were to be married.

Testing my generosity, Lucy can't resist adding. 'I'll borrow it next time.' She sees her Marine giving me the onceover and that perturbs her. 'Then my fellow over there will look at me like that.'

She stomps off when she hears two soldiers whistle at me as they walk by. I can't help but smile. I don't blame her. She doesn't want her Marine to like her big sister better. I acknowledge the compliment from the soldiers with a 'V for victory' sign and then wave with the other girls huddled on the platform as the servicemen get on the train and it rolls out of the station. Tomorrow there will be another train, more soldiers. The ladies and girls take turns, making sure every train is met.

Secretly, I'm clinging to the hope I'll find Jeff at the mill, tell him about the letter, and then I'll be back in my own time and he'll be with me. I sigh. A pipe dream, but it's nice to think about and one I'm not giving up. I'm here for a reason. Being given a second chance is a powerful incentive to do almost anything to make it happen.

The winter sun decides it's time for everyone to go home now the train has left. I pull up my fake fur collar. The mill is over a mile from the train station, so I start walking. I'm determined to find Jeff before something unexpected happens and I disappear as quickly as I got here.

\* \* \*

'Kate, wait up!'

I turn to see my friend Helen racing up the road behind me on her bicycle. She looks smart in her navy slacks, woolen blazer, and crisp white blouse with a patterned scarf around her neck blowing in the breeze. Her ebony-dark hair is covered by a snood.

'Helen,' I say with a warmth in my voice I don't hide when she rides up beside me. 'It's so good to see you.' We have a strong friendship, not the zany, sometimes combative, but loving relationship I have with my sister.

'I thought you were working today,' she says curiously. She gets off her bike and we walk together away from town, heading toward the mill.

'I was... I had something to do in town first.' A persnickety breeze blows off my hat. I grab it before it hits the dirt.

'Your *hair*, Kate.' She lets out a low whistle. 'So that's where you were. At *Maisie's*.'

The local beauty shop. Maisie has an eye for the newest styles, curling and frizzing ladies' hair as her glasses slide down to the tip of her nose.

I smooth down my hair, surprised to find out it's pulled up at the sides into long barrel rolls in the front with loose curls in the back. I smile. Victory rolls.

'You like it?' I ask.

'You look like a film star with that hairdo.'

Is that jealousy I hear in her voice? Helen always liked to show everyone she's the number one glamour girl in town. She had to do something to escape her mother's critical eye, seeing how she can never meet the woman's approval.

'I thought a new hairstyle would be fun for the holidays.' I put my hat back on before she can look any closer. I did get my hair done at Maisie's that day. Ma gave Maisie extra jam for her son to take with him when he left for camp and she wanted to do something nice for Ma. She offered to do my hair like she saw the movie stars wear in the magazines. I couldn't be happier with the new style. I wanted to look older back then – only a nineteen year old would wish that – and pretty for Jeff.

'I like it,' Helen says. 'Makes you look sophisticated, not like a kid, though you can pull off that "girl next door" look the magazines rave about better than anyone. You could be in the pictures.'

'Me? I'm a typist, not an actress.' I grin and can't resist adding, 'I'm thinking about becoming a writer.'

'You mean write racy novels?' She laughs. 'You'll have to use a man's name to get away with it.'

'I want to work for a magazine in the city.'

'Now I get it.'

'What?' I ask.

'The new hairdo. You want to get out of this town like I do and make something of yourself.'

I had ambitions to write back then, but they stayed under the radar because I was so deeply in love with Jeff. I couldn't imagine a future without him. I wonder, can a woman have it all? A man *and* a career?

Whatever crazy idea Helen has about my looks, it works for me. No one will question why I act more mature. I look the same as I did back then. Regarding any change in my attitude, they'll think it's the hairdo that makes me act more sophisticated. I breathe out. I'm still me. A more glamorous me, but me. I brush back the curls at the nape of my neck and wet my lips. I can't let the subject of working women drop.

'Someday they won't call women in uniform "petticoat soldiers" or look at women in management like we're ghosts. Women will make their way in the professional world,' I say, taking a big step forward and not apologizing for it. 'Which reminds me, Helen. Lucy looks up to you and she has this idea the soldiers who pass through here are hers for the taking. She's a charming flirt, but some guy may take it the wrong way.'

'She's got to grow up sometime, Kate.'

'Not in the back of the train station with the wrong guy with fast hands.' I have to say what's on my mind. 'You and I can take care of ourselves.' I fended off more wandering hands in the Holtford Company supply room than I care to admit. 'Lucy still believes in Santa Claus.'

Helen laughs, but I've made my point. 'Oh, how I envy your sister.'

'You do?'

'I never had anyone care about me like you do for her.'

I see a look of hurt on her face. It's quickly replaced by her familiar smirk. Helen is good at hiding her feelings about her mother. 'Don't worry about Lucy. She'll find a husband and have a bunch of kids and live happily ever after, while you and I keep chasing rainbows.'

'What is that supposed to mean?' I don't hide the surprise in my voice.

'Jeff Rushbrooke is a good man, but his mother will never allow her precious son to marry one of us.'

I look at her and to my horror, she believes she's helping me by saying that. 'You've been talking to Lucy.'

She smiles. 'I don't have to. I overheard the pernicious Mrs Rushbrooke talking to someone on the phone when I delivered her latest piece of hat frippery. Her back was to me, but she said in a clear voice that her boy Jeffrey was headed to Washington for big things before this war was over.'

'She doesn't know about us,' I assure my friend.

'Doesn't she?' Helen shoots back. 'Then why did she give me the third degree about you when she hung up the phone and saw me standing there?'

'What did she want to know?'

'If you were smitten with anyone, to use her words.'

I wince. 'What did you tell her?'

Helen throws her head back and laughs. 'That you're writing to so many boys overseas you have writer's cramp.'

'Oh, you didn't,' I say, panicked. 'What if Jeff hears about that?'

My mood shifts into pure terror, imagining my mission back in time dissipating like smoke if he calls off our marriage and never wants to see me again.

She stops her bike and grabs my hand. 'My dear Kate, if you could capture the look in that man's eyes every time he sees you, you wouldn't ask me such a silly question. He knows his mother and her hurtful games. I figured out you two were an item when I saw you together at the pictures, though you were trying to hide it. He loves you more than anything and nothing she says will change that. Be careful around that woman. Promise?'

I nod. 'I wonder...' A horrible thought hits me. Does his mother have something to do with Jeff's assignment overseas? Is she that hateful toward anyone she considers beneath her that she'll risk her son's life? Or is she so pompous she doesn't believe anything can happen to him? I let that thought simmer in my brain. 'She won't get away with her prejudices much longer,' I say with a fervent tone in my voice. 'Things will change after the war and she can't stop that.'

'You think so?' She wrinkles her nose, as if she finds that hard to believe.

'I know so,' I can't help but add. Women like Mrs Rushbrooke hate change, anything that threatens their pampered world where women of her class rule and don't want competition from girls like me willing to do what it takes to better ourselves. I fought hard to make my way in publishing, putting up with mundane coffee duties and hard stares from the male staff.

I pick up my pace. I want this conversation to end before I stick my foot in my mouth. Again. Any indiscriminate comment could set my compass pointing the wrong way. Everything I came back to change could go south. Fast. I know what happens when Helen makes good on her desire to leave town. My heart pings. I don't want to go there. Not now.

We walk along the dirt road, each lost in our own thoughts. I fret like a hen gathering up her wandering chicks. I can't keep track of every emotion, every fact that splatters my brain like changing hues of color. Some growing darker, others lighter. The good with the sorrow. I want to shut my eyes and a piece of me, a small piece mind you, wants to be back on that train heading home years from now.

Even my aching feet – which hurt more than they have in years from walking in pumps – don't stop me from going forward in this drama. I'm faced with a problem I never foresaw when I got off the train. Knowing the future isn't the utopia it's cracked up to be. It frazzles my nerves, upsets any sense of normality I have, and makes me want to cry like a baby because I know what happens to the folks of Posey Creek. Sadness, happiness... disappointment. Will I go through this insanity every time I run into someone I know?

Questioning whether or not I should tell them where they end up after the war?

I'm sinking deeper and deeper into a bowl of thick molasses, as Ma says. It's then I make up my mind to stop playing fortune teller. Settle down and do what I came back here for. Warn Jeff. I pray to God with all my heart I can set him off on a different course and save his life. Whether or not he comes home and marries me... I can't hope for everything. I can wish on those stars we saw in the dark sky, the two of us standing under the cherry tree and holding each other tight, that he *does* return. Wish for a life with him and if I can do good elsewhere while I'm here, I will.

I can't drive myself – and the town – off the edge into a dark abyss blabbing everything I know about the war and the people who live here. I'll either end up losing every friend I have or be packed off to the closest mental hospital. I can't take the chance of anyone stopping me from saving Jeff and that includes Pop. He doesn't approve of me seeing him. Pop is a supervisor on the factory floor and because there's a shortage of manpower to cut trees, his duties often take him to the timber camp down by the river to check on the supply of pulp wood. Most likely, he's there today. Still, I have to be careful. Which means I have to act like it's an ordinary winter afternoon in 1943 when I say goodbye to Helen.

Then I can walk through the front doors of the mill and into the arms of the man I love.

## 10

Jeff is nowhere on the factory floor.

Women wearing trousers and turbans scurry back and forth, some smiling, others serious, but all dedicated to their jobs. Their chatter blends with the melodic grinding of the raw materials needed for the war effort. I breathe out a sigh when I hear 'You'll Never Know' with a big band sound playing over the loudspeaker system. A way of reducing fatigue and increasing efficiency among the workers. Women are doing men's work and doing it well. I get a chill when I see the machines that made the pretty stationery and book bindings before the war replaced by the steel machines that turn out cardboard boxes to hold blood plasma bottles to save lives on the battlefield.

I keep looking, but I can't find Jeff. That surprises me. He often spent time down here with the workers giving pep talks, checking production times, and flirting with the female workers in his usual dashing style, making them feel special.

He was Mr Jeffrey to them to differentiate him from his father. They loved him and he could do no wrong in their eyes. He always made sure the wicker basket in the break-room was filled with apples and oranges. Fresh flowers placed in the powder room every day. Once a month, he encouraged them to have a 'turban contest' to see which woman had the most colorful turban on the floor. The winner got free passes to the Old Grande movie theater for Saturday night. A way to boost their morale.

All that changed when Jeff is declared MIA. I'll never forget the tremendous burden I felt. As if it was my fault, that somehow because he loved me, he was in the wrong place at the wrong time. That these women would never forgive me. It wasn't true, and though a few suspected we dated, no one knew we planned to spend the rest of our lives together. I often wonder how they'd have reacted if they did. Standoffish that I was no longer one of them? Or intensely sad, paying special attention to me and taking me into their private fold? I'll never know.

I walk the factory floor, the steady droning of the machines drowning out the tapping of my pumps. I look around the mill, the busy work atmosphere humming along in perfect rhythm. In my mind, all I can see is the entire work force devastated when they get the news weeks from now, that Jeff is missing. They'll be whispering to each other, grabbing hands and squeezing them. As if they can bring him home safe by sheer willpower. I remember how the ladies at Rushbrooke Mill held special prayer get-togethers for him, saying a rosary or reading Scriptures.

That was still nothing like when the news comes about him being killed in action. They were beside themselves with anguish. The women couldn't keep their handkerchiefs dry. The foreman suspended work for an hour, then the women returned in shifts, more determined than ever to do their job and get the mill's war goods out for shipment.

In the days that followed, they used up their sugar rations to bake cakes and pies and then take them up to Wrightwood House for the family as a way of expressing their grief and support. I doubt Mrs Rushbrooke noticed. More likely, she sent the proffered food downstairs to the servants' kitchen. I'll never tell them that.

Jeff didn't have time for dating when the mill was on a twenty-four-hour schedule but he made time for me, begging me to meet him down at the big ole cherry tree after work. He'd ask me about my day while he kissed my neck, tickling me and making me laugh. In late summer, the air was hot and still and the only breeze came from the swaying branches of the cherry tree when he pressed me against the trunk and kissed the tip of my nose. In winter, the air was cold and frosty and there was no breeze from the long, barren branches, but he held me tight to keep me warm.

I've never felt so special again. God, I have to see him.

'I need Mr Jeffrey to sign off on a memo.' I grin so widely as I take off my hat, I swear my lie would freeze my smile in place. 'Has anyone seen him today?'

The ladies stop, look at each other, and then shake their heads.

'No, Miss Arden, we'd be smiling if we did,' says one woman, nudging her friend who nods.

'Thank you, ladies.'

Before I give myself away, I take off for Mr Clayborn's office but not before I hear the whispering and giggling behind my back. They pretend to fix stray hair escaping from their turbans. I have no doubt they're gossiping about me. Will my new hairdo ever cease to be a source of amusement?

I check the foyer where the workers clock in, the familiar *Buy War Bonds* poster pasted where everyone can see it when they punch in. Everybody has a round badge with their name and picture to prevent anyone sneaking in who doesn't belong. Saboteurs are not unheard of, even in our small town.

Then I check the lunchroom where the mill kitchen staff serve fresh, nutritious lunches to keep up the workers' strength. Oh, have I missed these wonderful smells. Gravy and carrots and spice cake. I remember the fresh apple sauce and stews with hearty beans and fresh herbs from the Victory Garden planted on a sloping hill behind the factory. The ladies tended it during their breaks.

I also miss the camaraderie. We were insulated from a lot of what was happening overseas. The closest we came to seeing it up close was when the military trains sped through our little station without stopping, the flatbed train cars filled with tank after tank. The passenger cars would be over-flowing with soldiers hanging out of the windows, their faces grim but determined. No wonder we sat through hours and hours of newsreels at the Old Grande showing us what was happening over there. We wanted to feel what they were feeling. Everyone did their best to cheer the soldiers passing through, but I saw the anguish on the faces of the townsfolk. It was no secret the war had already taken a hundred thousand casualties.

I don't have the stomach to let on what I know about the husbands and sons who never come back. Daughters, too. One of the young women who left to join the Women's Army Corps is lost in a convoy sunk by the Nazis. She never makes it across the Atlantic.

I see the girl's mother, working the lever on a big

machine, doing her job. Head down, I do my best to avoid eye contact. No, I can't live with that knowledge eating me up inside. I'm so attuned to these workers, more so now, because this factory is my whole life during the war. So I do the unthinkable. I break a rule and it's a big one.

I spin around on my heel and head back to the woman.

'Have you heard from Carol Ann?' I ask her. She looks up, surprised I remember her daughter's name.

'Yes. I have her last letter in my locker.' Her grin is so huge, I want to cry. 'She's doing mighty fine, Miss Arden. She's a motor pool driver chauffeuring all them bigwigs around the Capitol, but she's itching to go overseas to help win this war. I don't know when, but the Lord does and He'll watch over her.'

Her words make me hesitate.

'I'm going to write her after work,' the woman continues. 'I'll tell her you asked about her.'

'Please do, ma'am, and when you write her, tell her...' I stumble, waiting to see if the floor rumbles beneath my feet, warning me, or a light flashes in my face. When it doesn't, I get a little braver, more confident I'm right in my thinking. I continue or I'll bust with misery and regret it for the rest of my life. 'Tell her our boys here need her, too. That what she's doing is as important as serving overseas.' I lean down and whisper. 'I hear Mr Jeffrey is headed to Washington to meet with the brass and he'll be disappointed if Carol Ann isn't there to drive him around.'

It works. The woman's eyes light up.

'Carol Ann will never forgive herself if she let Mr Jeffrey down. Yes, Miss Arden, I'll be writing her tonight and make sure she doesn't go volunteering for overseas duty just yet.'

I'm not surprised my words have the reaction they do. Jeff

has that much power over women. Including me. The only question is, will there be repercussions for my deed? I'll never know. It gives me more courage to tell Jeff about the letter. I breathe out a sigh of relief. I might have saved a young woman from death. Now to save my fiancé.

I finish my tour of the factory floor, my spirits lifted, but I can't find Jeff anywhere. I could go up to Wrightwood House and sneak in through the servants' entrance when the cook isn't looking. I did it all the time when I was a little girl. We'd often meet and he'd sneak frosted cakes and hard candy for us to munch on. What if Jeff isn't there? I have more of an opportunity to find out where he is here at the factory. Besides, I'm embarrassed to say I'm so filled with joy at doing good I take a few moments to enjoy my triumph. I swing my hips and hum a familiar holiday tune I heard on the radio last week. 'I'll be Home for Christmas.' Sure of myself, aren't I? Like I'm living a wildly romantic novel, except that instead of daydreaming, I have it in the palm of my hand. Until I run into the last person I want to see.

Timothy Rushbrooke.

'If you're not busy, Kate, we can go for a ride,' he says, baiting me.

'Sorry, Mr Rushbrooke, I have to get back to work.'

He acts like he doesn't know there's a war on.

'Too bad,' he says. 'I thought we'd drive over to Suttertown and take in a movie.'

*So your mother's spies don't see us together?*

It's no secret Timothy is a disappointment to Mrs Rushbrooke. He's lazy, irresponsible, gambles, and drinks too much. Jeff is her golden boy, which makes things worse for me. She's considered me a bad influence on him ever since we were kids. She hates me but, according to Helen, she doesn't know for sure I'm dating her son. God help me, she never will until we're married.

'I'm sure you have more important things to do, Mr Rushbrooke, than treat an employee to the pictures.'

'I'm supposed to be checking on production, but I find it rather boring.' He leans over and whispers in my ear. 'Let's get out of here. I won't tell, if you don't.'

'If I do... tell?' I don't back down. 'Then what will you do? Fire me?'

He knows that won't go over well with Jeff. He turns on his heel without so much as a leering look and leaves as abruptly as he came. No one on the floor likes Timothy. They see him as a privileged, spoiled brat. More than one female worker walks past him with her eyes down to avoid being the object of his attention. He sugar-talks the new girls into going out with him. The ones not smart enough to see through him end up with a bruised ego and a pink slip. His presence here bothers me. Something's up, but what?

I linger a few moments after he stomps off. I think about going after him, hoping to find out what's behind his sudden bravado to show up here at the mill, but it isn't my job to stick my nose into company politics. That point is brought home to me when I hear a gruff voice behind me bellow, 'Where on earth have you been, Miss Arden? Sipping tea with Mrs Roosevelt?'

Oh. No. My boss. Mr Clayborn.

His bark is worse than his bite, but today he sounds as angry as a big bear with his paw stuck in a spilled jar of honey. I stepped right into the mess. He never calls me Miss Arden unless Mr Rushbrooke Senior is within earshot. Did he see me talking with Timothy?

I turn around slowly, knowing this is a real test to see if I can pull off this charade. The man works with me every day from eight to five. He knows my quirks, my mediocre typing, and my penchant for daydreaming. Here we go.

'I've been right here on the floor, Mr Clayborn,' I say with a nonchalance I don't feel. 'Checking production schedules.' Luckily for me, he rarely notices what I wear so he doesn't give more than a quick glance at my silk suit.

'I don't care if you've been to Timbuktu and back. I want you in my office *now*!'

\* \* \*

I recognize the man from the train sitting in my boss's office. The silver-haired businessman seems amused yet puzzled. He says nothing, as if he's accustomed to being the man in charge and doesn't bother with office staff – though he's taken an interest in me. That worries me. What did I do? It turns out, it's what I *didn't* do.

'I sent you to meet Mr Unger at the train station, Miss Arden, but he says you walked right past him.'

'I... I didn't recognize him and then my sister Lucy came to fetch me.' I come out with a half-truth. I have to get out of this somehow.

'Family matters can wait.' He thinks a moment. 'It's not your ma, is it?' He's fond of my mother and I often thought he had a secret crush on her when they were younger.

'Ma's fine.' I wish he'd drop the subject so I can find out whether or not I'm fired. 'Lucy lost her ration card and wanted to know if I took hers by mistake.'

A lie, but it works. He nods, satisfied.

'Lucky for you, Miss Arden, the stationmaster directed him to the company car waiting for him.'

Mr Unger whispers something to my boss, which makes him nod his head up and down several times. He turns to me, but he doesn't look at me.

Here it comes. The heave-ho. How am I going to explain this to Ma?

'I'll deal with you later, Miss Arden. In the meantime, Mr Unger and I have important government business to discuss. If you'll excuse us...'

He ushers me out and closes the door. Leaving me wondering if I still have a job.

I have to admit my nineteen year old self is more efficient than I remember. Her desk is in order with each memo carefully marked and stacked, her logbooks are up to date, and her typewriter ribbons clean. Somewhere along the way, I developed bad habits in the workplace.

I fumble through the memos until I find the one from Mr Clayborn asking me to pick up this mysterious Mr Unger. It all comes back to me. After I had my hair done on my lunch hour, I raced off to the train station in the company car with Mr Rushbrooke's driver at the wheel and then jumped on board the train, going from car to car until I found him. Then, after making sure he was on his way to Rushbrooke Mills, I ran into Lucy and we spent the afternoon meeting and greeting the soldiers. It was our patriotic duty, so I got permission ahead of time.

I exhale, relieved to figure it out. So everything that happened already happened, except for the lively conversations I had with Lucy and Helen. So far, so good. I breathe out a sigh of relief when I find my purse inside the bottom drawer of my desk. I left the office without it, something I never do back in my own time. Amazing how our priorities change. I find my red lip tube and, using my round compact mirror, I apply fresh lipstick. I feel like me again. Now what?

I think about leaving my desk and asking Mr Rush-brooke's secretary where Jeff is – using the same excuse about needing his signature on a document – but I don't have that kind of freedom. I'm here to work, but I'm ready to jump out of my seat after spending twelve years without him. My need to see Jeff is eating at me because I know he's alive and I can't find him. He's my love, a man who fulfills my needs with every touch of his hand or every funny word he says. He claimed my heart and trapped me forever in a world where I want only him. I'm his and he's mine. So why are the fates toying with me like this?

I have to calm down before I do something stupid like walk out on the job when there's the possibility, a slight one I admit, that I'm not fired. I can't do that to Ma and Pop. They need my salary to keep us going and I willingly give it to them. Funny, when you're young you can live on love. As long as you have a good family.

I have the best.

To keep my mind occupied, I read through today's log, noting I penciled off this afternoon to meet the train so I don't have any pressing work to do. Which means I have to look busy, especially with the government man in Mr Clay-born's office. I have the feeling he's watching me.

I go about my work, though it takes me a while to remember where the stationery supplies are. I adjust the margins on the old manual typewriter and my fingers settle on the keys. Like a pair of old shoes, I slip back in time and start pounding them. Not easy. Several keys stick together.

What I wouldn't give for my new electric typewriter. I have a hard time keeping my mind on my work. I'm a better typist than I was back then, which raises an eyebrow or two. I notice other typists looking up in surprise when they hear my staccato typing. I smile. If they only knew.

I pretend I'm typing a business letter – I don't dare type anything incriminating, so I copy a recipe for meatless soup out of a magazine I find in the breakroom. My stomach growls. I'm hungry. How long since I've eaten? I don't want to think about it.

I keep looking at the clock. My rear end isn't used to sitting so long in a hard chair. I have to smile. I didn't notice it back then. All I thought about was doing a good job to impress Mr Clayborn so he'd send me upstairs to deliver the memos. Jeff's office is on the top floor and somehow I'd find myself going in that direction. I was so in love with him, it's a wonder I got any work done.

Now I go out of my way to avoid any office romance. I like my job and want to be a full editor someday. I spend a good deal of my day racing from the art department to the print department to taking meetings with the publisher. I'm beginning to appreciate the freedom I have.

Will my life in New York be gone if I save Jeff?

A funny feeling captures my brain. No, whatever happens, I'll write. I imagine myself the lady of a grand house in the future with three children running around while I bake bread and puddings all morning and write all afternoon until Jeff comes home. Then I'll make his favorite pot roast and fried potatoes and corn fricassee and we'll sit by the fireplace and hug each other after we put the children to bed after reading them a bedtime story.

All this runs through my head because I'm going crazy

waiting for my boss to call me into his office. I see him arguing with Mr Unger about something, which doesn't bode well for me. Whatever happens, it's my own fault. I embarrassed the company. I'm still trying to figure out how I got here. This is what I think happened. I took over the same space on the train occupied by my younger self when I went on board in 1943 to find Mr Unger. Because I was standing in the same place on the same train in the future, that strange coincidence brought me back here. Even the conductor didn't change. That has to be the answer.

I keep my eye on the goings-on in my boss's office. The two men go over blueprints and floorplans, nodding and making changes before they shake hands. Mr Unger looks pleased and nods in my direction as he leaves my boss's office with the blueprints under his arm. Unfortunately, I can't tell if he's forgiven me.

'Come in, please, Miss Arden.' Mr. Clayborn beckons me from behind his desk.

'Yes, sir.' I lower my head, trying to look contrite. I'm willing to fight for my job if I have to. Mr Clayborn doesn't ask me to close the door, which I take as a good sign.

'You're an excellent and skilled worker, Kate.' I relax. We're back to him calling me by my first name. 'Because of your actions, we almost lost that contract.'

*Don't panic. Not yet.*

'I'm sorry, sir,' I say in a firm voice. I don't back down. I'm not going to play the mousy secretary. 'I was wrong and I admit it. I promise you it will never happen again. We're in this fight together, but sometimes young people get carried away with the pressures they're not used to and make wrong decisions.'

'You mean Lucy.'

'No, sir. I mean me. All I'm asking for is another chance.'

'That's a very mature outlook, Kate, but it doesn't surprise me coming from you. That's why I couldn't believe it when I heard what happened.'

'Yes, sir.'

He looks at me with something in his eyes I can't read. Disappointment? 'You let the company down and if Mr Rush-brooke Senior hears about this—'

'Mr Clayborn, *please.*'

'He won't, Kate.' He smiles. 'It's our secret. Mr Unger won't mention it. He's on a tight schedule and must get back to Washington on the next train.' He laughs. 'In fact, he asked me *not* to fire you. He said you looked like you'd seen a ghost. He was concerned you were ill until Lucy found you and you two got off the train.'

I nod. I can only imagine what he saw. How *does* one look after traveling through time? Glassy-eyed? Disheveled? I feel a rumbling under my feet, alerting me to be careful. I got out of this mess, but I'm not done yet. I have to keep on my toes if I'm going to save Jeff. I'm about to thank my boss for keeping me on when a uniformed messenger from Western Union rushes by me and tips his cap to Mr Clayborn.

'Mr Harry Clayborn?' the boy asks.

'Yes.'

'Telegram for you, sir, from the War Department.'

Mr Clayborn doesn't move. His face goes ashen and he can barely raise his hand when the boy hands him the telegram. He digs into his pocket for a nickel to tip him. His son is serving in the Pacific. He rips open the envelope.

I wait for him to tell me what I already know.

## 11

'The telegram is from Mr Rushbrooke.' His voice trembles, but he quickly regains the steadiness I've come to expect from him. Then he heaves out a cleansing breath, the moment every father dreads pushed aside. For now. 'He won't be back in Posey Creek until early tomorrow morning.' He wipes off his forehead with his handkerchief, his voice filled with relief.

A bell goes off in my brain. I can't remember when, but I'm certain my boss received a Western Union telegram that changed him for the rest of the war when his son ended up in a POW camp in Japan. He'd have done anything to bring his son back safe, even go to war himself. I remember how he registered for the draft, mandatory military service, before they required men over forty-five to do so.

He's worried sick about his kid. I see the signs on his face. The deepening lines, the long stares out the window. The shuffling of his son's picture in his Navy uniform from one end of his desk to another, like he carries on conversations with him. But I know his boy came home in 1946, his body thin but his spirit strong.

I give my boss a moment to regroup. When I see him pick up some paperwork, I ask the question burning in my brain. 'Is Jeff with him?'

Mr Clayborn blinks. 'How'd you know?'

It all fits. Jeff going to the Capitol before leaving for his mission, what Helen overheard from Mrs Rushbrooke. Yet I can't let my boss suspect I know what's afoot.

'He told me yesterday when I saw him on the factory floor.'

'That's strange. I didn't hear about their trip to DC until this morning.'

'You know Jeff,' I say, laughing. 'He mentioned he'd be out of the office today.' I have to convince him nothing is out of the ordinary. 'He worries about the ladies on the floor and asked me to make sure they had fresh flowers in the powder room.'

Mr Clayborn accepts that because he has other things on his mind, like securing the government contract, but he's willing to share his thoughts with me.

'From what I gather, Kate, it's very hush hush. That boy is itching to get into the fight, but old Mr Rushbrooke is dead set against it.' He picks up a pencil and snaps it in two. 'I hate to think what will happen to the factory if he gets called up and Timothy is in charge. Production output, not to mention morale will go downhill fast.'

I bite back my words, pretending to think about what he said. Inside I'm ready to blurt out he's right. It's the beginning of the end for Rushbrooke Mills. If Jeff's father had put Mr Clayborn in charge, the mill might still be in business. I didn't think of it till now, but I have to make that happen for the workers of Posey Creek. If I talk to Jeff, will he listen to me?

I wipe the perspiration forming over my upper lip. My face feels hot. I'm beginning to find out how exhausting it is to keep up with the consequences of my journey back in time.

'Do you want me to send a reply to Mr Rushbrooke, sir?' I don't ask any more questions. We're expected to be fast, efficient typists but little more. Fortunately, I know Mr Clayborn isn't as strict as the other factory bosses and listens to my ideas. He enjoyed having a woman's viewpoint since he became a widower. Long after the war, I remember him as a kind and hardworking man who never got the recognition for his efforts to keep the mill productive during this time. Mr Rushbrooke gave Timothy the credit when the mill received an 'E' award for outstanding service to win the war. I'd like to change that, too, while I'm here.

Still, I have to know, why is Mr Rushbrooke in Washington at the War Department? Why is Jeff with him? Does it have anything to do with his mission in France? My throat tightens. Does Jeff already know he's leaving for an overseas assignment and there's no time for us to get married? I don't want to believe that.

'No reply, Kate,' Mr Clayborn says, interrupting my thoughts. 'I need you to type up the notes from my meeting with Mr Unger.'

'Yes, sir.' My disappointment shows on my face. When Mr Clayborn hands me the notes, he looks at me funny, as if he has something on his mind. 'No hurry, Kate. I planned to wait until tomorrow. I thought you asked for time off today to help at the canteen.' He scratches his head. 'I guess I was wrong.'

*No, you're not. I'm not supposed to be here in your office.*

That explains a lot. Why I don't remember this happening. It didn't. I blissfully spent this time getting ready for the holidays with Ma and Lucy, not knowing Jeff was in Washington with his father. He told me later he went to Philly to see about securing new equipment for the factory. I never questioned him.

Outside the office window, I see dusk slowly settling down like a filmy veil on what has been a long day and the next shift filing in, ready to work through the night. Production never stops, even with the holidays approaching. Which gives me an idea.

'What are you doing for Christmas dinner, Mr Clayborn?' I feel guilty for my mishap this afternoon. 'Ma would love to have you, and so would Pop.'

'That's swell of you to ask me, Kate, but I've got a place to go.' He doesn't say where, but I remember he drove to Suttertown on Christmas Eve. They had a canteen set up in the church community center for the servicemen and women. He volunteered to serve up Christmas dinner to the men so he could feel closer to his son. I don't try to change his mind. Some things in the past are best left as they were.

'Speaking of Christmas, Kate, we sure could use some help getting people to donate their old paper and not waste it wrapping Christmas presents.'

'*Mr Clayborn...*'

He takes a step back when he sees my arched brows. 'I'm not trying to ruin Christmas, Kate, but the military needs paper. We're on our way to a shortage.' He stops, calms down. 'Every piece of paper we save is a step closer to bringing our boys... my boy, home.'

I hate to see this wonderful, kind man so upset. He's right about people not giving a second thought to saving paper with the holiday wrapping in full swing. What we need is a catchy slogan to remind them. My work with the publicity department at Holtford gives me an idea.

'If you don't object, sir,' I begin, remembering an ad from the war I saw in a magazine when I researched a story last Christmas. 'What if I ask Mr Neville to take a picture of a female worker sitting on a big box wrapped up for Christmas?'

'Go on.'

'Instead of fancy wrapping paper, the box is covered with scrap paper or left bare and decorated with hand-drawn holiday decorations like candy canes, holly, and Santas. A way to encourage folks to make their own wrapping paper this year.'

'What a great idea, Kate.'

'Thank you, sir.' I beam. Score one for the local girl.

'I want you in the ad.' Tapping his fingers on the desk, he catches my eye. He's not joking.

'Me?'

'You're the prettiest girl we've got here.' He clears his throat. 'I'm sure I'm right in saying Jeff would agree.'

I blush. I have enough sense to keep my mouth shut. I can't hide anything from him. He knows about my frequent visits to Jeff's office to deliver memos. I never fooled him.

He isn't finished. Mr Clayborn rubs his chin. 'Too bad there's no spot for you in marketing, Kate. Mr Rushbrooke would never go for it. He hates the idea of women working anywhere but behind a stove.'

I give him a knowing look. 'Someday he'll be surprised what we women can do.'

I have to admit, I feel proud of myself for using my publishing experience to solve the problem, a way to show

Jeff's father I'm no slouch, that I'm a force to be reckoned with. I'm determined to change the past. Determined to marry the man I loved.

I type up the requisition in record time in spite of the sticking keys, and run it downstairs to the marketing department. Mr Neville loves the idea, assuming it's Mr Clayborn's. I roll my eyes. It never occurs to him I had something to do with it.

*Careful, don't get too smart. You've got a more important job to do.*

I have only a week to set things right between Jeff and me.

Heading back to my desk, I'm hot and sweaty from running up and down three flights of stairs. For all the adrenaline pumping through me, it's the lie Jeff told me that makes my heart pound. He knew he wasn't going away to basic training that day at the train station when we said goodbye. Even now, knowing what I do about wartime secrecy, I'm hurt. He could have given me a hint, a word. He didn't. Still, I can't let go of the idea that if I warn him, we'll be together and I'll have my perfect home and husband. Yes, I believe that because if I don't, I won't have the courage to tell him about the letter and how I got here. Of course, he'll say I watched too many outer space serials at the Saturday matinees when I was a kid, but when he sees how serious I am and I show him the proof, he'll have to believe me. I breathe out, slower.

When the factory whistle blows at five, I collapse, exhausted. But I have another hurdle to face before I see Jeff.

Something else is pulling at my heartstrings. A need to return to the nest. To rest my head against her shoulder. Tug at her apron and ask her to make me a cup of hot cocoa like she did before the war. With vanilla and cinnamon.

I need to see Ma.

\* \* \*

I'll never forget seeing three housewives huddled around the dinner table going over a huge map that covered a square wooden table from end to end, the smell of baby powder sticking to their clothes and the rich scent of kitchen grease clinging to their hair.

Posey Creek ladies, who before Pearl Harbor knew little about submarines or convoys, fought the war in their own way. Their crochet needles and balls of yarn would be put aside as they argued over where our Army would strike next. I forgot how serious these weekly meetings were with the women poking knitting needles into France or Holland and saying their piece with as much fortitude and surety as any general.

'I say the Allies hit Amsterdam next.' Mrs Bloom grabs a piece of hard candy out of the jar. Ma gives her a disapproving look. That jar is for servicemen when they get off the train. 'What with all them bridges the Nazis got hold of.'

'You got bats in your snood, Gert?' says Mrs Sims. 'I say we hit 'em hard in Poland.'

Ma grabs the candy jar before Mrs Bloom helps herself to more sweets. 'You're both wrong. Our boys will hit the beaches in France to win this war.' Then she smiles when she sees me. 'You forgot the candy jar for the soldiers when you left this morning, Kate.' Smoothing down her apron, she nods in approval. 'Maisie done right by you with the new hairstyle. Makes you look even prettier, if that's possible.'

'Thanks, Ma.' I beam. Her words reaffirm I look the same. Thank God.

That isn't what's making my heart race, my insides twist like a loaf of her braided bread. I miss her so much, it takes every ounce of my strength not to grab her and hug her close. Never let her go. My heart kicks me in the ribs as I study her closer. Eyes drooping, cheeks flushed, she looks tired. She's barely forty-two.

I try not to let my concern show. I hate how the years will take their toll on her. Her long, brown braid entwined around her head like a queen's knotted crown turns gray – she never cut it. Her lively hazel eyes dulled by loss. Her shoulders bent forward. Most of all, her hands. Fingers gnarled like tiny branches, but she never stopped putting up her jams even when she couldn't screw the lid tight on the glass jar. It hurts me. I vow to take care of her while I'm here, make her life easier.

"Course we won't have nothing left for them boys if Gert keeps feeding her sweet tooth,' Ma finishes.

'I'm as patriotic as you are, Mary Katharine Arden,' chimes in her friend. 'I donated my old girdles to the war effort, didn't I?'

'Because they don't fit no more,' Ma adds with a smirk. You can't get anything past her, but her war talk worries me. She's too close to the truth.

I take Ma aside so her friends can't hear us. 'What do you know about the invasion?'

'I might have heard something when I was up at the big house on the hill.' She winks at me. So Ma listens at keyholes, too. 'I saw that nice young Mr Jeffrey yesterday. My Lord, he was arguing something awful with his father. The minute he saw me bringing my jams, he stopped and smiled.'

'Did he ask about me?' I say, hopeful.

'No, child.' Her eyes dart around the room to see if her

guests heard. Fortunately, the two women are busy jabbing needles into the map, trying to outdo each other with their predictions. 'Is there something I should know, Kate?'

'No, Ma, nothing I swear.'

What can I say? *I want to marry him, but I can't unless I save him from a mission gone wrong.*

She'll never believe me. Dating Jeff isn't easy. We have to be careful what we say or do. He likes my mother, but he can't risk anyone in Mrs Rushbrooke's household asking questions about why he's chummy with her.

'I don't want to see you get your heart broke, Kate,' she offers in a voice colored so reverent, it's like a prayer. 'Mr Jeffrey is a good man, but he's not our kind.'

I clench my fists to my side. Now I know where Lucy gets such ideas. Doesn't anyone believe love conquers all?

'By the way, Ma,' I say, a mishmash of things going through my head with her sputtering about D-Day, 'don't go talking to anybody about our Army invading beaches in France, do you hear?'

'Why not?' She winces. 'It's the silliest idea I ever heard even if I did overhear Mr Rushbrooke muttering to himself about our boys landing on the sand like they're at the shore. What's the harm?'

'You don't want Pop to get fired, do you?' I want her to think about what she's saying so I bring it home to a place where she can understand the implications. 'Any talk about invasion isn't a good idea since he works at a war plant.'

'Of course not,' she says, horrified.

'Remember, loose lips sink ships.'

She zips her lips. 'You're right. I should have remembered that.'

'You're on the beam, Ma,' I say, using her favorite expression during the war. *Someday you'll know how right you are about those beaches*, I mutter under my breath as I hug her.

After her lady friends say their goodbyes, I spend the time before supper sitting at her side, rolling up yarn from her knitting basket, listening more than talking. About how cold the weather is but no snow, and if she'll have enough ration points for a Christmas turkey. Comforting, fuzzy moments that make me feel wrapped up in her love. Knowing I'll remember this afternoon with Ma and her neighbors conjuring up ways to win the war.

There's something else, too. The way she looks at me and smooths down my hair, pinches my cheeks, and then surveys me up and down like I'm a mannequin in a store window come to life. I swallow hard. I have the distinct feeling she senses something out of the ordinary about me. She'll never guess I'm her daughter from the future. A young woman so fiercely in love with a man, she'll do anything to be with him. Even travel through time to save his life.

I let the seconds tick by on the old Dutch clock, each *tick tock* not nearly as loud as the beating of my heart. I exchange a long, knowing look with my mother that makes me feel twelve years old again before I find the courage to say, 'You know I've been seeing Jeff.'

She nods. 'A little bird told me, though she didn't mean to. It slipped out when I reminded her to mend her socks and she grinned and said she didn't need to because you were giving her your stockings.'

I roll my eyes. *Lucy*. I can't be mad at her. In a funny way, she did me a favor telling Ma. I exhale loudly, relieved I don't have to conjure up a lie when we've had such a lovely reunion. 'I never could fool you, Ma.' I hug her close.

'That don't mean I approve of Mr Jeffrey courting you,'

she says, 'but you young people today have your own minds. It's not like when your Pop came round to woo me. This war's changed a lot of things.' She sighs deeply. 'I meant what I said. I won't let him hurt you. I expect your young man to pay Pop and me a visit before long.'

I freeze. Dating was one thing, but what if she knew we planned to elope before Christmas? No telling what she'd say. Pop, too. The two of them were like two tall corn stalks standing side by side in a field reaching for the sun. They followed a straight line and never wavered. I can't let her know the truth.

'It's not serious between Jeff and me, Ma,' I blurt out before I can stop myself, but it's too late. She arches a brow and gives me a look that says I can't fool her. She knows I'm lying. God help me, but we never had this conversation back then. I pray I haven't upset anything on the timeline.

'Nothing more to be said except go upstairs and wash your face. Pop will be home soon and I've got a kettle of stew on the stove. Now get on with you.' She grins and I want to die for deceiving her. I feel like I've committed a horrible sin I can never wash clean. Ma has that effect on everyone. That God put us here on earth to help each other and it's her duty to see you do.

I have no choice but to climb the familiar stairs to my room. I slide my fingers over the smooth bannister, noting the crack on the third step that never got fixed, the pictures on the wall of us when we were kids playing in the snow or picking berries. Happy days. Carefree.

I catch my breath as pangs of guilt stab me in my chest. I can't let go of the feeling that Ma caught me with my hand in her cookie jar. I don't feel like the confident career girl I was earlier when I got off that train. I have to adjust to being home again, a task I didn't see coming. Especially when my emotions pull me apart. I'm torn between being with the man I love and not disappointing my mother. I can't believe that thought didn't cross my mind back then. That I'll be hurting Ma by running away with Jeff. True, I was in love, but I was so wrapped up in my girlish desires, I didn't see her needs, only mine.

I half expect the stairs to shake before I get to the top step. They don't. That doesn't mean I haven't toyed with the past. Shaken a tile loose. I don't remember Ma catching on to the reason for my sullen mood swings after Jeff went missing and was later classified Killed In Action. She thought I was upset like the rest of the workers because we all adored him. She didn't know I was in love with him.

She does now. Even if I said I wasn't. That changes everything. She might let it slip out without meaning to when she chats with the cook at Wrightwood House or God help me, Jeff. What if his mother hears about it and forbids him to see me? Not that he'll listen to her, but it makes it harder for us to sneak out together. She might make it so difficult I'll never see him alone, never have the chance to warn him, make him believe I came back here to save him.

I bend over suddenly, holding my stomach. A bout of nausea hits me. I don't feel so good. I need to lie down and process what's happening to me. Make a plan. As I lie on my bed, thinking, my fingers digging into the familiar soft pink chenille spread, a kind of deep determination takes over. I managed to get this far without giving myself away, changing little things here and there. Small ripples that won't harm anybody. So why can't I save Jeff, too?

Fueled by this thought, I allow myself to succumb to a meditative state, like a fairy-tale princess with a spell cast over her. I don't fight it. I'm so tired. Part of me wants to jump up and explore my old room, go through my drawers, and yes, finally look into the mirror. That will come later. For now, I want to sleep.

I close my eyes and I hear Jeff's voice whispering in my ear, his arms holding me. We're standing by the big cherry tree, him nuzzling his face in my hair. My blood rushing through my veins, heart pounding, and I'm thrust into a joyful past with the man I love, the sight of his broad shoulders and black hair hanging in his eyes, their shiny sparkle catching the sun overhead.

Another thought hits me. How am I going to deal with touching him again? Running my fingers over his broad chest? Kissing his sensuous lips? How can I control myself after so many nights lying drenched with sweat, wrapped up in silk sheets and old memories?

My emotions jump from anticipation to a more subtle awakening of every nerve in me. I fall into a peaceful sleep, my hands clasped over my heart. My body still warm with need. For him.

Unfortunately, my respite lasts only a few minutes. Lucy is on the warpath.

## 12

'My whole life is ruined, Kate, and it's your fault.'

Lucy bursts into my room and throws herself across my bed sobbing. I don't remember this happening back then.

'What have I done?' It must be around six thirty. Time goes by faster since I got here.

'Just the worst thing you could ever do to me.'

'It can't be that bad, Lucy,' I say, trying to comfort her. I don't dare look her in the eye, fearful she'll see the flush of desire lingering on my cheeks thinking about Jeff.

'Oh, I wish you'd go away and never come back.'

'*Lucy.*' I don't know why her words shock me, but they do. I'm hurt. A kick to my ego I'm not expecting. This isn't the Lucy who begs me to come home for Christmas every year. What's wrong? 'Whatever I did, I'll fix it. Stop crying like a baby and tell me what happened.'

She sits up, huffing and puffing. Her holiday ribbon comes loose, so I pull back her hair and tie the ribbon into a fancy bow. She doesn't stop me. 'I'm in love with a soldier, Kate, and you ruined it.'

'How?' I've only been here a few hours, how can that be?

She blinks at me as if I asked her a silly question. 'You know what you did.'

'No, I don't. Tell me.'

I put my arm around her and let her talk, about how she met this dreamy-eyed boy from Ohio when he got off the train and he helped her distribute oranges to the soldiers. How they talked and talked. I smile. My heart melts at her girlish innocence, but also aches for her. I know what it's like to fall fast for a boy. Didn't I fall for Jeff when I was a kid? Somehow that seems different. I'll never tell my little sister that.

She promised to write to him, but before he gave her his address, I yanked her away and now she'll never see him again.

'How can you do that to me, Kate?' she begs to know. 'I told him I'd write to him every day. All he kept talking about was, "Who's the pretty girl I saw you with? Tell her to write to me, too."'

'Lucy—'

'My own *sister*! I'll never forgive you.'

'I'd never do anything to hurt you, Lucy. Why, I never even talked to him.' I don't want her to get hurt either. Then I have a terrible thought – did I mess up her future marriage with Jimmie? He's from Ohio, but they meet at a roller rink in the city and get married in 1946. Still, I have to be more careful I don't change anything without meaning to. 'I'm sorry, honest. What's his name?'

'Stephen.'

I breathe out, relieved. It isn't him. *Thank God.*

She sighs. 'He looked so handsome in his uniform. Tall with the biggest shoulders I've ever seen. Wait until I tell that

Gloria. She'll be so jealous he asked me to write to him and not her.'

She's more impressed with his uniform than anything else. For now, I have to keep her focused on flirting with the soldiers and keeping up their spirits, nothing more. Like falling in love.

'Think about what I said, okay?' I detect a slight acquiescence on her part, a quick nod, then she mumbles under her breath before leaving, her attitude still defiant.

I sit by myself next to the bay window, looking out at the plot of land we turned into a Victory Garden. It'll be ready for planting again after the thaw. We used to help Ma put up cans and jars of pumpkin, squash, celery, and turnips in the root cellar. I loved sitting here on the fluffy navy and yellow plaid cushions. Gossamer white drapes enfolding me like angel wings. When I was growing up, this was my favorite place to play with my doll, pretending she was a princess held in a tower waiting for her prince. Funny, how she found him and then lost him. Do princesses get second chances? I hope so.

I want to linger here, but Ma needs me to help her serve dinner. A one-pot stew simmering with onions, potatoes, corn, tomatoes, and lima beans. Dried parsley flakes dancing on top. She saved chicken stock for the base and added homemade noodles. Thick, sturdy noodles steamed to perfection in the soup, soaking up the golden broth and melting in your mouth. I'll add her noodle recipe and lima bean soup to my cookbook notes when I get back to my own time. I curl my legs under me and rest my chin on my hands. That's odd. That I assume I'm going back.

I waltz into the kitchen, my nose leading the way. For

now, I succumb to the overpowering smell of the stew driving me crazy. Rich and savory, I already tasted it twice.

I lick the spoon. 'Don't add any more salt, Ma.'

'Pop likes salt,' she insists.

I count to ten, praying she won't ignore me when I say something about how she cooks. She's a great cook, but heavy on the spices because that's what Pop wants. 'Please, it's not good for him. You want him to stay healthy, don't you?'

She regards me with a strange glance, as if the idea of him not being healthy never occurs to her.

My pulse races when I hear the front door open. Pop and Frank Junior. He waits for Pop at the bus stop most nights, the two of them enjoying time together without the females in the house. We called him Frankie later on. For now he's Junior.

A unique tenderness I have for the boy makes me stop and think. How can I look my brother in the eye knowing that he'll come home from Korea with wounds that don't show? That the battles fought in the subzero temperature, sleeping outside at night with his gun by his side, test a man's mettle in the hard winter. That it does something to his mind, the horrendous trauma of losing buddies, trying to save others, and then spending a brief time in captivity. That he'll spend years afterward going through the Veterans Affairs office to get benefits. That the doctors are still trying to figure out what to do with the men who saw action in Bataan and the Battle of the Bulge and have no time for him.

Which brings up another predicament I never saw coming. I'm on thin ice here. If I try to help him, I could make things worse. Especially now that he has a girl and a job. Do I want to take a chance on messing that up? I decide to keep mum and pray to God it's the right decision.

Then there's Pop. I settle in for what will be a difficult reunion.

Where do I begin? He's a tall man with shoulders little girls cry on when their doll's arm falls off so he'll fix it. He's the strong, silent type and so honest – he once walked three miles when he was twelve to return two copper pennies back to the grocer who gave him too much change. We were never as close as I would have liked, seeing how he was reared in an era when fathers took charge of their sons and mothers fussed with their daughters. We've had more than one heated battle over everything from me dating to leaving home. Yet underneath that stubborn, opinionated talk, a poet's soul burns. Ma confided to me Pop was quite the charmer with his sonnets when they were courting. Strange to think of my parents courting.

Stranger yet when we sit down to dinner and the talk turns to the war and the man I love.

Jeffrey Rushbrooke.

\* \* \*

'There's talk down at the mill that with the steel, power, and electric company strikes going on,' Pop says, tucking his napkin into his shirt, 'we could be next.'

My heart in my throat, I study the man who sat me on his knee when I was a little girl and read stories to me, who sneaked me peppermint sticks when Ma wasn't looking, and who showed me growing up that a husband can be strong but also tender with a woman. I saw that with how he was with Ma. And I wanted the same for Jeff and me.

Now I simply wanted to drink in this amazing man.

'I'm sure you're wrong,' I chime in, sparking the dinner

table conversation with my brash comment. Rushbrooke Mills had its problems, but the workforce was loyal and no strikes took place during the war. 'Everybody I talk to on the floor is happy with their jobs.'

There was curiosity in his gray eyes, a meandering that set the gears in his mind working. His little girl was talking shop with him? I admit, it was a fun moment, seeing my father in a different light. Made me realize I never really grew up in his eyes. Which explained his behavior later on, but for now I want to savor this time with him.

'You mean them female workers.' He grunts and Ma gives him a nudge in the shoulder to clam up. She loves her husband more than anything, but she's a firm believer in a woman's right to better herself and she lets him know it. Grumbling, Pop goes to work on his stew. In between bites, he lets go with a short speech about how the Allies are stepping up attacks on the German home front with the Brits bombing Berlin. 'Where are our boys?' he wants to know.

'Give them time, Pop,' I tell him. 'We'll be over the skies of Berlin soon.' I sip my soup, ignoring his hard stare. I never discussed military strategy with him back then, but the first American bombing of Berlin won't take place until March 1944.

He seems skeptical of my statement and goes back to what's really bothering him. 'How can our workers think about striking when we need all the manpower to run our factories?'

I note Ma's in the kitchen out of earshot when he uses the word *manpower*.

Clever going, Pop.

'Maybe they got a good reason.' Junior grabs two biscuits with one hand as Lucy sits down at the table. She doesn't say a word. She's too busy giving me the evil eye. I sigh. I don't need another war on my hands.

'We must defeat the enemy, son. Fueling our country and getting our boys up the air in those bombers comes first. That's what Mr Jeffrey says and he ought to know since he's taking over as plant manager.'

I choke on a carrot. *Jeff?* Is there a shift in power I don't know about?

'What do you mean, Pop?' I have to know. I don't care if I'm overstepping my place. 'Is Mr Rushbrooke turning over running the plant to Mr Jeffrey?'

I never call him Jeff around my father. He'd deem it disrespectful.

'That's the talk on the floor among us supervisors.'

I don't argue. Pop has worked at the mill since he left high school in the tenth grade to help support his mother. He got an apprenticeship at sixteen. He wanted to be an engineer, but the Depression put an end to his dreams.

Sitting back, looking at my father, I see him in a different light again. When you're a kid, you don't think about your parents having dreams because you're so wrapped up in your own. Pop long ago gave up on his and accepted his lot. He's a good welder and shaper and he knows what it takes to keep production moving. I've often wondered how far he could have gone if he didn't have us to take care of.

He smacks his lips and when he finishes his stew, Ma is right there with a second helping. She smiles at him and he gleams. He often says he's lucky to have a good woman and a good job, in that order. I never noticed their affectionate interplay when I was a teenager. I admit, I envy it now. The subtle grabbing of hands and a heartfelt squeeze. A smirk. A sideway glance. A smile. I realize how much I missed about being in love when I lost Jeff.

That only strengthens my resolve to save him. I hope I'll have with Jeff what my parents have. Like the kindness Pop shows toward Ma and the friendship they share and their love of words. Pop likes to write down his ditties and Ma always has a book in her hand when she isn't cooking or cleaning. I guess it's no surprise to them when I become a writer.

For the moment, I have to deal with this new predicament. The mill.

From what I can tell, Mr Rushbrooke has passed on disinformation to his staff about Jeff taking over the mill. Most likely to keep up morale among the workers. It is the direct opposite of what Jeff told me, that he's going to enlist in the AAF, the Army Air Force. No wonder he asked me not to say anything. I didn't. Back then I never questioned anything he did.

Not that I followed him around like a little mouse, but I couldn't see past my nose when it came to him. That he never forgot how I saved him when we were kids was a big moment in my life. I fell for a young man who treated me as an equal. I had no education, but he made me use my mind and encouraged me to think for myself. That was as exciting to me as him picking me up in his strong arms and carrying me up the hill to our cherry tree without drawing a breath. Which is why this news disturbs me. I feel betrayed.

I'm not dumb. Mr Rushbrooke is setting up Jeff's abrupt departure for overseas in everyone's mind. A simple but effective plan. They arrange for him to be called up suddenly and it will look unpatriotic if he doesn't leave for training immediately. They know Jeff is going on a secret mission. It has to look like he has no choice but to leave the running of the mill to his brother, Timothy. Nobody likes or trusts him.

Whether it's his father's idea or the War Department's, I don't care. They both get what they want. It's deceitful and heartless. Not just hurting me, but every worker at the mill. We believe in our heroes. Jeff is mine.

I have a strange thought then. That I've never seen him in uniform. Every girl loves her man looking so handsome and cavalier in his Army olive drab. I'm denied that moment of female swooning. When he left on the train that morning, he was in civvies. He never came back.

What he told me about joining the Air Force was a lie.

I drop my spoon and it hits the side of the bowl with a clatter. Pop thinks I'm angry, Junior pays me no mind, and Lucy ignores me, excusing herself, saying she has a headache. She glares at me before she disappears upstairs.

I don't care if my stew gets cold. Doesn't Jeff trust me? Would you trust a nineteen year old girl who isn't more than a kid herself? I thought I knew it all since I read a lot, but I had no life experience. Still, it's time I stand up for myself. Show everybody I'm no fool. That I'm smart, have ambition, and I can do more for the war effort than coming up with the idea of Miss Christmas Wrap. Starting with my own family.

I clear my throat and begin like nothing happened. 'I heard a certain congresswoman wants to draft women in the military,' I state with assurance. I've had the pleasure of meeting the esteemed politician after the war when she was on a book tour. 'I wouldn't be surprised if women serve in combat roles someday.'

Silence. Pop stares at me like I've sprouted horns. 'You mean, *fight*?'

'Why not?' I say, without batting a lash. 'Nurses serve on

the battlefield, so why can't women go into battle alongside men?'

'Fighting is for men,' Junior says, siding with Pop. I expect no less.

'A woman can pull the trigger on a rifle as good as any man,' I venture, sticking up for my sex.

'Watch your talk, Katie Marie,' Pop says, using his nickname for me. 'It's bad enough seeing those women working down at the mill doing men's work. I don't want to see my own daughter caught up in politics she doesn't understand.'

'Because I'm a girl?' I shoot back.

'Yes.'

'Girls have brains, too. Pop. Someday you'll see that when I—'

*Go off to New York and get a job in a big publishing company.*

I can't say it, though I want Pop to be proud of me. I see it isn't going to happen. He rarely includes Lucy and me in the conversation about the war. But deep inside me, I pray tonight is a breakthrough. Maybe if I'm lucky, he'll remember this conversation later on when I take off for the big city. I'll never forget that day. Ma was crying, but she helped me pack and made sure I had enough homemade cherry jam to last me a month. Pop wouldn't come home to see me off, but spent the afternoon down at the local tavern. It was an awful time in my life. He didn't talk to me for six months.

Now Pop waits for me to finish and get myself into more hot water. I bite my tongue. I'm ready to explode, but Ma, my angel in an apron, saves me.

'Why don't you help me serve the dessert, Kate?' she says sweetly.

I nod. That's her not-so-subtle way of calling a halt to family arguments at the dinner table.

'Sure, Ma.' I attempt a smile. I look at Pop. He pushes away his plate, though he hasn't finished his stew. 'What do we have tonight?'

'Apple pie.'

Her Victory Apple Pie glistens on top and can make the staunchest general get down on his knees. She sweetens it with less sugar than before the war, adding riced potatoes, and sprinkling it with cinnamon. My mouth watering, I slice up the pie while she sets down the tiny dessert plates with the daisy design she's had since her wedding day. Then she sits down with us. She lets out a big sigh and fans herself with her apron. I hate to see her so tired. She ate her stew in the kitchen. I wish she'd let herself enjoy dinnertime with us, but that's Ma. The family comes first, especially her man. Again, I feel a pang of envy when she insists he take the biggest piece of pie. She smiles at him and I see his eyes soften. Like I said, that's Ma.

The pie melts in my mouth as I eat every bite, and I would have a second piece, but it's all gone. Like the tension around the table. Ma's pie fixed that. Pop and Junior talk about the upcoming baseball games like the season starts tomorrow, while Lucy comes down and finishes her home-work. Words were said, but not forgotten. Still, I haven't enjoyed a meal so much in years and I make a note to write about Ma's Victory pie recipe in my food column when I get back.

Again, I have that feeling I'm not here for long.

'I'll help you with the dishes, Ma.' I gather up the empty plates.

'I'm fine, baby,' she says, her hands filled with dirty glasses and silverware. She stops, her brow furrowing like a caterpillar, her lips tight. She thinks a moment, leans over and whispers. 'Go into the parlor and sit a while with Pop while I clean up.'

Then she gives me that motherly nod I know so well when she wants us to make up. I balk. 'I will, Ma. Let me help you first.'

I'm not ready to take a step backward and give up the freedom to speak my mind. I thought I'd prepared myself for this dinner, that I'd got through the hardest part of my trip and substantiated my place here without arousing suspicion. I never expected the big kick to my emotions. I may have my differences with my family, but I'm proud of them, watching them do what's needed to win this war. Ma running the household on her ration books, Lucy and Junior sitting close together before dinner so they can both study using one light. Pop buying war bonds and stamps out of every week's paycheck. We're in the middle of a war hard fought and no one knows when it will be over. No one would ever talk about it, but there was no assurance we'd win. We suffered terrible setbacks, like the defeat at Corregidor, but we believed if every man, woman, and child did their part, even the smallest thing like saving paper, then our country would remain free.

I mull over these thoughts as I linger by the sink, shocked to see the steam coming off the hot water and Ma dipping her hands in it. No wonder she's hurting so bad.

'I'm getting you some lotion, Ma, to save your hands. No excuses.'

She pats my cheek. 'You're always looking out for me, Kate, but I don't need you wasting what little money you have left over buying lotion for your old ma. Get something for yourself. Like a new lipstick.' She raises her eyebrows at me. 'I noticed you're using up lip color faster than usual.'

I swallow and don't answer her. So she suspected I've been slipping out to meet someone, and now that she knows it's Jeff, she doesn't try to hide it anymore. This time I don't protest when she scoots me out of the kitchen. It's the only way I'll see that sparkle again in her eye. Ma likes her home to chime with a happy, clockwork rhythm. Any slip of the second hand upsets that rhythm. I'm already bending time to my will, so I do as she asks and join the family gathered in the parlor waiting for Pop's favorite quiz show to start. I have to smile when I see them all together. My heart pings and I let my frustration go. My father lighting his pipe, Ma with her ration books lined up on a small card table, stacking one on top of another, while Frank Junior pretends to study his history lesson and Lucy fusses and frets with her Christmas list.

So far, she announces in a bright, gleeful voice, she's asked Santa for two Army soldiers, a sailor, and one big strapping Marine. She keeps watching me out of the corner of her eye to see if I'll give her another lecture. I don't. I have something else on my mind. She opens her mouth to say something to Ma when she sees me grab my coat but Ma stares her down, surprising both of us. Ma doesn't look directly at me, nor does she say anything when I slip out through the back door. She has no idea Jeff isn't meeting me tonight, but her silence is a sign of approval. I'll cherish that for years to come.

I'll deal with Lucy later. For now, I want to be alone. Like an actor preparing for a play, mine is about to begin. Tomorrow Jeff will be back from Washington and I want to be ready. My body hums with a romantic tune too long unsung. I can't wait.

* * *

The deep shadows hovering under the eaves of the house where I grew up are more forbidding than I remember, the gravel crunching under my feet making me wonder how I ever got away without alerting Ma and her keen ear. I swear the night spirits shoot glimpses of light from their fingertips along the slippery path to guide me.

Until I come to the cherry tree standing proud on the knoll, its bleak branches swaying in the night wind, a hint of moonbeams tinting them silver-gray. I came here often after Jeff left. Holding my heart in my hands and not knowing what to do with it. I never gave it to another man, not completely, which was why I broke off my engagement. In the end, I buried my heart here under the tree. Let it return to the richness of the earth to heal. It was too fragile for me to keep. Now I'm here to reclaim it.

I can't control the spate of tears falling onto my cheeks. Soon I'll see Jeff for the first time since that painful day when he left to serve his country. That causes me more anguish than I care to admit, but I'm older now, wiser, and bursting with anticipation. I pat my coat pocket and the crackle of paper reminds me the letter is safely hidden there. I don't look at it, afraid I'll jinx it. Then I circle the pattern of the tree's tender bark with my gloved fingers, saying a prayer that the hours will go as quickly as the years disappeared on my journey back here. These moments are agonizing. I have to wait till morning, then warn him.

What if he doesn't believe me?

After my argument with Pop, I realize it won't be easy to exert my power as a woman in this time, though Jeff doesn't see me as the weaker sex. Quite the opposite. I'm his precocious Jelly Girl who stood up to his father. Still, I have to combat this wild scheme Mr Rushbrooke and a dodgy senator in the War Department concocted to take him away from me. If I fail, no telling what could happen. The worst things I can think of. Pop could get fired. Ma will get sicker faster from the stress. Frankie will lie about his age and enlist and Lucy will run off with the first good-looking serviceman who asks her.

Suddenly I'm afraid I made a terrible mistake coming back here. That the longer I stay, I'll undo the future in a frightful way I'll regret for the rest of my life.

## 13

I get ready for work, easing into my sensible black suede pumps and my navy-blue suit to avoid any more stares from the ladies on the floor. A uniform I wear to fit in with the other office girls down at the mill. Hopefully everyone will assume I wore a fancy suit and silk hat yesterday because Mr Clayborn had an important government visitor. I take more time with my hair, making sure the new style is just so, then put on my slip with the lacy trim. Jeff won't see it, but it boosts my confidence knowing I'm wearing something frilly.

Then I add a silver brooch to my jacket lapel with a tiny red ribbon for the holiday. I borrowed the slender piece of velvet from Lucy's ribbon box. She won't miss it. She's already fleeing out the door, her mouth filled with crackers and cherry jam. Nothing out of the ordinary here.

I beg off breakfast and Ma takes it as a sign I'm too infatuated with Jeff to eat. She has no idea of the excitement roiling through me. I toss on my red coat and old black hat and my feet move so fast to the bus stop, I swear I sprouted butterfly wings. I don't notice the cold wind coming up off the river, something we feel down here when the temperature drops. I button up my coat, all six buttons, reminding me the war hasn't yet taken my love from me. If I have anything to do with it, they never will. Somewhere on a distant mount, the gods of time are playing games with me. My desperation to see Jeff rattles my insides so much, I dash to make an earlier bus than usual. Seven twenty. Which means Mrs Canton is the bus driver.

If there is ever a character out of a Dickens novel bent on making my life miserable, it's Sarah Canton. She's a busy-body on wheels. She was pretty once, but her body softened like uncooked dough and her mouth contorted into a perpetual snarl no red lipstick can fix. She never keeps her opinions to herself and has nothing good to say about the young women who ride her bus to the mill every morning, including me. She can't wait to comment on my new hairdo.

'You expect me to drop you off at the factory with that hair?' She slams the door shut behind me with a loud bang. She took over the bus driver's job on a temporary basis when her husband went to sea before the war. Talk is he signed up on a freighter to get away from her nagging. When the war started, she stayed on, much to her riders' dismay.

'Maisie said Victory rolls are all the fashion,' I say with a casual nod, hoping to defuse an uncomfortable situation. I don't need a lecture, but I'm not going to let her take advantage of me either. I'm not as naïve as I was then. She seems particularly anxious to pick on me this morning.

The bus is nearly full so I take a seat in the back and fuss with my hair, trying to keep the big curls under my hat, planning what I'm going to say when I see Jeff. I let my thoughts ramble as the bus makes its way along the country road, stopping to pick up passengers. I'm friendly with all the girls, but this morning I don't participate in the usual chitchat. They respect that, but their curious eyes and hushed whispers tell me they find my conversation with Mrs Canton a welcome respite on what is usually a quiet, boring ride to work. As for me, I want to soak up what I missed when I moved to the big city. That rural perfume that revs you up in the morning with the bountiful scents of nature, so unlike motor oil coming up off the asphalt and the uniform smell of humanity on the move on city streets.

A thick forest surrounds Posey Creek on the east, while acres of farms cozy up to the south along the river where the mill has stood since the early nineteenth century. I love the ride through the thick forest with its unique earthy smells that somehow turn festive during the winter months.

How am I going to keep my emotions under control when I see Jeff? I can't do anything stupid, like blurt out something about the war that hasn't happened yet.

Mrs Canton won't let me be. 'You girls and your peekaboo hair,' she says in a loud voice so I hear her in the back. The other ladies on the bus hear her, too, and giggle. 'I bet your ma ain't happy about it.'

'Ma loves it,' I say sweetly, not letting her get the best of me. Several women shoot me the 'V for Victory' sign in approval. I can't resist adding, 'She's having hers done up like mine next Wednesday.'

*Screech*.

Mrs Canton slams her foot hard on the brakes and I lurch forward in the bus seat, a flash of darkness hovering over me, its tactile presence so acute, I feel cold fingers tap dancing up and down my spine.

I hold my breath, my hand going to my stomach, fearing a nausea attack. Nothing happens. I let it out, slow. I'm still here. All eyes dart to see why she stopped so suddenly, but I need a moment to compose myself. I smooth down my coat and adjust my hat. That was close. I can't explain it, but a tiny voice in my head keeps telling me that I'm hanging on by a delicate string.

I squint through the window, the glass smudged with my glove prints, and see a woman waving down the bus, her tall, slim figure wearing wide, gray trousers and a flannel coat fitted with huge shoulder pads, her reddish hair covered with a white bandana.

I smile. It's Mildred. The reverend's wife.

Her blue pickup truck is parked in the middle of the road to stop traffic.

I see why. Nearby stands a tall, broad shouldered man swinging an axe, trying to bring down a magnificent fir tree. Mildred flagged us down to avoid an accident if the tree slams to the ground in our path. I bite my lip; this man makes my heart race. He possesses an intensity that demands my attention. Makes me quiver all over. I lean in closer, my hand going to my mouth. No, it can't be. Can it?

The big strong man swings the axe easily, like it's a candy cane. Only one man in town has brawn like that. Jeff. He's taller than most men with muscles that ripple under his russet-tanned skin in the summer months. I never tire of watching his biceps bulge into big knots, especially when he grabs me around the waist, his smile so big and the man so sure of himself. When I can see that he wants to kiss me and pulls me close and twirls me around like a merry-go-round and I never want to get off.

His back is to me now, but even with the bulky wool of his jacket, I make out those broad shoulders. As he swings the axe, the scrape of metal biting into the thick tree, I note the back of his jacket is wet with the sweat of his labor. While I glory in the beautiful sight of him, he never stops until the grand fir tree topples over and lands with a loud thump. It hits the cold ground on a clear patch of earth off to the side of the road, its graceful branches swan diving down to earth with such precision, it takes my breath away. When he turns around, my jaw drops. I barely take him in without shuddering, my breath catching, my pulse racing so fast I suffer a sudden bout of lightheadedness. Oh, my God, he's magnificent. I stare at him far too long, for the forces at play here didn't prepare me for this moment. My brain goes into shock. He looks so young.

I forgot *how* young he is. Around twenty-two.

I don't know why that comes as such a surprise to me. An uncomfortable feeling wiggles through me. I expected to see a tall, sexy man who will carry me away in his strong arms. Angular jaw, deep, sexy eyes. Hands that hold me tight. Don't get me wrong, the young Jeff wielding that axe is a hunk of young manhood I'll never forget, his body hard-toned and muscular. That indefinable confidence that comes with maturity isn't there yet, only hinted at.

I sink deeper into my seat. Suddenly I feel old. How can I pull this off? It's one thing to convince my family I'm the same girl I was back then, but Jeff knows me in a more intimate manner. The curve of my small waist, the girlish laughter that rings with my innocence, my hunger to learn how to kiss. I'll never be able to duplicate that.

I can't let that stop me. Losing him cast a shadow over my life and in one beautiful, shining moment every tear I shed, every pain to my heart mellows out and drips away like the holiest of oils seething through a sieve. I *am* that young girl again. My skin tingles with the bloom no face powder can give back when it fades. I don't feel guilty for wanting to recapture my gregarious youth. While so many girls reach across the ocean with their thoughts to tell their man they love him, I reached across time. God put this man in my path and no way am I going to ignore that gift.

I have to see him... *now*. Ready or not, I stand up in my seat and walk to the rear exit of the bus. 'Open the door. I'm getting off here.'

The driver shrugs, enjoying her power over me. 'Nope. It's not one of my stops.'

'*Please*, Mrs Canton,' I plead. 'I need to get off this bus.'

'Sit down. It's my bus and you do what I say.' She revs the engine several times, grumbling to herself, then grinds the gears, getting antsy while she waits for Mildred to move her truck.

I didn't travel back in time to be thwarted by an over-stuffed strudel.

I blow out my breath, count to ten. 'I asked you nice, now I'm telling you,' I say, losing my patience and my schoolgirl manners. '*Open the door.*'

Loud gasps. Coughing. More whispering.

'You're like the rest of them girls who work at the mill. You think you can have everything you want.' She laughs like an evil cartoon character. 'Well, you can't.'

'Mrs Canton, *please*—'

Mildred's truck still blocks the road, but that's not the issue. Sarah Canton is insufferable. She's being obstinate because rumor has it her husband had romantic encounters with girls working at the factory. When she found out, he left her. I empathize with her feeling of loss, but I can't condone her way of dealing with it. I have to do something. Fast.

'I need to speak to Mildred.' I search for a reason other

than the truth. Not easy with every inch of my body on fire, sweat oozing up on the back of my neck, knowing I'm seconds away from reuniting with the man I loved and lost. This woman isn't going to stop me.

'What for?' Mrs Canton says, egging me on.

Every passenger leans forward in her seat, waiting to hear my answer. I don't disappoint them. Seeing the big fir tree gives me an idea. 'We need a tree to decorate down at the mill to keep up company spirit during the holidays.'

'Nope.'

My eyebrows shoot up. 'You'd stop us from having a tree?'

*Boos* come from the ladies on the bus. Mrs Canton smiles, enjoying her revenge. 'Yep.'

'Fine,' I say, baiting her. 'Wait until I tell everybody down at the mill you don't have any Christmas spirit, Mrs Canton… or should I call you Mrs Scrooge?'

She glares at me and I make another small rip in the fabric of my history. What I said is akin to saying she's unpatriotic. By the loud whispers and approving looks in my direction, I have no doubt our run-in will be all over Posey Creek by noon. How I called her out and embarrassed her on a bus filled with mill workers and housewives going into town. The cold, hard stare she tosses at me tells me I won for now, but she's not done with me. *There'll be a price to pay*, her eyes say. I ignore the burning on my cheeks, as if she slapped me.

'Go on then.' The snippy driver opens the rear exit door. 'I ain't waiting for you. You'll have to walk to work.'

I don't hesitate, don't bother with a flippant remark. I'm too excited. My heart pounds so hard in my chest, I can't breathe as I jump off the bus and never look back. I hear her stall the engine, then restart it with a loud grinding of the gears as she maneuvers the bus around the fallen tree and takes off down the road, smoke pouring out of the exhaust.

All I see is my man. I can't move. I've waited, dreamed for so long and now that I'm living the moment, I don't know what to do. It feels as though the film's stopped in the projector and it won't start running again. I can't hear the deep sound of his voice calling out to me, but I see the sudden light in his eyes when he catches the splash of my red coat. The way he looks at me, greeting me with a silent kiss, showering my spirit with lovely vibrations. I wait, holding my breath. If there's a time when I'm afraid I'll disappear as quickly as I came, this is it. When I don't, I exhale from the pure joy of it and in an instant, my ears pop and my world comes alive again.

For the first time in twelve years.

## 14

My entire theory about why I'm here is put to a test when I run toward him. God help me, I forget about everything but him, his eyes smoldering with desire at the sight of my poor errant soul racing across the dirt road, breathing hard, my face shiny with sweat. Dolled up in my red coat with the fake fur collar, I must look like the red-hooded girl in the fairy tale. He can't believe it.

'Kate, what are you doing here?' Jeff stares at me, a combination of both concern and need lighting up his face. The tenseness I saw moments before when he was swinging the axe is gone, his tall body slipping into the easygoing style I know so well. That certain swagger that says he's happy to see me.

'Jeff!' I call out. My throat is so tight, my voice breaks. Only a deep guttural sound comes out. I rush into his arms, not caring if Mildred stares at us with her mouth open. I want his arms around me and for him never to let me go.

'Hold on, Jelly Girl, I've only been gone for two days.'

'Jeff... *oh, Jeff*, I can't believe you're here. *I'm here.*' My lower lip trembles uncontrollably and the tears fall. It's nothing compared to the intense, hot burn working its way up my body. I grab onto his jacket sleeve and feel his forearm flinch. I have to make sure he's real. That moment spikes such a yearning in me, it sends every nerve in my body into a spasm. I fight hard to control it, lowering my head so he can't see the hidden thoughts that must be so obvious in my eyes. That I'm in an ecstatic state of bliss, a deep need never to let him go building in my chest. I'm at my most vulnerable when I'm close to him and if I'm not careful, I'll blurt out the whole, unbelievable truth about why I'm here and ruin everything.

I have to find the right moment, then tell him. Make him believe. Not yet.

He senses something is wrong in my world, but he doesn't ask. An unseen bond between us kicks into gear as it has since we were kids. When one of us was sad or hurt but didn't want to talk about it, we wouldn't ask. We'd hold each other tight until the other got past the moment. For me, it was usually something silly, like I was late to school or Ma had scolded me for something dumb I did. For Jeff, it was more than likely his father. I always had a feeling the verbal abuse and hard demands he made upon him never stopped.

My heart slows finally, my head cradled against his chest, my lashes crunched together with dried tears. His jacket, chilled from the cold, soothes the burn on my cheeks so I calm down, deal with a situation no one should ever have to, the rediscovery of a lost love but knowing things will turn out the same if I don't change it.

'You'll be late for work,' he says in a low voice, his fingers rifling through my hair and sending my hat askew. I don't make a move to fix it. The bus is gone, though I'm aware Mildred is doing her best not to notice his romantic gesture toward me. 'If I had my way, I'd give you the day off so you could spend it with me.'

'You know what Mr Clayborn says,' I mumble, getting myself back together enough to tease him. 'No one takes a day off until our soldiers come home.'

'He's right, Jelly Girl,' Jeff says, serious, then he leads me away from the fallen tree to the other side of the road. 'I guess he told you about my trip to Washington. The brass wanted to talk to me about a desk job.'

'Your father's idea, Jeff?'

He looks surprised. 'No, my mother pulled some strings to get me the meeting. My father was dead set against it until she talked him into it. Reminding him we need someone in Washington to keep those government contracts coming in.'

'Your mother?' My mind takes a step back. This is news. 'Why would she—'

*You know why. She hates you. Didn't she give Helen the third degree about you?*

'I didn't take the job,' he states flatly.

'Why not?' I grab his hand. A desk job will be dull, but he'll be safe. 'I can come up to Washington to see you. It's only a two hour train ride once I get to Philly.'

'I'm not a paper pusher, Kate. I want to do my part, fly bombers, and beat the crap out of those Nazis.'

His eyes bore into mine with a passion I can't turn away from. Dark and moody, but not cloaked with a lie. I take a step back in my mind. What if Jeff is tapped for the job with the newly formed intelligence agency before he leaves for pilot training? He wouldn't question why his orders came through that fast, but I bet his mother is behind it. The woman is a fool, thinking she's sending her son to a desk job, not giving it a second thought – doesn't she realize he could be sent overseas?

'My father will have no choice but to hand over the everyday production duties of the mill to Timothy.'

I feel the frustration emanating from his body as we continue our conversation on the side of the country road. No traffic. Jeff isn't pleased with the idea, but we both know the decision is made.

'That won't go over well with everyone on the floor,' I warn him, then add with a smile. 'Especially the ladies.'

'I'm depending on you to keep the home fires burning, Kate. You can trust Mr Clayborn to help you.'

We get quiet for a moment, words unspoken. We both know it won't be easy with Timothy running production. I intend to speak to my boss about what I know is coming in a subtle way and hopefully curtail the downfall of the company after the war. Which makes this seem like the appropriate time to tell Jeff what I came so far to say. 'Jeff, there's something I want to tell you.' I keep my voice low.

'No, me first.' He pulls out a long envelope from inside his jacket pocket and smiles.

'Can we go somewhere private?' I interrupt, working up my nerve. As much as I like Mildred, I can't let her know my secret. 'This is important.'

'More important than this?' He pulls out two train tickets and wiggles them under my nose. 'The 7.10 a.m. *Standard Flyer* to Washington on Monday next week.'

'Jeffrey Rushbrooke, what *are* you talking about?' I say, breathless. I feel my lips curl into a big smile, but I still need reassurance I didn't change the timeline with my impetuousness.

'I didn't spend all my time hobnobbing with the brass.'

'What do you mean?' I ask, my heart racing.

'I slipped away when my father was meeting with a special envoy from the War Production Board. I had a long talk with Judge Stevens. I swore him to secrecy, but the judge promised to marry us. We'll spend two, maybe three days in Washington. I got us a hotel room, thanks to the judge's brother-in-law, and we'll be home on Christmas Eve to spend it with the family as Mr and Mrs Jeffrey Rushbrooke.'

'Home on Christmas Eve... with the family.' I can't stop my hands from trembling as I stare at the train tickets, although my heart jumps with joy. This isn't what I expected. Jeff didn't mention train tickets and us eloping until the night of the holiday dance at the canteen. That's on Saturday. December eighteenth. Four days from now. Did I change history without knowing it?

'Aren't you pleased?' He runs his hands through his thick, dark hair. He doesn't understand my hesitation.

'Pleased?' I gush, overwhelmed. 'My Lord, Jeff, you have no idea. You've made me the happiest woman in the world.'

'That's my Jelly Girl,' he says, hugging me and then putting the tickets back in his jacket pocket.

'Hey, you two, time to celebrate later,' Mildred calls out to us. How long has she been standing there? Quiet, still as a statue, and God help me, she heard every word. 'We've got to load up the tree for the candle lighting ceremony.' She's grinning from ear to ear. The twinkle in her eye tells me she's happy for us.

'Gosh, Mildred, I don't know what to say,' I turn, my face flushed.

'Don't worry, honey.' She lays her hand on my arm. 'Your secret is safe with me.'

'Thanks, Mildred, you know how I feel about Kate.' Jeff

kisses the tip of my nose. 'She's the best thing that ever happened to me.'

Then with a squeeze, he lets me go and drags the nearly seven foot tall fir tree to the back cargo area of Mildred's half-ton truck.

I marvel at how easily Jeff handles himself, lifting the tree onto his wide shoulders and loading it into the truck, his dark hair falling into his eyes in such a sexy manner, I want to kiss him. He has no idea I haven't felt his lips on mine in twelve years. I can't wait much longer.

I pace up and down the side of the road, hoping he'll be so shocked he won't notice his Jelly Girl has learned a thing or two about kissing a man. I have no doubt I'll be familiar with his hot kisses. How many nights have I stood with him on God's acre of paradise under the cherry tree, his mouth pressed against mine? His breath warm, me digging my fingers into his shoulders to hold on because I'm so shaky inside, my knees buckle. A place where the stars drift like tiny boats in a sea of velvet.

I'd know his kisses anywhere, but this isn't the moment to find out.

Not with Mildred sneaking peeks at us, her eyes misting over, as if she's thinking about the reverend and remembering loving moments with him. Growing up, I was in awe of the powerful man with eyes the color of maple syrup swirling with questions. I can see why Mildred fell in love with the former boxer who found serving God and helping the needy a more fitting way to bring peace to his soul.

Mildred stayed strong when her husband went to war to guide and comfort servicemen with the word of God and fight alongside them. I adore the woman, admire her strength and gumption not to be a placid wife. She puts herself on the

line and gives her church members the courage to keep going
and lifts their spirits. She's a true heroine in my eyes. More so
now, knowing what she'll go through before coming out on
the other side even stronger. No one else but Mildred can
bring our little town together for the holidays, working hard
to set up the lighting ceremony with a tall Christmas tree in
front of the community center for the soldiers when they
come home on furlough. A place where they meet up with
their friends, have a cup of coffee and cookies and someone
to listen to them. Their families don't understand the loneliness they feel or the close bond they have with their fellow
soldiers. We can't replace that, but we can listen.

Jeff looks at his wristwatch. The tree isn't yet secure in the
back of the truck, but he's anxious to leave.

'Mildred will drop you by the mill.' He smiles at me,
having no idea the torture he's putting me through.

'I'll see you later?' I ask, hopeful.

'Not tonight, Kate. I've got to attend some social function
my mother planned. Tomorrow, I promise.' He helps me
climb into the cab of the truck, my pumps tapping on the
floorboard, a strange sensation underneath my feet. As if
whatever force brought me here is warning me I don't have
much time. I ignore it.

*Not now. Not with my man's hand around my waist.*

'How will you get to the mill?' I don't let go of his hand.
Not yet.

'I parked my roadster behind the ridge so I didn't block
the road. I'm going back to Wrightwood House first. I'm
expecting an important call from the War Department about
that new contract. Mr Clayborn met with the government
representative yesterday.'

'Really?' I act surprised and pray my boss doesn't give me away.

He shakes his head. 'I wish I could tell you more, Jelly Girl, but everything is top secret.'

'I understand.' *Oh, do I.*

I don't dare bring up how I almost lost that government contract. I want to tell him about my Miss Christmas Wrap idea, but I'll surprise him instead. After all, that never happened back then so I have no idea how it will turn out.

The seconds tick by. I run my gloved fingers over the rough fabric on the seat, toying with the design, while Jeff ties up the tree with a long, knotted rope, whistling a holiday tune, his sparkling eyes sneaking a glance at me through the back window of the truck.

'Is the tree secure, Jeff?' Mildred calls out the window. 'Can we go?'

'Not yet, Mildred.' He comes around to my side and motions for me to roll down my window. 'Don't forget our date next week, Jelly Girl.' His voice is dangerously smooth, which only ignites my need for him into a reckless state. He lifts my face like he wants to kiss me, but he stops. *We're not alone,* his eyes say. I'm not worried about the reverend's wife. She'll understand a woman's need to connect with her man, but I'm afraid to kiss him. Afraid it won't be as wonderful as I want it to be.

Or is it something else? Am I worried that I'll break down and start sobbing like a baby? Afraid I won't let go of him?

It's one thing to have my annual day of melancholy, to go through each moment with him during that last week with careful precision, enjoying the best parts, but relive it and lose him again? I can't. I'll break. Besides, I'm not satisfied with a sexy promise anymore. Not when I've come this far. I want the real thing.

I want him.

Before I think twice, I draw his head down to me, cupping my hands over his face so he can't get away, and then brush my lips with his, teasing him, hoping he'll forget everything but kissing me. I feel him stiffen, then a low growl from deep in his throat when I plant a big kiss on his mouth that deepens into something so hot, so passionate, he nearly loses control. My lips burn on his until I melt away his resolve and he kisses me back with a raw hunger, the same hunger seething inside me for endless nights. I didn't mean for it to go this far, knowing Mildred is sitting in the driver's seat, her brows raised, fingers tapping the steering wheel, but I don't know when – or if – I'll get the chance again to show him how I much I love him. I can't quell my raging desire for him, nor do I want to. Long, beautiful moments go by and this lonely girl from Posey Creek shows her man exactly what a kiss can do.

When we finally part, he lets out a low whistle, and then slicks back his hair like he doesn't know what else to do. 'You try a man's soul, Kate.'

That's it. Nothing more. I look hard into his eyes. They smolder dark and rich like golden honey mixed with molasses heated to a boiling temperature and he can't cool it down. Like he doesn't believe it. Then he's off. Taking long strides back behind the trees.

What is fascinating to my time-traveling soul is I find new courage this morning. I let my passion ride a wave that takes me not only back to this wonderful time in my life, but makes me more convinced than ever I came here for a reason. I can't fail to save Jeff. Not now. I'll never regret it.

Without a word, Mildred heads the truck down the dirt road toward the mill. I see a smile of approval curve over her lips. We don't talk about what happened. Or that kiss. I have no doubt my cheeks blush a fever red. Every nerve in my body afire. My senses are so acute, I smell the unique citrus scent of the fir tree drifting through my open window. I fill my lungs with the smell of crushed oranges mixing with Mildred's soft perfume. She glances at me sideways as she makes small talk, commenting on her husband's latest letter about how his men helped him set up an altar in the middle of a jungle using a big box of ammo. Kind soul that she is, she's affording me time to compose myself.

What can I say to her? *I love this man, but I'm going to lose him?* I don't have the heart to tell her the reverend comes home from the war a different man. It isn't until after Mildred drops me off at the mill I remember I didn't ask Jeff about getting a tree for the factory floor.

After the way I kissed him, I doubt he'd remember anyway.

## 15

My career as a pinup girl begins and ends on the same day. Wednesday, five days before Jeff and I are set to elope. I bite my lip, eyes fixed on the day ahead and the task I set for myself on the trip into town. I feel confident our lives are on track, as much as they can be in this hectic time. I have to keep things following a normal fashion so no one suspects what we're up to. That doesn't make it any easier. I want to be with him every minute. Kiss him, hug him. God Almighty, I just want to look at him. Breathe him in. Love him.

Basking in the memory of that kiss puts me at odds with myself. On one hand, I never saw a man smolder with so much desire or look at me with such fascination. His spine stiffened and the wheels in his brain turned in a different direction. Like he wasn't sure what happened to his Jelly Girl. Yet in the back of my mind is the pivotal thought: when to tell him about the letter?

If truth be told, I'm enjoying witnessing life through a different pair of eyes and also making my own history with today's photoshoot. I'm determined to do my best to get this poster done. Besides, it keeps me busy so I don't have to think about the fact I haven't seen Jeff since yesterday morning. I imagine his face when he sees me posing on top of a giant Christmas box to help the paper shortage. Holding me close, whispering in my ear he likes my idea, tugging on my hair like he does when we're alone.

I'm feeling confident when I enter the DB Baker & Sons photography studio situated on a cozy, tree-lined corner of Main Street. The classical brick storefront boasts an oak door weathered with time. That's comforting to me somehow. The studio is two doors down from Maisie's hair salon and across the street from the post office. Downtown is busy with everyone shopping, mailing Christmas cards (if they have any left over from last year) and ladies getting fussed over with manicures. Rich ladies from the west end of town with the big Victorian homes mixing with girls from the mill. Women with foxtails sitting next to cheeky girls with ponytails. A breeding ground for gossip.

There'll be plenty of news to go around when word gets out one of their own is joining the movie star ranks. I won't be surprised if my picture ends up splashed all over the local newspaper. I find the idea amusing. I can't help but think what the townsfolk will say if I put an ad in the Locals section of the *Posey Creek Courier* (people announce who's in town for the holiday or who's home ill) that '*Miss Kate Arden is visiting from the future to spend a week with family.*'

I snicker. Not likely, but I can use a spot of humor. Especially after my meeting earlier with Mr Neville. He kept repeating what a great idea it was to have a girl sitting on an unwrapped, big box decorated for Christmas. Already he's had calls from the local press and the city council wanting copies.

He insisted the factory setting isn't right for the photo-shoot, so we made the trek to the photography studio. He drove me into town in the company car, ranting on about if Mr Timothy starts running things, he'll cut the marketing budget. Along with his job. No wonder he convinced Mr Clayborn if he wants this poster done right, we must go to the best.

DB Baker has been the town's photographer for forty years but his grandson is home on furlough and insists on doing the job.

Flirty Freddie, we called him back in high school, because he liked making time with the girls before he got himself a gig as a photographer with the Army.

I'm impressed with the photos he shows us of his work. GIs going into battle, the fear as well as the courage reflected in every shot. He also caught them at their most vulnerable moments, like smoking a cigarette or writing a letter back home. He captured something in their eyes and on their faces in his photos that looks into the soul of each soldier and what they're thinking: home and Mom and their best girl. That's what they're fighting for.

Freddie is quick to add he's seen action in Belgium and Italy. 'Come Christmastime next year,' he tells me with a wink of an eye, 'who knows where I'll be? London, Paris?'

I put down the magazine and try to smile. I can't. I know where he'll be. In the Ardennes. At the Battle of the Bulge. It's not easy knowing the history of everybody I meet. Freddie was there in the dense woods, holding his position on the frozen ground in the snow, recording the bloody action during that winter of 1944 to 1945 when he got caught in the crossfire and took a hit. He came home with a bum leg, but he never gave up taking pictures and for that I admire him.

But that doesn't give him the right to turn my poster idea into cheesecake. I'm not the shy kid I was back then. I'm a magazine food editor back in my time. I've sat in and supervised several author photo and cover shoots. Watched the art director pose the model in a dream sequence and turn on the wind machine, marveling at the invisible wires attached to a floating goddess advertising heavenly butter. I know about lighting and angles and what Madison Avenue gurus call, 'Sell the sizzle, not the steak.'

Freddie wants more sizzle than I'm willing to give. 'Lift your skirt up higher, so we can see more leg.'

'How about we trade places and *you* pose on top of this box?' I pull down my skirt. I'm wearing my favorite blue sweater with the imitation pearl buttons and a dark skirt. I used leg makeup so I don't get a run in my last pair of precious nylons. 'It's cold sitting up here.'

Up here is a five foot high wooden box hastily constructed to look like a giant Christmas present. Mr Neville painted candy canes, holly, and a waving Santa along with cute elves on each side. The studio is cool so as not to waste fuel, but as soon as Freddie turns on the hot spotlights, a patina of sweat makes my face shine. Which brings the makeup girl out of the corner with her powder puff. A cute kid with braces and bobby sox, she dabs my nose and cheeks with loose powder that flies everywhere and makes me sneeze.

'Please, Miss Arden, try to look like you're enjoying yourself.' Freddie pops a stick of gum into his mouth. 'It's Christmas, you're supposed to be happy because you're helping Uncle Sam, not look like you're going to the dentist. Let's try something else,' he says, pacing up and down. Then he hits me with: 'Undo the top button on your sweater.'

'You don't give up, do you?' I slip the pearl button out of the slender opening not because he asked me, but because I see models do it to add sex appeal. Besides, anything to get this over with so I can go find Jeff.

'Now turn your right shoulder toward me... a little more.' He exhales, wipes his brow and spits out his gum. 'Think of something wonderful... like ice cream or a thick, juicy steak... or kissing a handsome soldier.'

By the smirk on his face, he means him, but my mind goes straight to Jeff. This time I don't try to dissect what happened when we kissed in the woods. I let it happen. Fill me up and take me to dreamland. The lovely, quivery feeling in the pit of my stomach when my lips pressed against his and my whole world lit up inside me like fireworks. Popping, sparkling sensations.

'Hold it. *Don't move.* That's perfect. Keep that smile coming... beautiful, baby, you're a star.' He snaps shot after shot, moving around me, standing on a ladder, shooting me from every angle and he never stops talking. 'By the way, gorgeous, who's taking you to the dance on Saturday night?'

'Who says I'm going?' I shoot back, wiggling my shoulders. I'm getting into this modeling thing. It's fun being on this side of camera instead of watching on the sidelines.

'Every girl in town will be there to meet and greet their favorite soldier. Which, if you're lucky, will be me.'

'Sorry, Freddie, I'm taking my sister, Lucy.'

Jeff asked me, but I can't tell him that. Hopefully we will get lost in the crowd and no one will notice the stardust in my eyes.

'You won't escape me. I'll tag you for a dance and afterward we'll go for a long walk in the moonlight—'

I hear a loud cough from Mr Neville. I almost forgot he's

there. He clears his throat. 'Did you get the shot you wanted, Sgt Baker? Miss Arden and I have work to do and must be getting back to the mill.'

'Sure thing, Pops. Miss Arden is easy on the eyes and a heck of a model.' He lifts me off the box and I swear he gives my waist an extra squeeze, making me flinch. I pretend not to notice. Freddie is a good-looking guy and fast with the compliments. I see why girls fall for his line. Every girl but me. Jeff is the only man I want. 'Don't forget, save me a dance.' Then he winks at me.

'With all the pretty girls in town, I doubt you'll have time for me.' I wink back.

'Oh, yeah? You're my type. The girl next door with class. We went to the same high school, right?'

'You never noticed me.'

'I am now, sister.' He whistles at me.

He takes a step back, giving me the onceover as if he can't figure me out. 'You're different than you were back in high school. Not so much the quiet kid who spent more time with her nose in a book than teasing the boys.' He looks me up and down. 'Baby, do I like it.'

'You, on the other hand, are the same Freddie Baker.' I poke him in the ribs. 'I *don't* like it.'

With that, I can't wait to leave the studio with Mr Neville trailing at my heels, huffing and puffing like he can't breathe. Neither can I.

'I've never met such an impertinent young man.' He wipes the sweat off his face and loosens his bowtie, something I never saw him do before.

'I have. The publishing business is full of them.' I don't bother to explain. 'He *is* good at his job.' I smile at Mr Neville, remembering Freddie's poignant and stirring photos of soldiers at war. I don't want to be too hard on him, putting himself in danger to capture the war on film for generations to come so I say with a smile, 'Don't worry, Pops. He got the shot. I'd bet on it.'

* * *

I'm counting the Christmas presents I bought for Ma and the family on this chilly December late Wednesday afternoon when I hear the telephone ring. It can't be for me, not with the whole block on the same party line. Still, it takes me a minute to recollect whether or not it's our specific ring. Two short rings. Two long.

That's ours. I'm curious, but Ma is the gatekeeper when it comes to the phone. Besides, Jeff wouldn't call me here (Mrs Widget might be listening). My friend Helen isn't allowed to use the phone in her mom's shop except for business.

Lost in my thoughts, I check over the presents my younger self put together. I line up the unwrapped gifts on my bed in a straight line like good soldiers.

I start wrapping bows around the presents, but the phone won't stop ringing.

It rings five, six more times. Where's Ma? Finally, the ringing stops. I breathe out. Good. She must have answered it.

I want to spend every precious moment with Jeff this week until that fateful morning when he gets on that train. I can't. He's busy with the mill production, so I relive memories with him more vivid because I'm here. Like the time I was at Wrightwood House with Ma delivering sugar cookies she made for Christmas Eve. I saw a young Polish maid in the kitchen, sobbing. She wasn't much older than I was. She didn't speak much English, but I took her hand and together we sat in the kitchen and sang Christmas Carols and ate sugar cookies. Imagine my surprise when Jeff showed up and joined us. It was my best Christmas Eve ever, the three of us holding hands and singing. I lost that part of me over the years. That the true spirit of Christmas is giving, no matter how small or how simple. To think it took a trip through time for me to get it back. Why was I so stubborn? I shouldn't have waited so long to go home for Christmas.

Thinking only of myself every holiday and my pain. I hurt Lucy, too. I'm determined to make it up to her when I get back to my own time.

Why am I so sure I'm going back? I rub my head, aching from the turmoil and confusion I experienced the past few days. My long rolls of hair come loose and keep falling in my eyes. I go back to what is a favorite ritual of mine during the holidays. Going through the presents I purchased, wrapping them up with pretty bows and anointing each one with a special prayer my family will use it well in the coming New Year. Gifts are hard to come by this season, but Pop and Junior are easy. My younger self traded two jars of cherry jam for Mr Evers' best tobacco in the shop, and a factory worker at the mill donated a used baseball mitt to our barter exchange I got for Junior. I found a fluffy, blue bed jacket made from brushed rayon for Lucy, and I crocheted wool rosette earmuffs for Ma so her ears won't freeze when she hangs up the laundry in the cold wind.

I sit back on my heels, thinking. I hoped she'd love the muffs as I much as I do, but Ma never wears my girlish gift. I find it years later with the bow still on. That's Ma, too practical for her own good. So I made a special trip to the drugstore and picked up a big glass jar of lavender scented hand cream. I have a feeling she'll like that.

The phone starts ringing again. More insistent this time. Whoever is on the other end isn't giving up.

'Ma, *Ma!*' I call out, looking down the stairs. No one is about. Lucy isn't home from school yet, Junior is at the community center playing ping pong, and Pop doesn't get off work until six o'clock. I glance out the upstairs window in the hallway and see Ma hanging up sheets in the backyard.

'I'm coming, I'm coming,' I mutter, taking two steps at a time down the stairs. I grab the receiver. 'Arden residence. This is Kate. Can I help you?' I say, using my best office voice in case it's for Pop.

'This is Mrs Ambrose Rushbrooke,' comes the stern, cold voice.

I cringe. 'Ma's outside, Mrs Rushbrooke,' I say in a pleasing voice even if she's mean to Ma and that irks me. 'I'll get her for you.'

'Don't bother, dear.'

Cold, territorial attitude. I feel a shiver go up my back. 'Excuse me?'

'I wish to speak to you.'

'Me?' I nearly choke.

'I'll get straight to the point, Miss Arden. You are *not* to see my son again.'

'I don't know what you're talking about.'

*Deny everything.* A practice I've seen my boss at Holtford Company use many times when something goes wrong with a book shipment that never arrives.

'You're a selfish, impertinent girl,' she continues as if she didn't hear me. 'You don't care about Jeffrey. If you did, you'd let him go so he can get over this silly fascination he has with you.'

'Is that what you think it is?' I don't deny her words since it's obvious she's found out somehow, though we've been dating six months. 'I'm in love with Jeff and he loves me.'

'You're a foolish girl, my dear, if you think my son could fall for you,' she says in that condescending manner of hers to make me retreat like I'm a bunny and she stepped on my tail. She isn't dealing with that nineteen year old girl. She's dealing with me.

I fight back. 'Jeff knows what he wants and he wants me. His love makes me feel alive.'

'What if I disown him, then what? Do you think he'll stay with you after the war when he has no family, no home?'

'Love is about sticking together, Mrs Rushbrooke, whatever the problems we face.'

'You surprise me, Miss Arden. I had no idea you had a head on your shoulders.'

'You don't know a lot of things about me.'

'That doesn't change my mind. If anything, it makes me more determined to make sure you don't see my son again. He could actually be in love with you and that only makes matters worse.' She pauses a moment, as if taking a long drag on a cigarette. 'You are to cease your involvement with my son immediately. Is that clear?'

'I can't. I love him.'

'You're too young to know what love is.'

'It's understanding and caring for somebody so much you'll do anything to be with them.' *Even travel through time*, I add silently. 'I know what it's like to torture yourself when you're not together. Knowing I'll see him soon is the sweetest torture. I've lived for such a long time knowing how easily I could lose him. You can't stop me from feeling what I do. Or Jeff either.'

'My son has no idea what's good for him.'

'You do?'

'I'm his mother.'

'Does that give you the right to choose his life for him?'

'Of course it does.'

'Where were you when he was growing up? Why didn't you help him through those painful times when he needed you?' I'm on a roll, but I'm not fool enough to bring up the physical and mental abuse his father wields over him. I can't be sure the woman is privy to what her son endures at the hands of his father and it isn't my place to tell her.

'I called you not to *ask* you to stop seeing my son, Miss Arden, but to *order* you, is that clear?'

'There's static on the line, Mrs Rushbrooke, I can't hear you.'

I take the coward's way out and don't acknowledge her threat. I don't want to say something I'll regret. The woman is mean and hurtful, but she's Jeff's mother and I'm naïve enough to believe I can have a civil relationship with her. I don't understand how a woman can be so self-absorbed she doesn't see how much she's alienating her son. Or doesn't she care?

The back door creaks.

I peek into the kitchen and see Ma coming in with her empty laundry basket and the late afternoon sun setting at her back. I swear she's covered in a holy light of orange-gold. I want to slam down the phone, but seeing Ma gives me new courage.

'What was that you said, Mrs Rushbrooke?' I ask. 'We have a bad connection.'

'I'm *ordering* you to stop seeing my son.'

'I'll do that,' I say, inhaling a deep breath, then, 'when Jeff stops loving me. Good day.' Then I hang up.

'Who was that, Kate?' she asks with her usual calm.

'Nobody important, Ma.' I say, forcing a light tone in my voice as I try to put on a brave front, but I can't stop shaking. My heart sinks.

'It was Mrs Rushbrooke, wasn't it?'

I spin around. 'How'd you know?'

'She called earlier when you weren't here and asked to talk to you.' She smiles. 'You gave her an earful, baby, didn't you?'

'I did, Ma.'

'Good for you. I don't like to speak bad about people in this town, but that woman had it coming.' She fusses with her apron, wringing her hands on the soft cotton. 'There'll be repercussions. She won't buy my jam for the holidays, but she'll come round by spring. She always does.'

*Not this time.*

'Ma, I—'

'You don't have to explain, Kate. You did what's right. I raised my girls to go after what they want and if Mr Jeffrey is the man for you, then nothing can stop it, not even Mrs Rushbrooke.'

She hugs me and gives me that look that says, *What's done is done and life will go on.* I'm so lucky to have her for a mother. I wish I could tell her the truth, but I'm already tiptoeing on top of a glass bottle. Who knows what might tip it over? I could lose everything if I dare taunt whatever forces brought me here with a careless word. I've already tempted them by giving Mrs Rushbrooke a piece of my mind just now, something the younger me never would have done, and that worries me. Nothing must interfere with me telling Jeff about the letter. I have time. He said he'll meet me at the cherry tree tonight. That was before his mother called. I don't feel so brave now.

'I hope you're right, Ma, about Jeff and me.'

'I feel it in my bones, child.' She looks down at her hands. Red, rough. Is she thinking about that hand cream I promised her?

*You'll have it for Christmas, Ma.*

'I've got a deep feeling you're anxious about something that's bigger than you are.'

'What do you mean, Ma?'

'You remind me of that gopher we had in our Victory Garden last spring. He kept popping his head up, sniffing around and looking for something nigh onto a week till one day he didn't pop up no more, like he'd disappeared deep down into the bowels of the earth.' She looks at me with a profound sadness etched onto her face. 'Promise me you won't disappear, Kate.'

'I promise, Ma.'

I feel guilty the minute I say the words. Whatever happens, I won't be the same girl I am now. Somehow, my younger self will have to deal with the changes I made in her life after I read the sergeant's letter and learned the truth about Jeff. If I'm successful in warning him, can I dare believe Jeff and I will be together after all?

Till then, I'm here. I won't give up these precious moments with Ma. She clasps her hand over mine. Its coldness sends a shiver through me. Or is it something else?

That I made her a promise I can't keep.

## 16

The misty frost coating the yellowish-green stalks standing in Ma's Victory Garden is the closest we get to snow this year. Christmas is only nine days away, but my time to elope with Jeff is four days from now. December twentieth. There's a chill in the air. I'm sleepy-eyed and nervous at work today since I was up for hours last night thinking about the earful Mrs Rushbrooke gave me yesterday.

I won't take back a word, but that doesn't mean I'm not fearful of what havoc that woman can wreak. I'm convinced I can handle her but seeing news about a train wreck in the morning paper sets a fire under me. What if I was in an accident and don't know it? What if this is all a dream and I lie dying somewhere?

I don't know why such a morbid thought hits me so hard. I'm beginning to have my doubts about changing the past. Every time I try to talk to Jeff, something happens to stop me. He didn't show up at the cherry tree last night. I waited until it got so cold I had to leave. No wonder I couldn't sleep, half of me believing he has a good excuse and the other half fearing he changed his mind about marrying me.

*Have you no faith in the man? You two go back a long way, he won't leave you hanging.*

And there's no telling what he's facing at home. To me, the war is over. Back here, the threat of invasion is a real thing as well as the fear of losing more lives in this conflict. Jeff has no idea what's in store for him, that if he becomes a bomber pilot there's a good chance he'll never return.

I start to cry. Soft tears messing up my cake mascara. Now I understand why he wants to marry me. He wants to leave me well cared for. I never thought of that back then. What teenage girl thinks about how she's going to fend for herself in the world? You figure there's always going to be a job you can do. I've seen it doesn't work that way. The funny thing is, even if I change history and bring Jeff home, I want to write. I've had a taste of independence and I like it.

I'm scared I've just made things worse with my meddling. Something tells me Mrs Rushbrooke isn't finished with me and it's my own doing. I did wonder if Helen was feeding her information about Jeff and me, but I was sure she wasn't.

And then I found out who it was when I jumped on the bus early this morning and saw Sarah Canton at the wheel, grinning and fussing with her new hairdo. Rolls of big curls sat on top of her head. The worst part was when she shot me the 'V for Victory' sign. A sick feeling rolled through me. She must have gone to Maisie's and although the shop owner won't gossip about me, I have no doubt Mrs Rushbrooke got her information about Jeff and me from one of her snobby friends. A busybody who overheard Mrs Canton complaining about how I made her stop the bus so I could hobnob with the boss's son. That woman will be the end of me. Worse yet,

I have no doubt Mrs Rushbrooke will do everything in her power to have me fired.

*So what are you going to do about it? Roll over or fight?*

I can sit here at my desk and wonder when I'm getting the axe. Or I can beat Mrs Rushbrooke to the punch. I choose the latter.

* * *

'I quit.'

'You *what*?' Mr Clayborn holds onto his desk for support. I catch him in a bad moment, pacing up and down in his office, snapping his pencil in half while he tries to make sense of a report he holds in his hand. My blunt statement does him in.

'I said I quit. I'm leaving the company, sir.' I keep my voice calm though inside I'm walking over coals, my skin hot to the touch. I don't wipe the sweat off my face, though I want to.

*Are you insane? Quitting your job? What's your younger self going to do when you go back to your own time?*

'Why in heaven's name, Miss Arden, would you do that?' he says in a blustery tone. Yet I can tell by the drooping corners of his mouth, he's hurt. 'Don't you like working for me?'

'Yes, I do. You've taught me a lot and someday I'll remember the skills I learned from you about office management when I work for a big publishing company. That's a long way off.'

*Stop this madness before you can't take it back.*

'Then why won't you stay?'

'It's a private matter, sir.' I don't want to say anything about Jeff and me.

He slumps down in his chair and pushes his coffee cup across the desk in frustration. 'Has Timothy made a pass at you?'

'No, sir,' I lie. No need to have the whole family against me.

'Timothy Rushbrooke tries to make time with all the pretty girls. I figured you could take care of yourself. So it must be something else.'

'I'd rather not talk about it, Mr Clayborn.'

'I'm missing something here,' he says to himself more than to me. 'You like working here, the other secretaries speak highly of your efficiency, and the ladies on the factory floor adore you.' He looks at me and I swear he sees right through my charade. I'm shaking and my eyes are misty. 'It's Jeff, isn't it? He's broken your heart.'

'Sir...'

'I'm surprised at the boy. I took him to be upstanding and a gentleman. I'm disappointed in him.'

'He doesn't know anything about my decision, Mr Clayborn.'

'Then why are you leaving?'

'There's a rumor going around about Jeff and me. Certain people saw us together and mistook it for something it isn't.'

'Oh, really?' He stares me direct in the eye. 'Miss Arden... Kate, you may not believe it, but I know a thing or two about women, though my late wife would dispute that when our anniversary came around.' He pauses, a deep, burning glow making his eyes shine at her memory. 'I've known for the past few months you're in love with that boy and he loves you.'

'Mr Clayborn...'

'I'm not blind, Kate. I see how you look at him and how he watches you when you're at your desk typing, or when you head off to deliver memos, your heels tapping on the floor. He comes into my office and asks me how you're doing, if you need anything, if you like your job. He cares about what happens to you and wants to see you happy. If you'll tell me who's spreading these rumors, I'll put an end to it—'

I gasp loudly and put my hand to my mouth. I can't tell him the truth. For once I don't speak my mind, but the look on my face gives me away. He reads me loud and clear.

'It's no secret Mrs Rushbrooke keeps a close eye on Jeff. Is that it?'

I nod. 'Now you understand why I have to leave.'

He taps his fingers on the desk. 'Your Pop is going to be heartbroken.'

'I might try modeling,' I say in a whimsical moment and striking a pose. It's a silly notion, but I have to say something. I try to smile, but my lower lip quivers and I can't stop the cold, clammy feeling running down to my toes. 'Freddie says I'm a good model.'

'You're not going anywhere, Kate.' My boss pounds on his desk with his fist. More dramatic than he intended, but it gets my attention. 'I need you here, do you understand?'

'It won't work, Mr Clayborn,' I say, my shoulders slumped. 'That woman dislikes me intensely.'

'You let me worry about Mrs Rushbrooke. She may run her husband, but she doesn't run the mill. Whatever she threatened you with, it won't go over here.' He clears his throat. 'We have an important memo to get out before lunch about that new contract. Get your pad, Miss Arden, and let's get to work.' He winks at me and the matter is settled. I'm not quitting. My spirits rise as a surge of confidence shoots through me. I know Mr Clayborn will look out for me and not only because I'm a good worker. I believe deep down he's a bit of a romantic. That makes me smile. Let Mrs Rush-brooke put *that* in her hat.

More important, I gain an ally in my determination to save Jeff, something I hoped for. I can't and *won't* let woman win.

I must admit, I'm relieved when Mr Clayborn sends me back to my desk with the understanding we never speak of the matter again. I see him in a new light, a man who is not only a good boss, but a good soul. Which is why I'm not surprised when he sends me into town that afternoon to the bank, me riding in the backseat of the company car, to deliver paperwork to the manager.

Jeff is there.

'Kate, what are you doing here?' Jeff whispers, leading me by the elbow toward the private office in the back. The bank is a fine old financial institution with mahogany desks with pearl-inlayed tops and life-size paintings of men in colonial wigs and tight breeches on the walls. One droopy Christmas wreath hangs on the front door as if to say money is a serious business and takes no holiday. The bank is as quiet as a library. It's a quarter to three.

'Mr Clayborn sent me.' I look every which way to see if anyone is watching us. The manager left, so I drop off the manila envelope with his secretary. She keeps looking at the big round clock on the wall, its ordinary, plain numbers a stark contrast to the ornate, historical décor. She smiles at me and then goes back to applying fresh lipstick. No doubt she's meeting the train this afternoon. She pays little attention to Jeff and me disappearing into a back office. I make no pretense about how I feel about him, smiling so big any woman will recognize the love for him in my eyes and the spring in my walk. Rest assured, there's no escape from any future gossip about us.

Jeff has no idea what trepidations simmer inside me. The poor darling gives me a guilty look that he sugars with a sexy growl. Testing the waters, he says. 'I hope you're not sore at me for not showing up last night.'

'I should be,' I tease, avoiding his dark eyes. *Playing games, are you? Be careful.*

'I couldn't get there until after midnight.' He turns me around to face him, his eyes never leaving mine, trying to read my thoughts. 'I had to drag Timothy home last night before he got himself in another jam.' He doesn't elaborate, but I can imagine. Women, gambling. The mill owner's son is an easy mark for the drifters and ne'er-do-wells looking to fleece money from him. As I watch, his worried expression makes deeper lines on his brow, unsettling me. I have no reason to play games with him, nor do I want to, but a little teasing doesn't hurt. I ignore that little voice telling me I'm playing with fire. Instead I touch his arm and I feel him relax, his expression softening when I say. 'I can never be mad at you, Jeff. Especially when I came so far to find you.'

He looks confused. 'I don't understand you, Kate. I expected you to stomp your foot and pout like you usually do.'

*I do that?*

He adds a sheepish grin. 'You look so cute doing it.'

My heart swells. Only a man in love would say that. 'I'm not that teenage girl anymore, Jeff. I've grown up.'

'You sure have.' His expression tells me he's referring more to my kissing technique than my appearance. Still, he has something else on his mind. He runs his hand through his hair, mussing it up more than usual. Jeff pulls me farther into the back corner office where we won't be seen. 'Speaking of you growing up, I want to kiss you right now.'

'You do?' My eyes widen. I can still play the schoolgirl. Again, I ignore the advice of my sensible self and keep flirting with him.

'Nothing's changed between us, Kate, though I admit you gave me something to think about the other day with that kiss.'

Here it comes. The consequences of my foolishness.

'About that—' I begin, shuffling my feet.

I have to tell him about the gossip before anyone else does.

The clock strikes the hour. One... two... three.

Jeff breathes into my ear, making me shiver. 'The bank is closed.'

'Are we locked in here?' I ask, curious.

'Would you mind, Jelly Girl?'

He confesses that when he saw the company car pull up outside and me get out, he checked to make sure the back office was empty. Rushbrooke Mills is the bank's biggest customer, so no one will question him if he lingers here after closing time to go over the bank's books.

We're alone. I let out a heavy sigh when he draws me close and presses me against his broad chest. Hidden behind a bookcase filled with massive handwritten tomes my worlds collide under the branding of his kiss. Burning desire consumes me, my lips on fire when he deepens the kiss and my knees wobble. This is no boyish fling with a pretty girl, but the raw hunger of a man turning me into a pool of melting passion. He can't hold back and I do as I've wanted to do so many times. I surrender to him, digging my nails into his fine, wool tweed, knowing he'll soon trade it for the leather of a bomber jacket. Not for long. There's no uniform for a spy except the band of courage steeled into his bones.

I can't send him off to war unfulfilled. I don't protest when he picks me up and sits me on the fine mahogany desk empty except for a quill pen and bottle of ink. I should, since he's put me in a compromising position. My younger self would tremble and the sheer look of innocence in her eyes would stop Jeff from going any farther. He'd pull back, not wanting to hurt me.

I push that thought aside as his hands roam up and down my ribcage, his mouth holding mine captive in a long, long kiss. I should say something before I lose all sense of reason. I can't. I revel in his unexpected move, his zealous push to do what my eyes begged him, what my kiss promised. That he'll find me all woman and ready to love him back in ways he never imagined.

He nuzzles his face in my hair. 'With luck, they won't find us till morning.'

'Yes... morning.'

Before I contemplate that unsettling thought, his hands are everywhere on me and I thrill to his touch like I never have. That little voice warning me finally gets through when I knock over the ink. It spills. Making a big dark splotch on the gray blotter. Reminding me I can't go through with this, that like the ink soaking deep into the blotter, I can't take back my actions. I'm still a young woman in this time. I can't ignore that little voice in my head telling me I have no guarantee I can change the future. We can't do something we regret later.

I push him away. Gently. A push nonetheless.

'No, Jeff, we can't.' To my surprise, he nods.

'I know, Kate, but I wanted you all to myself for a little while.' He pulls off his tie, which is half-undone as usual. That makes me smile. 'I'm sorry I lost my head. I got carried away when I saw you, knowing no one will spy on us here.'

'About that...' I say, knowing I have to tell him about the phone call. 'I've caused an awful mess, Jeff. It's just I love you so much and I'm afraid of losing you.'

'You're stuck with me, Jelly Girl.'

'Oh, if only that were true.' I sigh. 'Not everyone thinks so.'

'You mean my mother.'

'You heard.'

He smirks. 'She lectured me for an hour this morning about my responsibility to the Rushbrooke name. I told her that's why I fell in love with a girl like you.'

I gulp. 'She knows about our plans to get married?'

'No. That's our secret, but I'm tired of sneaking around and pretending not to notice you when you're the most wonderful girl in the world.'

'I think you're wonderful, too, Jeff, but we don't want to upset your mother. We should respect her feelings. She's trying to protect what she sees as her legacy.'

'I love you for saying that, Kate. Once we're married, she'll have no choice but to accept you. Till then, we have to be careful.' His arms tighten around me and he presses my head against his chest. 'Monday can't come soon enough for me.'

'Me, neither.'

He lets me go, that indefinable grin on his face making me smile, too. 'I'll pick you up for the dance on Saturday night.'

'Do you think that's a good idea?' There's no telling what his mother will do if we show up together. 'I can go with Lucy and meet you there.' I don't mention Freddie and his precocious advances and wanting to dance with me. It isn't a big deal, so why worry?

He nods. 'I'll be working at the factory late seeing how we've stepped up production, but nothing can keep me from dancing with you. Not even Goebbels himself.'

He's trying to make me smile but his words chill me, reminding me of the horrors to come.

'Please believe me, Jeff, when I tell you we have many months before this war is won.' Do I dare tell him more? 'Many battles will be fought in the air over Germany and ground troops will fight hard to make advances in Italy... lives will be lost both in Europe and the Pacific. In places like Anzio and Iwo Jima.'

He looks at me like I'm crazy.

'You've been watching too many newsreels, Kate. We'll have those Nazis whipped before next Christmas. We'll win in the Pacific, too.' He regards my outburst with a strange cast in his eyes. 'I don't know who's filling your head with this stuff. The government needs you to do your job here at home and leave the fighting to us.'

I'm upset. 'You haven't been called up yet.'

'No, but I heard rumors swirling around Washington that something big is in the air. I'm hoping they'll speed up the pilot training. Fourteen months is a long time to wait to get in a cockpit, thunder down the runway, and take off to show those Nazis they can't destroy us.'

'Oh, Jeff, if you only knew what you're getting into.'

'Knew what?'

I lower my eyes. 'I'd tell you, but you won't believe me.' I suck in a sharp breath. 'We need to have a serious talk about us.'

'I know.'

I look up. 'You do?'

He grins. 'Sure. Enough war talk. I asked you to marry me and I don't even have a ring to give you. Don't worry, I'll get you the prettiest wedding ring when we get to Washington. You can pick out anything you want and when we come home to Posey Creek, I've got a place picked out for us. A two story house near the river fixed up with new plumbing, nice and private. It used to be a refuge during colonial times for patriots hiding from the British. My family has owned it since then. No one uses it anymore. It'll be swell.'

'Yeah, swell.' I clasp my hands together tight, my voice going up an octave, maybe two.

I can't believe my ears. We never had this discussion back then and for once, I forget I'm supposed to be a more mature me and simply stare at the man. I'm filled with the joy and anticipation of a woman soon to be a bride. My own home? Is it possible? I grew up in a big old house with Ma at the helm and rightly so. Then in New York, I moved from one tiny brownstone to another, places where the sidewalks heat up in summer and become slippery decks in winter. No trees or flowers except for the tiny pots on my windowsill filled with geraniums and fresh herbs. A piece of home, even if I won't admit it.

My heart swells. I always wanted my own home. Jeff knows it. He often commented on how his Jelly Girl should have her own kitchen to make his favorite jam. I can barely believe it, my mind whirling with the dream of us being together back in my own time. In that house. Of course I'll find a job here in Posey Creek, hopefully writing for the *Courier,* and who says I can't continue as a contributing food editor for a New York magazine? Send in my stories by mail. The stakes are even higher now, things moving so fast my head is spinning. I want to be near him, for he touches my soul like no other.

I let the urgency to tell him about the letter go. It stands between us, but without it I never could bridge the years between my time and now. He's so excited about the future, he won't believe me anyway. What catches in my craw is that saving him isn't as simple as I first believed. I feel as though we're worlds apart and I'm not sure we can close the gap between the girl I was then and who I am now. No man wants to be told how to run a war by a woman, even his fiancée. Unsettling, but I can't let that stop me. I'll have to tread carefully when it comes to revealing what I know. The problem is, while my heart sings with the joy of being a bride, my practical self reminds me I won't be a bride if I don't convince him I'm from the future. That I love him so much, somehow I found my way back to warn him. That my love for him is that strong. I have to bide my time, knowing I don't have much of it left.

We plan to elope on Monday morning. Early. I have to tell him before he gets on that train. Make him see the danger and grab onto it, use it to save his life. Then we can have that house by the river.

The night watchman lets us out via the back door – he minds his own business, but I see he's curious – and then Jeff drops me off at my house. He can't promise, but he'll try to meet me at the cherry tree tomorrow night. He leaves the engine running while he kisses me, long enough to stir intense feelings in the pit of my belly and make it hard for me to let him go. I needn't worry, he's gone before I catch my breath. It doesn't matter. The damage is done. I see the curtain on the second floor move. Lucy saw us. I don't care. I'm going to marry Jeff.

Nothing can stop us.

* * *

'I saw you kissing Jeffrey Rushbrooke,' my kid sister blurts out the minute I come through the front door. 'Are you crazy, Kate?'

'So?' I say quickly. 'We're getting married.'

'I don't understand you. You were so secretive before, now you're kissing the man right outside our front door.' She peeks through the curtains. 'You know that snoopy Mrs Widget never closes her drapes.'

'Girls, set the table for supper.' Ma shoos us into the kitchen. 'Kate will tell us about it when she's ready.' She smiles at me with the biggest twinkle in her eyes, one I haven't seen since she won the blue ribbon for her geraniums before the war.

'Thanks, Ma.' I hug her.

She lets out a sigh. 'I hope you know what you're doing, Katie Marie.'

I wince. Now Ma is using my nickname. That means she isn't as easygoing about me marrying Jeff as she pretends. I see the corners of her eyes wrinkling into deep creases.

'I do, Ma. You'll see.'

'How come you're so easy on Kate, Ma?' Lucy huffs and puffs, getting the silverware. 'When I want something like my own face powder or get my hair done up, you say I'm too young. Whatever Kate wants, she gets.'

'Your time will come, child,' Ma says, fretting. I see how

upset she is, something she never shows. Do her instincts tell her that her elder daughter is in over her head?

'When, Ma?' Lucy insists. 'Girls my age are getting engaged every day. Sometimes to more than one soldier.'

Ma sets the dinner plates down on the table so hard, they rattle.

'Lucy Arden, do you think this is a game you're playing? Pulling on the heartstrings of these fine young men like a siren with a harp?' Ma sits her down on the kitchen stool like she used to make us do when we were little and our feet couldn't touch the floor. I keep quiet. I had no idea my mother has such thoughts. 'It's time we had a talk, young lady.'

Lucy and I both groan. Now that we're grown up, it doesn't mean we're too big for one of her lectures. It's a doozy.

'I'm proud of my girls, how you put up the jams for the soldiers and greet those boys and girls serving our country. Tonight I'm ashamed, Lucy. The holiest of nights will soon be upon us and when those men are camped out under the stars, their rifles by their side, their God in their hearts, they'll be thinking of the girl back home. Seeing her face in the stars like she's an angel of victory. Seeing your face.'

'Ma—'

'I'm not saying don't write to these young men. They need letters from home to comfort them. They don't need false promises from girls who have no intention of keeping them.'

'I do,' she protests. 'Then I meet another soldier, and I like him, too.' She stares at Ma, puzzled. 'What am I going to do?'

Ma smiles. 'Don't be in such a hurry to grow up, Lucy. Be the girl next door, their friend. Don't try to be every soldier's sweetheart. You can't. For their sake and yours. Don't fight with your sister. Kate's going to have a rough time with her young man if things don't simmer down. She doesn't need you stirring the pot.'

'Ma's right, Lucy, let's not fight,' I tell her, trying to calm her down. The irony is Lucy will find her man and have a good home and three kids, while I lose Jeff in the war. I have to set the stage for her meeting her soldier and if she runs into trouble back in my own time, I'll fix it. 'I promise you'll meet the handsomest soldier and live a wonderful life with him and have three beautiful children. A boy and twin girls.'

I wait for the winds of time to blow open the back door and send a scolding tempest my way. All I hear is the shrill whistle of the tea kettle. Ma turns it off. Then she goes back to her macaroni and cheese casserole finishing up in the oven, adding more paprika as she keeps her ear attuned to what I'm saying.

'Twins?' Lucy's eyes spark. 'You're making that up.' The smile on her face is so real, she wants to believe me because I described the life she wants so badly in her heart.

'I wish I could tell you how I know,' I say. 'Maybe someday I will. For now, you've got to trust me.'

I've said more than I should, but I'm so frustrated at fighting the war alone, I can't hold back anymore. Ma has already guessed something is afoot even if she doesn't understand it, but she accepts it. Like a frost in late May or sun-warmed sprouts poking up out of the earth in the dead of winter. Like nature is playing a trick on her. She's a wise, God-fearing woman, and if He's behind it, I imagine her telling herself, who is she to doubt it?

Lucy needs more convincing.

'You act different, Kate. The way you talk, move, your interest in the war news and what's happening overseas. Like you figured out what's going to happen before it does. A quirky sense none of us have, but you do. You were never like that before. I don't know why you've changed. I guess I'm too young and too dumb to figure it out.' She unties the ribbon in her hair and lets the soft curls fall around her shoulders like a mantle of womanhood. 'For some crazy reason, I believe everything you said.'

'Then stick by me like Ma says, because I know what's coming, little sister, the biggest heartbreak any woman can experience, and unless I change it, I'm going to need you more than ever.'

She must have read something in my eyes I can't hide. A desperation that turns them dark and melancholy, for I swear she grows up at that moment. Never again is she the innocent bobby-soxer.

'Oh, Kate, I'm so sorry. I've been a mean, horrible person. Whatever it is, we'll get through it together. I promise.'

She hugs me tight and I hear her catch her breath. I look over my shoulder and I see Ma smiling. Dabbing her eyes with her apron. Today is Thursday. The clock is ticking.

Reminding me I don't have much time left.

**17**
_____

I almost give away my secret life when I meet up with Helen the next day. Friday, the day before the dance. My friend is strangely quiet when we rendezvous in front of the post office. The community center is a short walk away and although the air is crisp, I don't feel the cold.

My thoughts bounce back and forth between the past I'm living now and the future I'm so set on changing when I push through the big double doors of the center. The sweet, sticky smell of pine invades my senses, a gentle reminder Christmas is in the air. Prickly cones strung on wires and interlaced with holly berries hang from the rafters, making the scent overpowering. It makes me dreamy-eyed. I enjoy the poignancy of revisiting the holiday season at a time when I'm young and filled with hope, such feelings heating my skin.

I try to focus on the task at hand but I want to jump out of my clothes, a romantic thought that doesn't surprise me since I daydream often about Jeff's strong body pressed next to mine after we're married. Maybe even more often now I'm back here because I know I'll lose him again if I take a misstep. That thought haunts me mercilessly, making me shake and, at the same time, fuels my determination to make things right, wake up with him in the mornings and kiss him. Call him my husband. I so blindly believe it isn't impossible, if I've come this far it has to be. The moment to tell him about the letter will present itself, like finding a flower blooming under the snow.

It takes your breath away.

Until then, I have to pretend everything is normal. That means decorating the community center. Mr Clayborn insisted I leave work early to help out. True to his word, we never speak of our conversation again, but I know he's cheering for me to be with Jeff.

Because I'm feeling so sure of myself I let my guard down around Helen. My journey is almost over, so I speak without thinking. It starts when Helen lays a bombshell on me.

'I overheard a telephone conversation,' Helen says, 'between Mr Rushbrooke and some bigwig when I delivered a package to Wrightwood House.' She seems both intrigued and puzzled. Like she knows it's important, but she doesn't know why. She confided in me that she gets a secret thrill spying on the Rushbrookes, as if she's helping my romance. She has no idea what harm her eavesdropping can do if it goes any further than her telling me.

'You got my attention.' I keep my voice casual. 'What gives?'

'I heard him say our troops are dropping in on the Nazis very soon and have the men and supplies lined up and ready to go.' Her eyes settle on me. She's clearly interested in my reaction.

I don't answer her right away. This isn't good. She picked

up top-secret information about government plans to help the French Résistance.

'I doubt if it means anything,' I say, smiling and looking around. The center is humming with volunteers, women and girls, chatting and laughing as they set up tables, chairs, and a big coffee urn. White ceramic cups are lined up row after row on a green felt card table.

'You can tell me, Kate. Is Jeff in on it?' she whispers. 'Is that why you're acting so strange?' Her blue eyes glow with curiosity, daring me to give her an answer. I have no choice but to impart on her the harsh reality of what the consequences are for leaking intelligence.

'You must never repeat what you heard to anyone, Helen,' I beg her, knowing she's trying to help me. What she told me is the beginning of preparations for D-Day. 'If that information falls into the wrong hands, civilians as well as Résistance fighters will die.'

'Jeff told you that?'

'Yes,' I lie, hoping I'm not going to regret it. 'According to news reports, several Frenchmen were killed by the Nazis in reprisal for the deaths of two German soldiers.'

Too late I catch myself. Yes, it happens. In January 1944.

Helen looks puzzled. 'No wonder you haven't been yourself lately.'

I don't deny it, but her observation gives me a jolt. As much as I want to, I can't share with her that I've come from another time to save the man I love because I can't live without him. That Jeff will be among the men and women dropped into occupied France and other countries to train the locals for the invasion that's coming.

I have to divert her attention. 'I can't keep the news from you any longer, Helen,' I say, seizing the moment.

She arches a brow. 'Did he pop the question?'

I nod. 'Jeff asked me to marry him in the spring when the cherry blossoms bloom. You know how much he loves Ma's cherry jam.' Thankfully, a career in wooing advertisers and dealing with fickle authors has taught me how to think fast and come up with excuses so good they sound real. Helen accepts my explanation, teasing me about having Mrs Rushbrooke for a mother-in-law.

'I bet she looks into her magic mirror every day,' she says, 'but it's afraid to talk back.'

'Are you sure she didn't see you at Wrightwood House?' God help us both if the woman finds out Helen is spying on them.

'The butler said she wasn't home.'

'She's probably out buying a new mirror,' I joke.

We both laugh and I relax, letting her think about it. That will take her mind off the explosive information she heard about the drops into France and Belgium.

Meanwhile, we get the decorations underway for the dance tomorrow night along with the other volunteers. The large public room is flanked on either side by smaller rooms used for club meetings. I hear the loud chatter of women engaged in a discussion over the latest pamphlet about air raid precautions, along with who wore the most outlandish hat to the wardens' meeting. I smile. Everything is rationed but hats.

Helen and I are in charge of the Victory Booth. Or as it's known among the servicemen, the kissing booth. The sturdy wooden structure is designed with the top board scalloped to look like a canopy. Every year somebody adds a fresh coat of red paint and more gummed star stickers than the year before. A 'Buy War Bonds' sign hangs on the front of the booth.

While the other volunteers string up the lights, Helen and I hang a six foot long green garland of tinsel over the kissing booth. It shimmers like a trail of stardust fallen to earth, its once perfect foils droopy and tattered from being dragged out every Christmas since the Depression. I get up on the stepladder and fasten the tinsel onto the wooden frame with thumbtacks, getting a special joy in remembering how popular the booth was that year. We couldn't keep up with the demand for soldiers wanting a kiss every time they bought a war bond or stamps. I did my share of kissing and to my surprise, Jeff encouraged me, telling me these boys deserved a kiss but after the dance, those kisses belonged only to him.

Was I that naïve back then? To think he wasn't jealous? I smile. I'll make sure to stay away from the kissing booth. No way do I want him to think I have eyes for any man but him. I can't jeopardize our relationship. He has to believe me when I tell him about the letter. I don't need anything else clouding his mind.

I'm daydreaming about my wonderful man and the joy I get kissing him when I catch a glimpse of the ladies leaving the wardens' meeting. I nearly fall off the ladder when I see the raging storm in a mink lined coat with a matching pillbox hat coming my way. A huge feather waving in the air like a battle flag. Mrs Rushbrooke.

Oh, Lord, what have I done now?

'I see you paid no attention to what I said, Miss Arden,' purrs the elegant woman, not caring who hears her. 'A pity, since it's so close to Christmas.'

What does she mean by that?

'I suppose your spies told you Jeff and I were together yesterday.' I smirk. Brazen words on my part, but I refuse to allow this scheming woman to get the better of me. I imagine the night watchman couldn't wait to tell anyone who'd listen over a beer at the tavern. Words spoken in such places have a way of spreading like bee's pollen to a poison flower like Mrs Rushbrooke.

She curls her lip. 'Mark my words, my son will have nothing more to do with you.'

'I don't wish to argue, ma'am,' I say with as much courtesy as I can. Every woman, from her cronies to the girls stringing up the lights, hangs onto our conversation like we're giving away ration stamps. 'As you so aptly put it, it's close to Christmas, so let's speak of goodwill toward our fellow...' I pause, then add, '... women.' Whispers. A few handclaps. A '*Merry Christmas*' or two.

Mrs Rushbrooke ignores my heartfelt gesture. 'I hear there may be an opening down at the mill soon,' she threatens. I ignore her. I'm not worried about my job. Mr Clayborn will stand by me.

'Sorry, Mrs Rushbrooke, Helen and I are busy hanging tinsel for the dance.'

I turn my back on her. Too late I realize I broke my own rule. One I learned my first month as an editor at Holtford Company. Never *ever* let the client think you're ignoring them. They always come back at you with a stinger – and this one is a good one.

Mrs Rushbrooke clears her throat. 'I hear we have too many superintendents on the floor.' She fiddles with the feather on her hat with gloved fingers. 'Your father is a superintendent, is he not?'

*No, not Pop.*

I climb down the stepladder, taking two steps at a time. 'What are you up to now, Mrs Rushbrooke?'

'Me?' she says, keeping her expression blank, as if she found a note in a bottle and she's floating with the tide. 'I merely suggested to my husband the company could cut production costs by retiring unnecessary workers from the floor.'

Retire? Pop is in his forties. Even if he could, he has no intention of retiring and never does. He stays on the job till the mill closes. What she means is *fire him*. She's trying to pull a fast one. I smile in spite of the woman's meanness, marveling she thinks she can get away with it.

'You mean retire him with a year's severance pay and a full pension,' I come back at her like a bullet. Straight to her heart, though I doubt she has one. 'I'm sure the union will be very interested in the company's change of policy to let men go because of your whims.'

Her eyelids flutter. She's a clever woman when it comes to making people's lives miserable, but she has no idea how the mill runs. Or that I know anything about the power of unions and the hard-won benefits Pop and the other workers spent years fighting for. They can't let him go because she doesn't like me.

Besides, my father loves that job. It's his life and his workers speak highly of him, bringing him homemade goods on his birthday every year, though everyone knows no one can cook like Ma. It's a tribute to Pop, the man and the superintendent. Not to mention that job is my family's security. He needs to keep working because that union pension keeps Ma in our house after Pop passes.

I stare her down. Her lower lip quivers. The woman is bluffing. That doesn't mean she's finished with me.

'You think you're a clever young woman, Miss Arden.' She takes a step forward and for the first time I notice she barely comes up to my shoulder. I think of her as being much taller. 'I'll see to it you never set foot in my home again. You have my word on it.'

What she's saying is she won't allow Jeff to marry me.

I bite back the words aching to spill over my lips. I can't tell this woman what I think of her. I can't blurt out we're eloping in a few days. Anything I say will only make things worse, so I say nothing. It kills me not to fight back. I want to tell her off in not-so-nice terms, but I won't do anything to jeopardize saving Jeff's life. Even if she's right and he never marries me, I want with all my heart to keep him safe.

The woman taps her foot, waiting for my comeback. When it doesn't happen, she takes my silence as an affirmation of my defeat. I have no choice. She's Jeff's mother and I hear Ma in the back of my head telling me to respect her, even if she's wrong.

Helen, on the other hand, has nothing to lose. She jumps right into the fray and lets her have it. 'I saw snakes in the grass when I was a kid, Mrs Rushbrooke. How they come crawling out of their holes with sharp fangs to feed their egos. I never saw one strike out with so much venom.' Hands on her hips, she cocks her head to one side. 'You should apologize to Kate.'

'Apologize?' She lifts her chin. 'What gives *you* the right to speak to me like that? You're nothing but the daughter of a woman from the wrong side of the tracks.'

Helen takes another step forward. Mrs Rushbrooke doesn't back down. 'You leave my mother out of this.'

I lay my hand on Helen's arm. 'She's not worth it, Helen, let her be.'

Mrs Rushbrooke is in fine form and eager to redeem herself with her cronies hanging on to her every word. 'We all know what your mother was before she came to this town. I believe they have a word for it.'

There are gasps and whispers around us. No one ever says it out loud, but we all heard the rumor Helen's elegant, beautiful mother worked in a dime-a-dance joint raided for illegal gambling before coming here. Thankfully, the good womenfolk of Posey Creek dislike Mrs Rushbrooke so much, they don't give a hoot what Mrs Linder did in the past. She has other talents that far outweigh her nefarious reputation. There isn't a woman in town who doesn't own at least one hat crafted by her hand.

With the excitement over, Mrs Rushbrooke leaves the building quickly, her cronies dutifully following her like ducklings wearing fur lined coats. I refuse to acknowledge her when she swishes by me and continue decorating for the dance. I wonder if I'll pay for my folly.

Helen pulls me aside so no one can hear us. 'I'm done in this town, Kate. I'm tired of the petty talk and stupid hierarchy that puts women like Mrs Rushbrooke at the top of the heap instead of good, God-fearing ladies like your ma.'

'What about your mother... she'll be devastated.' I implore her not to go.

She manages a weak smile. 'She's not my mother.' Her voice is steady but emotionless. She lets her shoulders slump, as if her admission took a weight off her back.

'Then who is she?' I ask her quietly. Helen never revealed that information to me. Why now?

'My real ma worked with Nadine – that's what I call her when we're alone – as a dance hostess. She died when I was born. I never knew my father and Nadine promised her she'd raise me. She's done her best, but it's time I move on.'

Helen was never a quiet girl. Indeed, quite the opposite, so I understand how difficult it is for her to keep her past hidden. I feel guilty for not sharing my story about how I came back here, but telling her will only complicate this turn of events. So I listen, nodding my head up and down when she speaks to me in low tones, volunteering bits and pieces of information. From what I can gather, Helen's father paid off Nadine rather than cause a scandal. She brought the girl to Posey Creek and opened a shop. It also explains why I never saw any family resemblance between the two women.

'Where will you go, Helen?'

'I'm headed out west as soon as I get a ticket on the next train.' She squeezes my hand, her eyes upon me. 'Don't let that woman stop you from being with your man. I know her type. She's capable of doing anything to get her way.'

I should pay more attention to her ominous words, but I'm still reeling over the news my best friend is leaving town. I don't judge her; if anything, I admire her spunk. When I think back, I remember Helen went out west to California in 1944 to work in a defense plant and she married a Marine. He was killed at Saipan. Last I heard, she entered a convent. Now my meddling spurs her to leave town sooner. Does a different outcome await her? I hope so. That Marine, too.

My coming here also changes something else in my universe. When I get back up on the stepladder, a rumbling vibrates beneath my feet. My pumps wobble, my footing unsteady. A new crack in the walls of time is vying for my attention.

I learn no one in my family is immune.

## 18

'Where'd you get that shiner, Junior?'

I catch my brother poking around the icebox to see if he can find something cold to put over his right eye. Deepening in color into a black and blue wonder, a reddish shade circling his eye with a droopy lid.

He must be in a lot of pain, but he doesn't make a whimper. He doesn't answer my question either. He lowers his head and won't look at me. He takes his time shuffling around the icebox. He draws his lips together so tight, they nearly disappear. I know that look.

*Go away, you're a girl, you don't understand.*

Back then, the other me didn't think much about his standoffishness. He was like a shifting wind. You couldn't predict what he'd do next, or if he'd bother to notice he had two sisters who care about him. Like the time he got lost in the woods when he was six. Lucy and I spent hours looking for him until we found him sleeping under a tree with his pinewood model airplane clutched in his hand. The wings broken off. His arms and legs bruised. His nose bleeding. He never said what happened. He carried his mental pain from Korea the same way.

'You get hit by a baseball?' I grab ice chips from the bottom tray. Luckily, Pop used his overtime pay to get us a new icebox before the war. We marveled it had a light inside. Now that light shines bright on my brother's black eye as I wrap the ice in a dishtowel and hold it over his swollen lid.

He won't tell me what happened – back then I'd have hugged him and let it go. Not now. Something about the guilty look on his face makes me dig deeper.

'Who were you fighting?' I ask straight out.

He looks up at me, not denying it.

That takes me by surprise. My kid brother is into sports, not looking for fights, though during the Korean War he will earn a purple heart and several medals for marksmanship.

'You know Ma will get it out of you,' I urge, 'so spill it and save her the trouble.'

'I can't, Kate.'

Finally, the boy talks. I won't get it out of him unless I keep probing. I won't fail him, even if I have to be harder on him than I like.

'Listen, Junior, Ma's awful tired and Pop has an extra load down at the mill to carry, so you're stuck with me.' I grab more ice, applying it gently to his swollen eye. My younger brother is tough, but at the moment he's as fragile as a blackbird with its wing broken. 'I won't bite your head off, I promise.'

'You won't?' He stares at me, wanting to make sure.

'Promise.'

'Even if it's bad?'

'Cross my heart.' I mean it, but I don't like the way he keeps staring at me, as if we're on unfamiliar territory here with our relationship and he's testing the waters. Did he also figure out I'm different?

'You're not going to like it, Sis.'

'For gosh sakes, Junior, what's going on?'

'Me and Skip were hanging out at the soda fountain in the drugstore, when two hoodlums came in and acted tough and tried to take over our booth.'

'Was it just you and Skip?' I tease him.

'No, we were talking to the Butler twins.'

I nod, remembering the cute sisters who giggle a lot. 'Go on.'

'I recognized them fellows right away. They got caught last week slashing the upholstery in the seats at the Old Grande. They do stuff like that to impress girls.'

I nod. *Thrill saboteurs*, delinquents who steal purses and try to derail trains by putting stones on the track.

'They tried to butt in and when we said no, they started calling us names and saying we were trash.' Then he gets real quiet and huffs up his chest, snorting out hot air from his nostrils. 'Then one of them said…'

'Go on.'

He sucks in a big breath. 'One of them said you were doing stuff with the boss's son so that makes me trash, too.'

'They said *what*?' I collapse onto the kitchen stool, landing on my rear with a thump. 'No, don't tell me what else they said, I can guess.'

'I'm so sorry, Kate. I didn't know what to do.'

'So you socked him.'

'We took it outside the drugstore and started arguing, them yelling awful, disgusting words. I yelled back it weren't true, but they wouldn't give up.' He buries his head in his hands. 'I did what Pop said, I *tried* to reason with them. When the bigger one took a punch at me, I couldn't take it no more.'

Cool perspiration breaks out over my upper lip. *Oh, God, what have I done by coming back here?*

'Then I did what Pop would want me to do,' Junior continues, fired up. He slams his fist into the palm of his hand. 'I laid him out on the pavement and then went after his friend. He chickened out and ran, so I dragged the creep to his feet and—' He stops and glares at me, his eyes searching. 'It ain't true, is it? What they said?'

What do you tell a fifteen year old boy who looks up to his sister?

'I – I, uh...'

'I don't believe it, Kate. Not you and that slimy Timothy Rushbrooke.'

*'Timothy?'*

'The jerk said he was boasting down at the pool hall you went out with him. Talk is any girl who goes out with him is easy.'

I want to laugh, but my kid brother won't understand my sudden mirth. Instead, I grab his hands and hold them in mine. They're cold, but they warm as I speak to him in a calm, clear voice. I tell him I've never gone out with Timothy, but I'm seeing Jeff and it's serious between us. Is that okay with him? I can't believe the light shining in his eyes, even if one is droopy.

'Jeez, Kate, that's swell. Pops says Mr Jeffrey is the greatest.'

Then Junior grabs me around the waist and hugs me, a first from a kid brother who never shows his emotions around me or anybody, who is too inward to reveal what's bothering him. Tonight he has come out of the woods and fought back the demons that cloud his mind.

For me and himself. That's a good thing.

* * *

'*Mm...* kiss me again, Jeff.'

I close my eyes and lean against the rough bark of the big ole cherry tree and wait for his lips to meet mine. It doesn't happen. Jeff has something on his mind, but what? Instead of the blistering hot kisses I can't get enough of, my lips sting with the chill of a night so deep and dark my mouth turns blue. I shiver.

Not every scene, every moment on my journey back is perfect – far from it – but my time with Jeff is sacrosanct. I forge new memories with him every time we're together that are warm and sweet, like the sun-kissed cherries we savored as kids. The flavor ripens to the best of delights and I want more. Tonight is no exception. Still, he says nothing.

We met under the cherry tree after I had dinner with the family. A talkative affair with everyone doing their part to assure Junior we stand behind him. Ma made sure he had extra apple butter with his bread. Not as sweet as before the war, but it's her way of coddling him, knowing it reminds him of how he stirred the apple butter kettle for her when he was growing up. He was chattier than usual and it makes me wonder if I'll see a different Frank Junior when I return back to my own time.

I don't think about that now. I yearn in this young woman's body for my love's touch, my female instinct fine-tuned by time and experience. Something is in the air. It isn't good.

With a thumping heart, I open my eyes. 'What's wrong, Jeff?'

'I don't know how to say this, Kate, but—'

His expression is troubled. I see a longing in his eyes. He wants to kiss me but doesn't. Why?

'But what?' I lean against the tree, its uneven bark digging into my shoulder. Pricking my mind as well as my flesh. I refuse to panic. I thought everything is falling into place. Tomorrow night is the dance, then Sunday at home with the family. On Monday morning, off to the train station to play out that painful scene and the end of my journey. I honestly believe that afterward, I'll find my way back to my own time. It's a strong feeling I have, like when you think you've been somewhere before and you're walking through the motions.

Then a new fear replaces that thought. What if his mother gets to him beforehand and Jeff doesn't want to marry me after all?

A serious faced young man looks me straight on, trying to get the words out and shaking his head. 'I can't go to training school, Kate. I can't become a bomber pilot.'

I choke. That's the last thing I expect to hear.

'You passed the exams. You'll be called up soon.'

'You don't know the power my father wields in Washington. He'll fix it so they take me off the list.' He smirks. 'God knows my mother will be thrilled. She can run the pants off any senator if she puts her mind to it.'

'Why? What's changed?'

He takes several moments to think about what he wants to say, staring at me as if he's not sure I understand. I flap my hands against my arms to keep warm, feeling my insides churning, a subtle shift in my world making me nervous. I have mixed feelings of elation and confusion.

Is this my undoing? Or my salvation?

'It's simple mathematics, Kate. I can't leave the mill and run off to play flyboy.' The tone of his voice resonates with roiling anger and pent-up frustration. 'My father isn't feeling well and I can't trust the everyday factory production in Timothy's hands. He's irresponsible and in more trouble than I thought. He owes money to a numbers syndicate and there's talk he's involved in other dealings that if they ever come out, will tarnish the Rushbrooke name.'

I keep quiet and listen while he expounds further on how bad things will get at the mill if his father falters and Timothy takes over. I don't tell him about Junior getting into a fight because some boys spread rumors about me going out with Timothy. I don't want to fuel the fire any more. I don't need to. Jeff is on a rant, exposing his soul to me with such fire and passion, I can't stop him.

'We'll lose our government contracts and have to lay people off. We won't do our part to win this war.' Something in the way he says it triggers an emotional understanding in me I wouldn't have picked up back then, making me uncomfortable. The words tumble off the tip of his tongue with a harshness that assaults my ears. 'I can't go. We'll be bankrupt in six months.'

I understand. While he's doing his part overseas, he'll lose everything he cares about back home.

'I know the responsibility of running the mill is tremendous, that you won't have time for us, but I'll wait for you, Jeff,' I say softly. 'No matter how long it takes.'

*Even twelve years. Yes, twelve long years. I'm not giving you up now.*

'Without you, Jelly Girl, I have nothing.' He kisses me, not with a hot passion, but something deeper, more meaningful and that touches me. He needs me, and the tremor I feel go through his body when he holds me tight tells me he's torn between staying here and going off to war. It's up to me to make that decision for him.

I'm glad a dark cloud passes over the waning moon so Jeff can't see the spark in my eyes. It will take a lot of maneuvering to bend time to my will. If Jeff stays here in Posey Creek, that letter won't exist. Everything will be the way it should be. Won't it?

We'll be married and living in the house on the river. We'll have children and lovely picnics in the summer and tree decorating fun at Christmas. My heart skips. I hold in my hand the power to change everything, *everything*. A selfish move, at best, but if I go along with his idea to stay here and then marry him, he'll be miserable and hate me for it. I can't take away from him what he was meant to do. Help the French Résistance win this war.

Swallowing hard, I hate myself for thinking of my own needs and desires that don't amount to a hill of anything in this war. True, I gloried in the idea for a moment, but I never felt such strong emotion tearing me up inside when I tell him what's on my mind.

'Mr Clayborn can take over running the mill, Jeff,' I say in very quiet tones. 'He knows every facet of the operation and he's a good, honest man.' I pause, let my words sink in. 'Pop thinks the world of him,' I conclude as a final testimony to his qualifications.

He perks up. 'Would he want the job?'

'I work for the man. Believe me, he'll jump at the chance to keep the mill in tiptop shape. Go on, ask him, please.'

'You're smart, clever, and did I mention beautiful?' he

says, his lips brushing mine. 'You're going to make some man a wonderful wife, Jelly Girl.'

'Oh, really?' I tease him. 'You got anybody in mind?'

'Yeah... this fellow who's about to kiss you.'

I put my heart and soul into that kiss even though I've given up the sure chance of having my man by my side and making those lonely years go away. My trip back through time just got a whole lot stranger. I can't forget what that letter said:

What we did that night stopped the Nazi flow of men, arms, and tanks into Southern France for months. Helped the Allies with the invasion yet to come. Jeff forged so deep into the underground, cavorting with the Vichy, I forgot he wasn't French. He became one of them so he could get the information we needed. Without him, it never would have happened.

Yes, he has to pull off that mission. Is it asking too much to want him back with me afterward?

Jeff doesn't say much after kissing me, but the expression in his eyes indicates the wheels in his brain are working overtime, making plans to keep the mill at full production. The promise he made to marry me fills the silence between us. I don't have to ask him if he's changed his mind about us eloping because I have no doubt he'd have said something if he did. We hold hands as he walks me back toward the house, not caring if Mrs Widget sees us. The woman never sleeps, her eyes on the alert for anything suspicious. *It's the war, you know.*

After a quick squeeze to my waist with his big strong hands, he's off. I stand there for a while, thinking. Time, I discover, can be very cunning and capricious. It doesn't run in a straight line like everyone believes. You can bend and shape it with a word, a deed. That doesn't make it the right thing to do. In the end, I have no choice. I'm driven to do the honorable thing, what makes Jeff happy *and* help win the war. If the forces that brought me here think they can push me around, tempt me to go against the grain, they're wrong. They can't. I feel compelled to follow what's right. If I want to save the man I love, I must listen to my heart.

Ma left the porch light on, so I have no doubt Mrs Widget is watching. I turn and wave to her. A window slams across the street. I smile to myself, then walk inside the house. The quiet calms me, but the stirrings in me make me tense. Only two days remain until that morning when Jeff will leave on the train and I'll never see him again. That's all I have left. Two days. I've laid the groundwork and very soon now, I'll have to leave.

I start up the stairs when I hear the soft creaking of a rocking chair. Then I hear the strike of a match and a candle flickers on. Ma. Her wise eyes turn toward me. She's waiting for me. She's staring, questioning, hurting. She clears her throat.

'It's time we have a talk, Kate.'

My mother was born in a time when ladies cinched themselves into special corsets at bedtime and a married woman never wore her hair down. She knew no other man than Pop, never wanted to, and her children are God's bounty to her. She cherishes each of us like we're ripe berries about to be picked, but not until the earth fills us with its nourishment. The sun warms our souls. The wind sets our sail. Make us ready for the world. In Ma's eyes, I'm not ready.

'You're too young to get married, Kate.'

I swallow hard, the fervor inside me squeezing my feelings up tight into a ball. I can't unravel. Not now. No telling how long my mother has been watching me, her quick mind putting things together about Jeff and me. Though why she's bringing this up tonight, I don't know. It sends curious shivers through me that shake my confidence. But no matter what she's got on her mind, I won't back down.

'I'm nineteen, Ma.'

*Going on thirty-two.*

'No matter, child, I don't see why you need to run away and get married. Wait until you have a fine blessing from the reverend when he comes home from the war.' She rocks back and forth, taking her time with what she has to say. 'There's no more beautiful bride than you, Katie Marie, and your dear old Pop will be so disappointed if he can't walk you down the aisle.'

In the light of a single candle, I see my mother's face, the pleading, wistfulness, hope. It makes me feel guilty, fosters my fear she's suffered in silence, worrying about my involvement with Jeff. I can't lie to her. 'How long have you known Jeff and I are going to elope?'

Her eyes twinkle. 'I didn't... until now.'

'You're a sly old fox, Ma.'

She chuckles. 'I have to be where you children are concerned.' She rocks back and forth in her chair, twining fuzzy strands around a red ball of yarn. If she isn't cooking or cleaning or mending, she's rolling yarn. Usually with a cup of hot tea beside her. Tonight her cup is empty. Like her heart will be if I leave home and get married. 'I have my hands filled with Lucy and Junior. I never thought I'd have to worry about you.'

'You don't, Ma. After Jeff and I are married, I'll be here every day to help you, I promise.'

She laughs. 'Somehow I can't see my daughter living at Wrightwood House and putting up with that chatterbox, Mrs Rushbrooke.'

I look at her, surprised. Ma never says anything bad about anyone. This is more telling than her staying up to wait for me, especially since she's always first in line at the butcher shop on Saturday at 7 a. m. with her ration books neat and folded. Yes, she's very upset.

I sit down on the tweed ottoman frayed at the corners from us kids jumping on it so much. A suitable place to have this conversation, putting me at her feet. Like when I was a little girl and I sat cross-legged while she read fairy tales to me.

Now she eyes me with suspicion, and then hands me the ball of yarn to hold for her. Yes, this is going to be a long talk. It's time she knows everything. I take a deep breath and begin to speak. Of Christmas, lost love, and trains.

By the time the candle burns down to the wick, Ma knows as much of my story that I feel comfortable telling her. By the sheer intensity of her silence, the rigid manner she sits in her stilled rocker, I have no doubt my wild tale stole the breath from her. Like she's suspended in space and doesn't know where to land.

Before she knew my story or after.

Whether or not she believes me, she'll never be the same. I don't regret my decision. After holding it in for so long, my heart jumps with joy sharing it with someone. Ma above all. That as crazy as it sounds, I came back here to save Jeff.

'I wouldn't be here if Lucy didn't beg me to come home for

Christmas and I got on the train to come back to Posey Creek.' I'm grateful for the darkness covering us like a fuzzy blanket. The truth comes more easily in the dark. Nothing to stop me from unburdening my soul, like I'm floating between different times. I hear her gasp when I tell her about the letter.

'Have you shown it to Jeff?' she wants to know.

'Not yet.'

'What if he doesn't believe you?'

'He will, Ma. You always tell me God has a plan for us. Well, His plan for me is to save Jeff.'

'I pray you're right, child.'

'Ma...'

'Yes?' she says, her voice calm though I swear she's breathing harder. I imagine how difficult this is for her to take in.

'Don't be scared if I'm gone on Monday morning when you get up to pack Pop's lunchbox.' She tends to the day's chores long before the birds flutter around her windowsill, looking for their morning crumbs.

'You made plans to meet Jeff... to elope?'

'Yes, it's all set, Ma, but it won't happen. I promise you. I can't explain why, I've already said too much. I have a feeling that when the girl in the red coat comes home, her eyes red and swollen from crying, it won't be the girl sitting with you now.'

A long silence. I hear the Dutch clock ticking, reminding us that time doesn't stop, but has a way of going on and we will, too.

'Your Irish grandma was a storyteller, Kate.' I hear the crack in her voice, that uncertainty, she's found herself in a situation she doesn't understand. She's used to protecting her brood from the devil himself if she has to. For the first time, she can't. 'I'd sit with her by the fireplace here in this house and listen to her tales of selkies and fairies and elves.' She pauses a beat. 'I believed her and I believe you.'

'You do, Ma?'

'Yes. Now go to bed, Katie, my child. Know in your heart your ma is praying for you.' She squeezes my hand. 'Don't worry, when your other self returns from the train station on Monday, I'll be here to comfort her. As God is my witness, I'll never say a word to her about our talk.'

She never does.

## 19

Whatever else happens to me on this sentimental journey through time, I will never forget the Christmas tree lighting ceremony outside the Posey Creek community center.

From where I stand, I see the townsfolk gathered around the big fir tree rising up like a symbol of peace and freedom, their faces shining with anticipation. Some arriving on foot, others using precious gas rations to make the trek into town from neighboring farms. I feel the wonder of the holiday season in their hearts, inhale the scent of the fresh tree wafting through the air filling our lungs. Sweet and comforting like memories past.

Saturday night and the air is crisp and cold like many December nights during the war. Tonight, it's as if time stands still. Everybody feels it. That we're all united in coming together to remember the good in man and that good endures even in times of war. A chance to let go of the everyday stress of ration books, shortages, and waiting for telegrams we pray never come. It's the hope for peace that unites us.

I have no qualms about being here tonight. I came back to save Jeff and this is my chance to tell him about the letter, to change the future. I didn't go to the ceremony back then. I stayed home primping and fussing with my hair, my dress, while everyone else was here. There was no one to spy on me since I had the house to myself. I showed up later to attend the holiday dance.

Tonight I follow a different path. I join the family in the short walk across town, lifting up my chin, head high as Lucy and I lead the way. Under my red coat, I'm wearing my favorite holiday long gown: a crushed sapphire blue velvet, very sophisticated with red and blue and silver sequins adorning the wide shoulders. Tight belt at the waist with a sequined buckle. Ma looks right smart in her favorite blue and plum paisley (the first time I've seen her not wearing an apron since I've been back), while earlier Lucy balked at wearing my old pink taffeta prom dress with angel sleeves. She insisted she looked like she was sixteen. I pointed out she *was* sixteen and that she'd grow up to be a lovely woman. A wary look crossed her face at my prediction but she forgot about it when I chatted on about how pretty she looked when I removed the chunky fake flowers at her waist. Next, I pulled down the cap sleeves so they were off-the-shoulder and she smiled. An instant makeover that makes her look at least eighteen.

Chatting with familiar faces I haven't seen for years, I pray I don't say something I shouldn't. This is what I missed back then. The last Christmas before my heart was broken. I believe with my whole being I can fix it. Since the moment I arrived here on the train dressed in my favorite red coat and deep blue silk hat, I've been possessed by one thing: save Jeff from certain death. It scares the heck out of me and thrills me at the same time.

Still, I have to be on my toes. I already changed a few things, like posing for the Miss Christmas Wrap poster, but I can't let anything stop me from meeting up with Jeff at the train station on Monday morning. Bright and early.

I step back and take a breath. Till then, I don't want to miss out on any opportunity to be near him. I see my man standing near the tall fir tree, watching me, his broad shoulders filling out a long topcoat, his strong figure drawing my eyes. I can't help but imagine cuddling up against his chest as Mildred greets me with her beautiful smile and kind words. Wearing a long jersey gown the color of aqua mist, the sweetheart neckline peeking out of her honey-colored, camel hair coat with three big buttons, she looks very much the reverend's wife. Confident and feminine.

'So glad you came, Kate.' She glances over her shoulder at Jeff. He winks at her and she laughs. She whispers to me she enjoys being privy to our secret. My heart skips when a tall Army chaplain approaches her. When he moves into the light streaming from the community center, I see it isn't Reverend Summers. Mildred introduces him to me. 'I want you to meet Captain Danvers. Captain, meet the charming Kate Arden.'

'Captain.' I acknowledge the man of God with a thankful smile for these brave men who risk their lives in combat zones. Many die giving comfort to the wounded, often in the line of fire. What's he doing here?

'You look familiar, Miss Arden.' He gives me a big smile and a long stare. 'Have we met?'

Did we meet back then? This is the first time someone knows me and I don't remember them. That's strange. Unsettling. Then I see the mischievous grin on Mildred's face.

'He saw the poster with you sitting on the Christmas box,' Mildred says without batting an eye. 'You're a pinup girl.'

'You have the poster?' I gulp.

'Freddie Baker brought a print by the rectory and asked me to hang it up on the bulletin board. The captain was with him and we got to talking about what's happening over there and well, you'll see.' She pokes me in the ribs. 'Think how you'll brighten up Sunday prayer service. Why, half the town will save every scrap of paper.'

'You mean the male half.' Then it hits me. 'What if Mrs Rushbrooke sees it?' I try to take this in. Patriotic or not, I have the feeling the woman will use it against me.

'She wouldn't dare put up a stink and make the mill look bad.' She leads me away from the chaplain greeting folks with his friendly smile and finds a quiet spot behind the tall tree. She takes a moment to compose herself. A furrowing of her brow makes me think she has something else on her mind. 'Kate, you know how deeply I care about our work here, the reverend's and mine.'

Since we were talking about a certain society woman, an awful thought invades my brain and I don't hold back. 'Don't tell me Mrs Rushbrooke is poking her nose in God's work, too?' I wouldn't put it past her.

She smiles. 'No, nothing like that. Something has come up that has me a bit befuddled about my duties here.'

'Like what?'

'What would you think if I left Posey Creek, Kate?' she whispers low enough so no one can hear her.

'Leave?' I ask, not understanding. 'Why?'

Mildred is a woman I look up to and admire. I can't imagine this town without her. Or the reverend. Watching this elegant couple is a beautiful thing. I remember seeing them together, her laying her hand over her husband's and looking at him like he was her universe. How well I understood that.

'I'll explain later,' she insists, watching the crowd. Loud chatter catches her attention. They're getting restless. 'Do you think the town will feel more comfortable with a real pastor living in the rectory during this war and not a pastor's wife?' She lets go with a deep sigh. 'No telling when the reverend will return.' I know he suffered mentally and physically during the war, losing forty pounds, his body broken, but not his spirit. Mildred told me he owed that to his training in the ring. I can't let her lose hope; I need to encourage her to stay strong and confident in her role till he comes home. But even angels have their moments and this was one of them.

'Replace you, Mildred?' I shake my head. 'With all the work you do for everyone? Picking up children from school, working at the canteen at the train station, visiting the sick, not to mention giving a fine Sunday sermon when we don't have a visiting reverend from the circuit.'

'I never thought of it that way,' she says with that funny smile of hers. 'I wonder if the others think the same way.'

'I often hear Ma and her lady friends talk about how lucky the reverend is to have you here in his place while he's gone.' I don't have a chance to find out more because there's a shift in the wind. A northerly gust coming down from the hill that's no evening breeze. With her foxtails flying over her shoulder, Mrs Rushbrooke rushes over to Mildred, demanding to be introduced to the captain. Her husband is home with a cold, she says, fawning over the good-looking Army chaplain, and she needs an escort.

I sneak away before she catches me in her crosshairs. Besides, I feel a rumbling under my feet, which makes me wonder if I've done something to change things again. I have no idea. I take heart from knowing I made the right decision to come here tonight.

I stare up at the first burst of stars and a half moon providing a backdrop to this evening and make a wish the heavenly messengers must have memorized by now. Then I take my place with Ma and Pop. Lucy and I link arms, and Junior stands next to Pop. He has bruising from that black eye, but I swear he stands taller than before. I see Jeff over by the big fir with two soldiers next to him, ready to help him turn on the generator so the Christmas tree lights go on. I don't see Timothy anywhere, which doesn't surprise me.

Mildred stands at the podium, the choir from St Mary Cecilia's orphanage behind her along with the high school choral group, their numbers sparse since several boys enlisted and are serving overseas.

I lock eyes with Jeff, the first of several times since we gathered here at dusk. Townspeople and servicemen and women. Soldiers home on furlough, others returning with wounded bodies. What a moment it is.

'When I first met the reverend in high school, he was a senior and already had a flock following him,' Mildred says, smiling. 'Every girl in the freshman class. Including me.'

Everyone laughs.

'We drifted apart after he graduated and it wasn't till years later our paths crossed again. It took hard work and dedication for him to find his way, but this lamb never lost faith in him and will happily follow him to the ends of the earth. You all know my husband as a good, kind man with a strong heart and not afraid to get his hands dirty. Especially when it comes to doing our Creator's work.' She pauses, her words catching in her throat.

No one moves or makes a sound.

She clears her throat. 'He has a new flock now. A platoon of Marines caught up in the fierce fighting somewhere in the South Pacific. From what Reverend Summers tells me, the men haven't lost their Christmas spirit. They picked up used tin cans tossed out from the mess tents and then cut long strips of tin to make tree ornaments.' She points out several twisted strips hanging on the tree. With the shiny side out, they look like icicles. 'I decided to go one step further and use the tin cans I planned to donate to salvage to make a silver star.'

She holds up a wavy star made from tin and glances over the crowd. 'In honor of every man and woman from Posey Creek in the service, I want to place this star at the top of our Christmas tree.'

We get misty-eyed as Jeff helps her use a short ladder to fasten the star at the top of the great fir and then he turns on the lights. Blinking lights deepening in reds, blues, yellows, and greens as the sun sets and twilight waves her magic wand to make them glimmer.

'I wish I had a tin star for each of our boys and girls serving overseas,' Mildred continues, 'but I like to think of this star as the guiding star that brings them home. To help make my wish come true, after the holiday we'll donate the tin ornaments for metal to make the planes, tanks, ships, and weapons to bring this conflict to a peaceful end. Let's bow our hearts for a moment of prayer.'

I bow my head, deeply moved by her heartfelt sermon. The woman is an extraordinary female for her time. She helped the reverend climb back up the hill from hell to a normal life not once but twice, first when he lost his soul in the ring and then later after the war. I'm so proud of her as she leads us in prayer. When the last 'Amen' is heard from the crowd, she grabs the sides of the podium and takes a moment to look at each and every face. As if she's searching for an answer to a question on her mind.

'I have some exciting news.' Hopeful gasps. *War news about our boys and girls?* 'Captain Danvers has asked me if I'm willing to volunteer as a chaplain's assistant and go overseas.' Murmurs from the crowd, asking questions she quickly answers. A fine night mist settles on folks' faces, or are those tears? Mine included. Posey Creek will never be the same without her. I don't remember her mentioning this back then. I pray for a Christmas miracle to keep her here.

I stand on the sidelines away from the crowd and watch the unexpected reaction erupt. Neighbor whispering to neighbor, nodding their heads, coming to terms with what she said. Then again, maybe not. I hear people in the crowd call out:

'We need you here, Mildred.'

'The reverend speaks to us through you, Mrs Summers.'

'You're our guiding light while Reverend Summers is gone. Please stay.'

'I'm deeply touched by your faith in me,' she says, her voice catching. 'Thank you. Your heartfelt words have convinced me to stay in Posey Creek. God bless you all and Merry Christmas!'

The high school choir bursts into song, singing traditional Christmas hymns with everyone joining in on 'Silent Night'. I raise my voice in song, scarcely believing such a lovely moment can come out of this war. How every soul here, wrapped up in harmony and a fine winter chill, is united with their neighbors in coming together tonight to honor our boys and girls fighting overseas.

Unfortunately that moment of moment of peace and goodwill doesn't last. Not by a long shot.

* * *

After the Yuletide tree lighting ceremony is over, I keep my eye on Jeff. He's watching me, both of us letting down our guard. He has eyes only for me. I ignore Lucy pulling on my coat sleeve.

'Mrs Rushbrooke is scowling at you, Kate,' Lucy whispers, dragging me away. I feel her shaking as if she senses this woman is a demon closing in on me and she's trying to protect me.

'She knows when she's beaten,' I say with confidence, even if I don't believe it. I don't trust the woman, never will. I doubt she heard one word of Mildred's moving tribute to our servicemen and women. I won't let her ruin a beautiful ceremony, the Christmas tree lights twinkling like tiny stars, as if each light is a prayer sent overseas from a special family member.

I smile again at Jeff, edging nearer to him and closing the distance between us. Lucy lets me go, knowing she can't stop me, but I can't blame her for trying to help.

I suck in my breath, knowing Jeff and I have to be cautious as everyone breaks up into small groups before crowding into the community center for the dance. God help us, if anyone else catches hold of the wild attraction between us every time we get close to each other. Our emotions are so raw when our fingers touch in passing, I swear an electric current goes straight through me. I whisper, 'Merry Christmas, darling,' hoping no one hears me, then, as if on cue, Mildred switches off the lights on the big fir tree. Government rules dictate no outside lights after dusk.

Inside the center, we find a Christmas Wonderland. Soldiers, sailors, Marines, *everywhere.* Laughing, flirting, letting go for a few hours like they're kids again in Santa's village. Hard to believe we're in the middle of a war. Garlands of tinsel and sprigs of holly hang across the rafters. Big band music plays over the PA system and low lighting casts a romantic hue over the dancefloor. The Victory Booth shimmers with the green tinsel Helen and I hung over it, while the glow of the holiday lights strung up around the wooden frame melts hearts and opens wallets.

Especially with Helen manning the booth. She's already engaged two sailors into buying War Bonds. She looks happier, her lipstick bolder. She's wearing one of her mother's – Nadine's – designs. A backless, black rayon crepe gown with a peplum short in front and hanging down to the floor in back. She's definitely making a statement. Good for her. I wonder when she's leaving town. I'll miss her.

I check my red coat in the cloakroom and look around for Jeff. After our brief encounter I lost him. Ma and Pop join their neighbors – including Ma's lady friends, Mrs Bloom and Mrs Sims – for a potluck supper in the backrooms, leaving the jitterbugging to the younger people. Date loaf cake, chicken salad, pickles, cookies, popcorn balls for the kids. Ma made hors d'oeuvres, both sweet and tangy. Holiday cherry jam as well as cheese with olives and pimentos served on crisp crackers.

I give a silent *thank-you* when Mrs Canton ignores me and heads for the food table. Maisie and the girls from her hair salon chat up Mildred's mother, making the woman laugh for the first time since I've known her. Even fussy Mrs Widget can't complain when Ma presents her with a jar of cherry jam.

There's Mr Clayborn in a deep conversation with two young sailors, drinking punch and hanging on to their every word. The young men keep eyeing the girls flitting by with cups of coffee and plates of cookies. My heart goes out to my boss, keen on gleaning news about the war in the Pacific so he can feel closer to his son. I wonder if he's said yes to Jeff's offer to take over running the mill. I get my answer when he waves to me and gives me the 'V for Victory' sign. I smile. The mill is in good hands now.

Behind me, I hear my sister's laughter. She's hanging onto a Marine, while an Army lieutenant tosses a nickel into the air to decide who will dance with her first. The Marine wins.

I peer over the crowd of military uniforms and party dresses, but I don't see Jeff. Where did he go? Instead of watching everyone else, I should pay more attention to the advancing army on my rear. My heart quickens when I hear a familiar twang.

'You were seen speaking to my son after the ceremony, Miss Arden,' Mrs Rushbrooke can't wait to comment, sniffing.

Spying on me again?

'It's a free country, Mrs Rushbrooke,' I say with confidence. I spin around and look her straight in the eye. I'm not afraid of her. 'Isn't that what we're fighting for?'

She ignores me. 'You always were a precocious child when you came with your mother up to Wrightwood House. Now you merely annoy me.' She smiles like a Cheshire cat wearing a pillbox hat. 'Not for long. Good evening, Miss Arden.'

Then she's off. Swishing her foxtails around her like it's her own tail.

I try to settle down, but can't. She thinks she won. The idea drops into the pit of my stomach like a rock. I hate the feeling, that in spite of the good I feel here tonight, someone like her wields such misery. She irritates me. There's something sinister in that smile that sets my nerves on edge, yet I feel secure the woman left for the night, her message delivered. She isn't the type to hide in dark corners and snarl at her prey. She'd rather do her dirty work out in the open. She said her piece to me like she rehearsed it, using the right words to make me anxious. That the stakes are raised in this scenario and she dealt me the losing hand.

I can't allow that. I mull over her words, trying to figure out what she's up to as I make the rounds of everyone at the dance, wishing them a wonderful holiday. I linger at the punch table, scooping up the tasty fruit drink with the long silver ladle, while at the same time I try to find Jeff. I look so hard, I feel lightheaded. Nerves. I have to guard against letting myself get so wrapped up in living every second I have left here, in case I get careless and do something stupid to lose him.

Especially when I see Mrs Widget following me around. No doubt she eavesdropped on every word. To hear Jeff's mother tell it, I'm a shameless hussy chasing after him. I don't want to give my neighbor anything to chat about, so I remain off to the side. A flood of warmth hits me when I locate him, surrounded by ladies from the factory vying for a dance with him. He beams when he sees me. I swish my long velvet skirt around in a circle, as if inviting him into my secret world. I don't dare move as I watch him mouth the words, '*Meet me outside.*'

I nod. As I start for the back-door exit, I feel Mrs Widget's curious eyes staring at us, waiting to see if he follows me. I freeze when I feel a hand slip around my waist and a jazzy baritone whisper in my ear, 'How about that dance you promised me, Miss Arden?'

I spin around so quickly I nearly lose my balance, not to mention dying of embarrassment.

*Freddie.*

I look up into my admirer's face and see a soldier intent on his mission. Me. How can I explain his boldness to Jeff? I don't dare look in his direction, imagining him storming over here and dragging me away. The younger me would find it very romantic having two men vying for my attention, but I'm too wise not to know such goings-on can have dire consequences. Which means I have to choose between them. Whatever I do, I can't win.

Oh, Lord, if there's ever a moment I want to disappear in a poof of smoke, this is it. My heart races so fast, I can't get the words out to turn Freddie down. I can't say no to a boy who will never dance again after the war. I can't tell Jeff that. I'll have to find another way to explain.

'C'mon, beautiful,' Freddie insists, pulling me out onto the dancefloor before I can protest. 'Let's take a spin around the floor.' He leans down and whispers in my ear, 'Then I've got a surprise for you.'

'One dance, Freddie, that's all,' I mutter under my breath, not daring to breathe when he takes me in his arms and we slow dance to a popular song. His hands feel so strange holding me, but I can't pull away without causing a scene. I feel the hard stares following us and God help me, is Jeff seeing this? Or has he left, not believing his Jelly Girl is dancing with another fellow?

How am I going to explain to Jeff why his girl went off with a soldier?

This is not going well. I can't finish my dance with Freddie. I pull him off to the side, but he takes my actions as meaning something different.

'You sure know how to send a soldier off to war.' He nuzzles my ear, his lips brushing my cheek.

'Please, Freddie, you've got me all wrong.' I'm dying by inches. 'I'm – I'm engaged.'

'I know,' he says, exhaling in a voice so low I barely hear him. Like he isn't surprised.

'You do?'

'What other reason is there for resisting me, Freddie G. Baker, the best damn photographer in the US Army?' His words are carefree, but he watches me with a silent pain clouding his eyes. He leans closer and whispers in my ear, 'I wish it were me.'

'Oh, Freddie, you'll never change, will you?'

'Maybe I have.' His voice is low, repentant.

I look closer. It's true. He isn't the same boy I knew in high school. I sense a deep, emotional stabbing at his heart, dug deep in him by what he's seen. He tries to hide the scars, but they're there in the tightness around his mouth, the deep sorrow clouding his eyes. I didn't see them the other day at the studio. I was too concerned with my pinup debut. I do now and it scratches away at my psyche, urging me to give this boy a fighting chance.

Will it hurt to help a friend one more time?

'Keep your head down over there in the woods.' I choose my words with care. 'In the Ardennes. Watch your back and stay alert so you don't get caught in the crossfire. You don't want the enemy sneaking up on you ~~on~~ when you're trying to get the shot. Promise?'

He gives me a wide-eyed stare. 'Sure, Kate, that's swell of

you to give a guy a break.' Then he chuckles, not sure what to make of it. 'Anything for my pinup girl.'

He leads me back to the Victory Booth, but it isn't a kiss he wants. He grabs a rolled up poster he left with Helen, unfurls it, and then holds it up for everyone to see. 'Drumroll, please!' he announces to the crowd hovering around him on the dancefloor. 'May I present Posey Creek's own pinup girl. Kate Arden, Miss Christmas Wrap.'

My hand flies to my mouth when I see the three by four foot poster of me sitting atop the big Christmas box. Is that me? Freddie caught me smiling, my eyes dancing, but it's the glamour of wartime pinups he captures so well with his camera. Lights and shadows that hide every flaw and yet show off the curve of my body in such a way there's an innocence in the sexy pose.

The girl next door. *That girl is me.*

I don't think my younger self could have pulled it off. The sway of the body, the lift of the chin, chest jutting out. I learned more than I thought at those photoshoots. In a funny, patriotic way, I'm proud to be Miss Christmas Wrap. Showing everybody they can have decorated packages for the holiday even if they don't have any paper wrap. The big question is, what will everybody think?

'Oh, Kate, you look beautiful,' Lucy says, holding on to her Marine as she rushes over to me. 'Like something out of a dream.'

The Marine lets out a low, wolf-whistle. 'Your sister is a real knockout.'

'What about me?' she says, miffed, but I see the pride in her eyes when she sneaks a peek at me, like she's not really jealous.

'Are you kidding?' He squeezes her hand. 'I'm the envy of every guy here. C'mon, baby, let's dance.'

I see the stars in Lucy's eyes and for once, she isn't competing with me. *I'm* competing with me. My poster, that is. It's the talk of the dance. I find the whispers and giggles amusing, but I should have known it wouldn't take Mrs Widget long to head up a committee of one to take it down. She makes it clear to anyone who will listen she disapproves of the poster.

I ask for the music to be lowered and go into my 'save the Christmas poster' speech. 'President Roosevelt started the USO, United Service Organizations, to give servicemen and women wholesome entertainment and a reminder of home,' I say in a clear, steady voice. 'That girl on the poster isn't me, Mrs Widget, she represents every soldier's sweetheart. Now, are you telling me you'd go against the President's wishes by taking it down? A poster that encourages all of us to save paper during this holiday season?'

'Well, I never...' she blurts out indignantly.

My impulsive speech doesn't go unnoticed by the onlookers and dancefloor couples who gather in closer to see what the commotion is all about. My patriotic plea hits a nerve and the servicemen and townsfolk start cheering and whistling.

Mrs Widget whisks past Ma without saying a word. My mother smiles. Pop doesn't look too happy about the poster until Ma says, 'It reminds the boys what they're fighting for.' Even Junior is proud and keeps telling everyone I'm his sister. Helen begs me to help her in the Victory Booth, seeing how I'm surrounded by soldiers, sailors, and Marines, all wanting to dance with me or buy a War Bond so they can get a kiss. I

let Helen do the kissing for me. I have to admit, to this thirty-
one year old woman, it's flattering.

Until I see Jeff pushing through the crowd. There's a
heated air of wildness about the way he moves. He shoves
aside his usual controlled demeanor and replaces it with a
stubborn male pride. He unbuttons his wool jacket, his tie
hanging, his crisp white shirt open at the collar. His jet-black
hair mussed as usual, but it's his eyes that set me off my
course. Black and piercing. He flexes his body like an incred-
ible marble statue come to life, all sinew and muscle, and
ready to claim what's his. Me.

Until he sees the Miss Christmas Wrap poster stuck up on
the side of the Victory Booth. His eyes dart from the poster to
me and then back to the poster. I'll never forget his penetrating gaze, as if he's seeing me for the first time. He keeps
his distance and doesn't say a word. He's uncomfortable with
the attention I'm getting from the servicemen. He turns on
his heel and leaves the community center. My jaw drops. I
don't remember him being jealous. Or maybe I never saw it.
Whatever, I can't stand here and do nothing. My whole life
just walked out that door.

Fear grows in me, becoming more powerful by the
second, and a fierce denial of what's happening holds me by
the throat. The Jeff I fell in love with is a virile young man,
used to having his way. Women adore him and I accept that. I
don't think he ever dreamed the shoe would be on the other
foot. I have to keep reminding myself we're kids caught up in
a wartime romance and it's up to me to talk some sense
into him.

Everybody is watching, waiting to see what I do. Whispers. Giggles. Even a few sighs.

I grab my red coat from the cloakroom and dash outside. I

don't care who sees me or what they think. My younger self will have to deal with it later. If I'm going to save my relationship, I have to patch things up with Jeff before it's too late and I lose him forever.

For a second time.

## 20
_____

I slow my pace as I make my way down the familiar path toward the cherry tree, hoping Jeff will be there. I can't shake away the cold sweat sweeping down my back. Not to mention my jangled nerves. I step carefully, my heavy velvet gown wet and grimy around the hem from running through the grass looking for him, and then kicking up dirt on the old road. I'm tired, out of breath, and discouraged. The night surrounds me, pulling me in deeper and deeper as I leave the dimly lit town behind me. I know the way. Oh, do I.

I traveled this path so many times over the years whenever Ma chewed me out for dawdling with my chores, or Pop had a talk with me about my arithmetic grade. I wish I was that kid again and I could make things better by going to the corner candy store, plunking down my four cents, and going home with a bag of Irish potatoes. Cinnamon covered, coconut candies that look like little spuds. Sweet and sticky, I loved them so much, I ate two at a time.

Life was so simple then. A fistful of candy, a good cry, and everything went back to normal.

Not tonight. I drew attention to myself in such a way the whole town is gossiping about me. I took a chance and stood up for myself. God knows where it will lead.

The chilly night air makes the back of my neck prickle, slicing through my coat. I keep walking, hands in my pocket. I hold onto the comfortable feel of the letter between my fingers, the sweat oozing down my neck making my hair wilt and my Victory rolls come undone. Like me. I can't believe my whole relationship with Jeff is at risk because I danced with Freddie and posed for that silly poster.

I can't leave things alone, can I? The plan was, show Jeff the letter, convince him he can come back safe, then we'll get married and have kids. No, I have to go around saving everybody else first. I kicked up the stakes by coming back home and set this little patch of earth known as Posey Creek off on a quicker axis. Making it spin so fast, folks weren't ready for it. I realize now you can try to change the past, but you can't predict human nature. When you think you've made it to the other side of the tightrope, the wire breaks. What a fool I am.

*Give me another chance, God, please.*

Chin tucked down to my chest, I keep going. I pass the cherry tree and no, he isn't there.

I turn back toward home, trying to make sense of everything when I hear a car engine coming from somewhere nearby. I spin around, trying to see who it is. The road is flanked by woods thick with trees and night creatures scurrying through the brush. Then, like out of a Gothic novel, I see low, dimmed headlights with black tape over the top – a wartime precaution for night driving – creeping closer toward me. I can't see who it is, but my heart pounds and I cross my fingers.

*Please, God, let it be him.*

I'm not disappointed. '*Jeff!*'

He pokes his head out the window. 'We have to talk, Jelly Girl.' His voice is low, almost a monotone, like he's lost part of himself. Seeing the anguished look on his face wrenches my heart.

I'm too shaken up to move as he parks his roadster along the side of the road and jumps out, his hands sliding around my waist. Heaven and I are in sync again. We stare at each other, the dimmed lights playing with the shadows carved onto our faces, but I see the pain in his eyes. His gaze never falters, searching for answers I can't give him. Not yet. We have to straighten things out between us first.

'I'm sorry I danced with Freddie, Jeff.'

'I'm not.'

'He corralled me and I couldn't say no—' I begin, then. 'What did you say?'

'I'm a hotheaded fool, Kate. I see it now. Trying to keep you all to myself, letting my mother have her way because I didn't want to upset my father. The old man isn't well and though I should hate him, I don't. You see, he's—'

'Please, Jeff, you don't have to explain.' I know about his father's heart problem. No need for him to feel uncomfortable telling me.

'I do. I've been selfish making you keep our relationship a secret. I can't blame the servicemen for wanting to dance with you. You were the most beautiful girl there tonight. I'm so afraid of losing you, that you'll fall for some guy in a uniform.'

I cut him a big grin. 'Never, Jeff, unless it's you.'

He exhales. He likes hearing that. Then his eyes turn serious. 'I don't know what's going to happen to me, to us, but I'm through not shouting to the world how much I love you. I wish we could run away tonight, drive to the city before anyone can stop us and get married.'

Tonight? Will that solve everything?

No. I have to tell him about the letter. Another question looms. What if us getting married tonight changes something in the past I haven't counted on? Like what if Jeff isn't called up for the secret mission? What if he goes to pilot training school and is shot down over Germany?

Can I afford to take that chance?

No. I can't risk it. We have to get through the next two days so I can warn him and pray that he believes me. Still, I have to know what's on his mind. I couldn't bear it if anything stopped our plans for eloping.

'Why did you run off when you saw the poster?' I ask with caution.

'I was ashamed,' he admits. 'I realized what an idiot I am. That you're doing your part for this war while I sit here twiddling my thumbs, waiting for orders to report to pilot training school.' He holds me tight by the shoulders. 'I'm determined to get into the fight, Kate, but not sitting behind a desk when I can be dropping bombs.'

'Please be careful, my darling,' I breathe, sputtering words I shouldn't. 'I pray you're not shot down... lost somewhere in Germany or...' I swallow hard. 'France.'

He cocks a brow. 'What made you say that?'

'Nothing.' I avoid his eyes. 'Too many newsreels, I guess.'

'They don't do this in newsreels.' He kisses me and this time the passion threatening to erupt from every pore in my body is barely contained. The temptation to let this go as far as it can makes it irresistible. I try to pull away, but can't. My heartbeat is keeping time with his, flooding my ears, my nerves coming undone in slow, pleasurable waves and I'm powerless to stop it.

'I want you to never stop kissing me, Jeff.' My words are a mere murmur, my breath as soft as my lips melting under his power. 'First, there's something I must tell you.'

'Can't it wait?'

I shake my head. 'No, Jeff, can we go somewhere and talk?'

'At this time of night?'

'Please, Jeff—'

'The house where we'll live when we're married after we return from Washington isn't far from here,' he says with caution. 'Down by the river where the two big oaks stand side by side. We can be alone there. I won't try anything. I promise.'

I'm sitting on a fence that has no greener side. I trust him, but being out late with him is against the social norms of the time. Whichever side of that fence I end up on, there'll be a price to pay, either back in this time or in my own.

No. I have to tell him about the letter. I smile, then whisper in his ear.

* * *

Headlights dimmed, it doesn't take us more than ten minutes to drive down the side road following the course of the river to a secluded spot where Posey Creek empties into the main body of water.

The limestone house sits close to the riverbank, protected by tall oak trees and the ghosts of those patriot soldiers. Nothing has changed since the days when they hid here from the British. In the pale ivory light of a half moon, the two story home welcomes us like an old childhood friend, the pine door boasting an ancient wooden latch. Unlocked, which doesn't surprise me. Here in Posey Creek folks look out for each other.

'I can hardly wait till I carry you over the threshold, Jelly Girl.'

'Why wait?' I tease.

'You want me to break tradition?'

'It's wartime, Jeff, *please*.'

He laughs and scoops me up in his big strong arms. 'Like I said, you try a man's soul.' Jeff shoves the door open with his boot and carries me across the threshold. No, the roof doesn't fall in.

'See?' I hug him around the neck. 'We're safe. Nothing happened.'

'I'll protect you,' Jeff says in a voice so warm it melts my insides like honey folding into cream. 'I'll never let you go, but I'll understand if you changed your mind about coming here tonight.'

'I trust you, Jeff, that you'll marry me like you promised,' I say as he puts me down. 'Now you must trust me when I say I love you so much I have something to tell you that can't wait.'

'I admit, Kate, you caught me by surprise.'

'I'm full of surprises.' My voice breaks, knowing what I have to tell him, but he doesn't notice.

After giving me a playful kiss, Jeff gets a fire going, the logs giving off a pleasant smell that speaks of hearth and home, love and companionship. As if the stately house waited for us to light the old fireplace. I slide my legs together and bring them to my chest, resting my chin on my knees and watch him. It isn't the heat from the flames that makes trickles of sweat roll down the back of my neck. His closeness burning my flesh and the raw tones of his voice urging me to join him on a wonderful adventure. Marriage. Where we won't have to hide. Where we can be true and honest in each other's arms.

'Times have changed, Jeff. Women make their own decisions now.' He wrinkles his brow. I brush his lips with my fingertip. 'I don't expect you to understand. Men never do. Know that being a powerful woman means I can also be soft and wanting and willing to express myself because I believe in us. In our love.'

*I've waited twelve years to find you. I don't want you to leave on that train without you knowing how much I love you.*

'Gosh, Kate, you're making me crazy. I'm going to miss you so much. Pilot training is over a year.'

'You'll be home on leave.' I can't wait much longer to tell him what awaits him. He doesn't know he'll be called to Washington to join the OSS at the last minute.

'It'll never be long enough. I hate being away from you.'

'Me, too,' I say between kisses. 'There are so many like us, waiting for this war to end so they can be together. We've got to do our part. For me, I have to stop you from getting killed.'

'What are you talking about?' he asks, puzzled.

I kiss him long and hard, forgetting about playing a blushing bride-to-be, and showing him how much he means to me. Then I'll tell him about the letter here in our house, the place I hope to return to when I go back to my own time. For fate won't be so cruel as to keep me here in this time if I don't change the past, make me relive every painful year, every moment without him.

He'll come home after the war and we'll have all those wonderful years together. Children. Here in this house. I feel him go completely still as he returns my passion, his good boy behavior gone. I let my body go limp, enjoying how his lips find mine in a hot kiss, arousing something in me I can't stop. We kiss and kiss... I forget where we are... I put off telling him about the letter as a ghostly, deep chill permeates the closed-up house and makes us hold each other tighter, his body covering mine. No one has lived here since Jeff was a boy and the house creaks and groans as if waking up from a hundred years' sleep.

That doesn't stop my pulse from speeding up. I stroke his cheek gently. 'Let's not break *all* the traditions,' I say, catching my breath. I have to remain in control of the situation. 'Why don't you show me the rest of the house? Then we'll... talk,' I tease him.

'Now?' he croaks, jamming his hand through his hair and making it stand up.

'Yes, my love.' I run my fingers up and down his muscular arms. I feel him shiver. 'Now.'

It's amazing how powerful anticipation can be. My poor darling unbuttons his topcoat and tosses it on a brocade covered divan the color of sweet maple and draws the blackout curtains. Not before I peer over his shoulder and catch the view of the river in the moonlight from the front parlor, its multi-framed windowpanes so clear I swear I see through time. Nothing has changed. The open field along the riverbank looks the same back in my own time. At least it did on my last trip home for cherry harvesting.

We both stop to listen when we hear the shrill whistle of the train in the distance, most likely a convoy train carrying men and supplies. Shining its bright bream of light as it flies through the night. I look at Jeff with a longing that speaks of my love for him. A train brought me here, a train will take him away. His face holds no knowledge of what's to come.

*Tell him before it's too late.*

I have time. My mind snaps back to the moment when he turns on a lamp with a rounded mosaic shade. I had no idea that before tonight he readied the house for us to live in after we're married. The electricity is turned on. We keep the lighting minimal, the mood romantic. I link my arm through his and Jeff takes me on a tour of the country style home that has stood here for over a hundred and seventy years.

I never dreamed of a house like this. Deep-colored, wooden floors that shine like copper pennies stained with cherry juice. Luxurious rugs with intricate patterns are a focal point in the main rooms furnished with antique pieces of furniture I'm afraid to sit on. A large kitchen with modern appliances in a pleasing buttermilk tone and a bathroom with a claw foot tub and fancy spigots.

I marvel at the walls with the original paint. A smoky blue that deepened with age but retains a certain calmness. I resist the urge to gaze into the gilt-framed mirror hung over the fireplace. Tempting, but afraid of what I'll see. A woman about to lose her love. The man who towers over me, boldly confident in everything he does, but not afraid to show his tender side and to admit when he's wrong.

I enjoy the moment, the thought of living in this house tugging at my heart in ways I can't put into words. Not that I don't love our old clapboard house, but this will be my realm. Like Ma rules hers with Pop at her side. Now I understand the sense of female empowerment she enjoys in her home. How it gives her purpose and makes her whole. I envy her that.

I've spent twelve years trying to find it behind a typewriter. Not that I don't love my job, writing my stories about the delights of food and the fascinating people who create those dishes occupies a special part of my soul. Yet I never dreamed I could have a home with a man who loves me and someday children, a place where a woman can live happily… it's too much. I can't lose that chance, not now. Not after I've come into my own. Found that special place where in the midst of war, peace is mine. Indulgent, yes, but if my plan to save Jeff goes wrong, this night will be the memory that lasts me till the end of my days. No way am I going to give it up. The man I love has never left me. I think often of that day when we were kids and he slid down the bannister and into my life. His expression didn't falter then and it doesn't now when he kisses me again and I let go with a deep sigh. He takes that as a sign I don't want him to stop. That I want him to make love to me.

'I always dreamed it would be like this, Jelly Girl,' he says biting my ear with a playful nip.

'Me, too, Jeff.' An undeniable ache builds low in my belly, making me squirm as I take off my red coat but I stop there. For all my big talk – and I'm no prude – I'm afraid to let myself go. That undressing in front of this man will seem more like a striptease than a soon-to-be-bride giving her man her heart and body. Jeff will never understand a saucy bra strap dipped over a bare shoulder or a bottom leaning over and wiggling out of cotton panties. Because back in this time, a girl doesn't do what I'm doing. Well, she does, but no one talks about it. I'm nervous; I'm not ashamed of my body – I forgot how flat my tummy is and my breasts are high with pert nipples – but fidgety with worry about how this will turn out. I'm breaking every rule, not only changing the past, but changing my life. My body. I'm willing to take the risk.

Jeff has no qualms about undressing in front of me and he's magnificent.

Oh. He takes my breath away when he unbuttons his shirt, revealing his bare chest. He lays me down on the divan and presses his body against mine. What I've dreamed about for so long is revealed to me when I run my hands up and down his strong body. A male dripping with raw sex appeal with every defined muscle. Broad shoulders. Flat stomach, lean hips that move with the grace of a jungle cat. Long, muscular legs. There are no walls between us as he holds me tighter. He doesn't grab me roughly as a young man wild with desire might, but aligns my body to his, pressing himself against me just enough to make my toes curl. He has the presence of a man who knows women, knows what they want, and his earthy scent confirms it.

I stifle a groan. We never got this heavy before. He draws in a sharp breath. I feel my blood rising to flush my cheeks already hot from the fire. Yes, we fooled around in the private office in the bank, but not like this. We never rubbed our bodies against each other. Never let it go this far. Maybe this is a mistake. Maybe it's better for him to keep the illusion of his Jelly Girl. I'm playing with an eternal fire – ignited by the friction of our body heat – that has haunted me for years. Kept me awake at nights.

Sweat trickles down my spine. I can't give him up now, but every good-girl instinct Ma ever taught me urges me to put a stop to this madness. He wants me and I've waited for so long, I don't stop him when he puts his hand under my gown and touches my bare skin. The instant skin against skin contact brands me his. He exhales loudly and stops. The pressure of his fingers against my inner thigh intensifies the delicious arousal of our senses, but he goes no farther. I understand what's happening here. We're both waiting.

Daring the other to cross the line we haven't done before.

Jeff groans, then looks at me with those smoldering, wanting eyes, giving me a heart stopping glimpse into his soul. His gaze never falters, but I see a tenderness in those eyes that assures me he'll hold back, wait till I'm ready. I don't know how long I can stall him while I suffer the anguish of whether or not to go through with this insanity, my emotions riding wave after wave of excitement, then exhilaration. Still, I hesitate. Do I even have the right to decide for my younger self?

I know what *I* want, always have. Him, taking me as his wife in the most precious way, but my younger self wouldn't dare cross that line before marriage. Again, I'm at war with the girl I was and the woman I am now.

The question is, who will win?

## 21

I don't want Jeff to get the wrong idea about me, but when he's under fire from the enemy or holed up in a French farmhouse trying to elude capture by the Gestapo, he'll remember this night. A night with a woman who adores him, wants him. Who never stopped loving him. Even if he doesn't have a picture of me in his wallet, he'll have one in his heart.

I want that picture to be the girl next door. A girl he can be proud of and respect. I make my decision because it's the right one. I can't make love to him. Not here, not now. Yet I fear I've already gone too far. The hunger in his eyes is so intense, the deepening fire in those eyes dominating everything in the room with a hypnotic spell he can't break, much less understand.

'You're so beautiful, Kate.' The words come out husky, yet filled with a reverence that surprises me. He doesn't make a move to go any farther, moves I know so well from nights filled with passion. Nights when I tried to make myself believe I was in love with the man trying to please me, when all the time I pretended that man was Jeff. A short lived pang of guilt shoots through me because I never gave them a chance. Because no one can take his place in my mind.

And now he's here, leaning over me, his muscular frame overpowering me with his masculine presence. He's holding back, barely. Waiting for a signal from me. I can't. I lie here and stare at him. Memorizing every sculpted plane of his broad chest, those strong arms bulging with muscle when he flexes his biceps, folding his hands behind his head, his glance penetrating, questioning, while he tries to decide what to do next. His flat stomach rippling, and that face. Awestruck. The deepening fire in his eyes dominating every-thing in the room with a hypnotic spell that even he can't break, much less understand.

*I want you, Jeff, yes, but we have to wait. Oh, you don't know how much I want to marry you.*

I mouth the words, for I'm afraid if I speak them aloud, it will break the spell. We're here together on the soft divan in a house where patriots' boots once trod in their pursuit of free-dom. I seek freedom, too. From the pain that has consumed me for so long. I arch my back to quell the sensation, pleasur-able as it is. The reaction on Jeff's face sends me farther along on my way to losing control. I almost change my mind, abandon my plan of self-righteousness for the overwhelming temptation of a riotous ride with him kissing me, touching, probing. Sending me to a place so long denied me. Hot tears well up in my eyes. I teeter back and forth in my mind for arduous seconds, my body aching for fulfillment. Sweating. Eyes misty.

Jeff isn't helping, panting hard, his bare chest shining with sweat. He's a man in need of release, but his love for me makes him refrain from going any farther. The hot desire in his eyes gives him away, but he doesn't push me. The way he holds me when he pulls me into his arms is protective, noble. My heart swells. I never loved him more than I do at this moment.

I want us to embrace our union of man and woman when it's right, in the future. There's only one way I can make that happen. I can't wait any longer to tell him about the letter before we both lose control and do something we regret.

'Jeff, there's something I want to tell you.'

'I know, Jelly Girl. I've known for a while.'

'You do?' He isn't making this any easier for me, kissing the back of my neck.

'What you got me for Christmas. Socks, right?' Breathing hard, he holds me tight and I study his face burning a golden bronze against the flames in the fireplace, his eyes penetrating, questioning, while he tries to defuse the situation with a light moment and quell his passion. I sense he's accepted what I didn't put into words. That we have to wait. 'Every soldier going overseas gets socks.'

'What if I told you I know things about this war others don't?' I ask him.

He looks at me strangely. The hollows in his cheeks deepen, his eyes flutter, like he didn't sleep a wink last night. 'Snooping at keyholes again?'

'No... and it's not because I watch the newsreels every Saturday. I *know* what's going on over there. How our government has been sending tanks, guns, and ammunition to help liberate France. That will happen in August which means France is a dangerous place for anyone working with the underground... like a pilot who could be shot down.'

I let my voice drift off, as low as the whisper of an angel on the holiest of nights, expecting him to say something. He doesn't move, but snuggles me in his arms. I wait for him to refute my words, challenge me, demand to know where I get these insane notions. There's enough truth in what I'm telling him reported in the newspapers to make him believe me.

I saw a small column on the front page earlier about how the German high command believes an invasion is coming from England. A hint at the upcoming Allied advance on the beaches of Normandy on June 6, 1944.

The bigwigs in Washington need intelligence to make that plan work. No wonder they pull Jeff out of flight school and plunk him down right in the middle of a nest of Nazis.

I rack my brain on how much to tell him. What if my plan doesn't work and he's captured and tortured by the Gestapo? In my awkward attempt to warn him, I may have planted a seed in his brain that will be his undoing. How can I explain to him he's in danger?

Jeff is strangely quiet. He must think he's marrying someone else, not his Jelly Girl. That I've morphed into a different woman. My emotions rule me when I'm nineteen, setting my body on fire whenever he touches me, kisses me. I know nothing of the world or the workings of the war machine of Washington. My emotions also rule me now, but the stakes are higher. I'm sweating but the primal need burning low in my belly has turned cold. Making love to him isn't on my mind. I'm desperate to save him. In doing so, I can lose him.

I shudder as if I've jumped off a precipice, thinking I can fly. I went straight down into the abyss and I'm still falling. My mind tells me I've gone about this all wrong, that presenting facts to this man is plain stupid. Most likely, he's been briefed in Washington and knows more than what I laid out. I have to try another approach, but what?

My guilt for having said too much is surpassed only by

my cowardice to nudge him and ask him his thoughts. I cuddle up against his chest, waiting for him to say something. Anything. I notice his breathing is slow and steady. Is he thinking about what I said? Or is he upset with me and he wants to break off our engagement?

The embers in the fireplace are still warm. A shiver makes me tremble. I pull away from him and smile when I see his eyes are closed. A loud, mood shattering, beautiful snore breaks the silence.

I smile, then kiss his lips and take up my position cradled against his chest. Lovely, just lovely. He's fast asleep.

I doubt he heard a word I said.

* * *

Jeff is gone.

I awake with a start and feel the empty space beside me, the divan cover wrinkled and cool to my touch. His body heat long gone. The fire smolders, giving off little warmth. I fell asleep. The last thing I remember is rifling my fingers through his hair, enjoying looking at him, when I drifted off into a Neverland and floated through one beautiful dream after another. Jeff kissing me... touching me... when the first sprinkle of dawn dances over my eyelids in spite of the blacked-out windows.

I jump up, smooth my gown, and pace around the room, every nerve in my body alert. I try to shake off this groggy feeling. I can't. Where is he? Does he regret bringing me here? Or did something else happen? Has what I feared come true? What I dread, what I can't face. That somehow I've come back to my own time?

I run outside, throwing my red coat over my gown,

leaving it unbuttoned, eager to see if the landscape has changed. If the dirt road has become a highway or houses have been built. I see in the daylight what I couldn't see in the dark last night. It strikes me with awe. The early morning sun tints the windows with a light shimmer, the wind sweeping over the grassy lawn, sprinkling dew on its shiny blades of grass, while a pink-gray sky slowly peels off the black glove of night holding it tight in its fist. As far as I can see – over beyond the woods, then down the dirt road leading back here to the stone house – nothing has changed.

My heart beats faster when I see Jeff standing by the river, tossing stones into the rippling water. He hears me approaching, but he doesn't turn around.

'Someday I want to redesign this house with big picture windows in the back so we can sit here every night and watch the river,' he says, his voice deep and heavy with emotion.

I smile. So that's why he added it to the drawing.

'Swirling with rough whitecaps in the winter,' he continues, 'and smooth and calm on a warm summer evening.'

'Sounds wonderful, Jeff.' I link my arm through his. 'I'd like that, too.'

I don't tell him the house sits empty for over a decade, overgrown with weeds and time. I never forgot how we'd drive by the place in his roadster and he talked about the good memories he had here. Over the years, the tall oaks held their place like good soldiers, their limbs bending under a great sadness. The leaves falling from the trees scatter as quickly as they fall, as if they can't bear to linger in a place where there's no life, no hope.

I came here after we got the news about Jeff being killed. I walked and walked for what seemed like hours after Mrs Rushbrooke threw me out of the memorial ceremony. I didn't know then that he planned for us to live here, but I was sure this was the house in the drawing he did of me. It was a good walk from the mill, but I remembered the way. I didn't dare get too close, fearing Mrs Rushbrooke would get me for trespassing. I had a special feeling about the place back then. Like I could hear Jeff's faint voice in my ear, telling me he loved me. Now I know why.

He has no idea what I'm thinking. 'I came here often when I was a boy with my French nanny, Aline.' He tosses another rock into the river. 'She had a big hearty laugh and blue, doll-like eyes. She was hardworking and loyal, and I never saw her without a fresh yellow flower pinned to her black and white uniform.'

He smiles.

'We'd spend time here during the summer when my mother filled Wrightwood House with her snooty friends from the Philadelphia Mainline. Timothy got shipped off to summer camp, but I liked it here. I fished in the river and built rafts and sailed my boat and drew while Aline told me stories about her life in France. How she followed her father and brothers skipping over russet tile rooftops in Paris, going from house to house with a ladder, long black brush, and sack for collecting soot. Her father was a chimney sweep, but he wanted something better for his little girl.

'Aline found work as a ladies' maid for a countess who encouraged her love of books. She showed me pictures of buildings in Old Paris with sloping roofs and medieval gables. Ancient gateways that led to thieves' dens. Stately mansions with courtyards and bubbling fountains that ran red during the Revolution with the blood of aristocrats.

'Hearing her speak about the grand market of Les Halles and the majestic white beauty of Sacré Coeur set me on a course to explore the need in me to design and build. That's when I became interested in architecture, a foolish notion according to my father. Aline never discouraged me. She became a fierce protector of my work and hid my drawings from him here in the house.'

He becomes quiet and I see a pleasant memory wash over him, then a smirk on his lips. 'I dreamed of redesigning this old place and living here when I finished architecture school. Aline encouraged me to study in France, insisting we speak nothing but French when I was growing up. Because of her, I easily adapted to the French way of life when I traveled there with my father.'

I've never heard a more fascinating story.

'I never forgot Aline and her laugh,' he goes on. 'I played hide-and-seek with her, running through the house and sneaking into the tiny secret room where Washington's men hid their weapons and writings of independence from the British. That's where she hid my drawings.' He holds my hand. 'Those were the best days of my life until I met you, Jelly Girl, and you introduced me to your cherry jam.' He nuzzles his face into my hair. 'Now I can't get enough of it.'

'What happened to Aline?' I ask, snuggling up close to him. It doesn't get any better than this.

'When I went off to boarding school, she went back to Paris to nurse her father when he became ill. An incurable disease from inhaling the smoke and tar from cleaning chimneys.'

'She never married?'

He shakes his head. 'The boy she loved died in the trenches of Verdun. I'd see her take out his picture from her missal and kiss it goodnight.'

'Oh.'

I can't hold back the mistiness settling on my cheeks. How my soul aches for this remarkable woman who reared the boy with such a fine hand. I wish I could tell her how wonderful a man he is. I also want to tell her I understand the pain as only another woman can. Losing the man she loves. I think about what Jeff was like as a little boy, the lonely hours he spent here because his mother didn't want him around. My heart bleeds.

A light drizzle dampens the earth around us, soaking up the past while I weigh my options for the future. Jeff is in a melancholy mood, the weight of the world on his shoulders. This is not the time to tell him about the letter. I still have time to convince him he's in danger. I have a better chance of him believing me after he gets the telephone call that his orders are changed and he gets called up sooner to report to Washington.

My fears that he slept through my plea last night are confirmed a heartbeat later when Jeff takes my hand in his, his voice deep and gravelly as he says, 'The next time we come here, Jelly Girl, we'll be married.'

I pray that's true.

## 22

Pop is livid with anger when I sneak in through the back kitchen door, chewing on his pipe, pacing up and down, demanding to know where I was all night. With the servicemen looking for a good time, he says, *anything* can happen. Ma calms him down with a few well-placed words and then turns and gives me a look that says, *Don't say a word.*

'Kate spent the night at the rectory with the reverend's wife.' Ma leads him over to the kitchen table and eases him down into a chair. She slides an empty saucer in front of him so he can dump out the burnt tobacco from his pipe. A classic move from Ma. This is her territory, so he doesn't protest. 'The poor woman needed company,' she continues, 'what with her emotions spilling over and everybody going home afterwards and her all alone.' She stares straight at me through clenched teeth. 'Right, Kate?'

'Yeah, Ma. Mildred needed someone to talk to.'

Ma plays her role with the skill of any Broadway actress, fiddling with the stray hair getting into her eyes, wringing her hands on her apron. 'Kate told me where she was going, but

when we got home, I was so tired it slipped my mind.' Ma
shoots me a hard look. There's no question in her eyes, only
disapproval. She doesn't have to ask if I was out with Jeff, she
knows.

After our talk, she also knows I'm not her little girl and
whatever her personal thoughts are on the matter, she has no
choice but to accept my decision to spend the night with the
man I love. She can't change it, so she does what Ma does
best. Keep the family intact, no matter what she has to do.
Even if it means telling Pop a fib. Something I never saw her
do in my whole life. Ma is as straight up as a Sunday sermon.
Whatever she says, you never doubt her.

Her piece said, she cajoles Pop into having an early breakfast before Sunday church services. Then, like she does for
Junior when he needs pepping up, she serves him something
special. Pancakes with apple butter. Hot coffee. A little cream
she traded jam for from the milkman. Then she sits down
and reads the latest war news to him before they get ready for
church.

I hustle upstairs to change before Lucy and Junior come
down to breakfast. Ma closed my bedroom door, so they don't
know I didn't come home last night. She was up waiting for
me when Pop came down to check on her and I barged
through the door. The sight of me disheveled and my gown
stained with dirt told the story. His daughter was out all
night. No wonder Pop was fit to be tied. I've hurt both of
them, and it isn't a good feeling.

I want to thank Ma for what she did when I come back
down dressed for church. She won't look at me and there's no
mistaking that pain in her eyes. There's no undoing what I
did. I debate whether or not to try to explain to her later.
That I tried to tell Jeff about the letter, but we fell asleep and

nothing happened between us. I pray she comes around and believes me.

Lucy has no idea what's going on when she pops down for breakfast, neither does Junior. She babbles on and on about how many soldiers, sailors, and Marines she danced with last night.

'Twenty, maybe twenty-five,' she says, helping herself to pancakes. 'All tall, dark, and handsome.'

Junior has a different opinion. 'There weren't any girls left to dance with, what with them servicemen taking them all.'

'You're too young for girls,' Lucy says with her mouth full.

'I'm a year younger than you are.'

'Girls mature faster.'

'Now, children, *please*.' Ma tosses down the newspaper, startling everyone. 'Let's have a quiet breakfast. We're all very tired this morning.' She rubs her eyes and she won't look at me. Tears wet her cheeks. It's the worst moment of my trip back through time. I'll never forget it. My selfish actions hit me hard when I see how deeply I've hurt Ma. Her tears are a sign of both anger and relief I came home safe. That I don't doubt, but it doesn't change anything. I broke a cardinal rule in her eyes. Good girls don't spend the night with a man. Still, she knows I'll soon be gone and my instincts tell me she views that, in a strange way, as akin to losing a child.

We don't speak much after Ma's outburst. The rest of the family does their best to help her out, though I don't think Lucy and Junior grasp her sadness. Pop does. I see him eyeing me. He has something on his mind, but I can tell he's holding it in.

*Ma's had enough to upset her for now*, his eyes say.

My heart skips later that morning after church services when Mildred thanks me for helping her. Pop is within earshot and smiles. Luckily for me, he has no idea she's refer-ring to our conversation before the tree lighting ceremony – for which I say a special prayer of gratitude.

Then Mildred pulls me aside and whispers her concern in my ear about the Rushbrooke family pew being empty. Not even the help came to church today, which is unusual. I wonder about that, too, since Mrs Rushbrooke always attends church, if only to show off a new hat or spread the latest gossip. Then Mildred tells me she heard the news about Jeff and me eloping.

'I'm so excited for you, Kate, you'll make a beautiful bride.' She adds that Jeff asked her to pick me up tomorrow morning. Monday. Early.

I take a step backward in my mind. 'He did?' I let go with a shiver, my shoulders shaking. This is a good thing, right? Back then, I rushed to the station because Jeff didn't show up like we planned and I was scared like crazy I'd miss the train. I ran into Mildred by chance. Now I've set my compass – and hers – on a new course.

'Yes. Jeff said his mother was in a fit earlier about some-thing to do with a call from Washington. He paid me a visit to ask for my help so nothing goes wrong with your elopement plans.' She squeezes my hand and can't stop smiling at me. I can't be more pleased at having her as a co-conspirator, but I also can't forget the flat tire we had on the way to the train station the morning Jeff and I planned to elope.

I ask, 'Are your tires okay?'

She nods. 'I had them checked at the gas station since I'll be doing a lot of driving with Christmas visits coming up. I appreciate your ma making sure I have apple cinnamon preserves to give to the families. Believe me, the sweet helps with the pain.' Her smile takes on a more determined look, her mouth tight. 'I have more Gold Star families to visit this Christmas than last.'

More to come before our boys come home. Next Christmas, too.

I can't tell her that. I've already brought home enough sadness for one day.

'You did it, Katie Marie Arden, didn't you?'

Ma slams down the bread dough on the wooden board and begins kneading it like it's made out of shoe leather. She wipes the sweat off her brow, but she refuses to look up at me. Tuesday is her regular bread making day, so for her to drag out the flour and yeast and her precious sugar means she needs to find comfort. She finds it in making bread.

I freeze. I raided the icebox for a glass of homemade berry juice when I found her in the kitchen. I don't try to escape. I'm no angel with invisible wings. I expect she won't let me go without a talking to. I deserve it.

'Ma, I—' I start to explain. She'll have none of it.

'You spent the night together before you were man and wife, hoping I'd bless you.' She pounds the bread dough harder to make her point. 'It goes against everything I hold dear. Against the teachings I learned my whole life.'

'I'm not a child, Ma. You'll find out in a few years I do well for myself in the city, working my way up to editor. It's lonely at the top when you have no one. I longed for years to be at Jeff's side. For him to hold me in his arms, kiss me without the fear of prying eyes, embarrassing moments. Would you deny me that happiness? To spend one night with him? I swear to you nothing happened. Jeff kissed me, nothing else.'

'I'm trying to understand, but I can't.' She puts the dough in a big round bowl and covers it with a piece of cheesecloth to let it prove. Then she breaks down, her shoulders shaking. '*I can't.*'

'I need you, Ma. Listen to me, please,' I plead. 'Think what you will of me, but don't turn your back on your other daughter, the one waiting in the shadows. I'll be gone soon, back to my own time. I feel it in my bones. Please don't shut out my younger self when she returns. Give her all the love you can because she's going to need it.'

'Even if you save Jeff,' she says, finally looking at me, 'how do you know he'll marry you?'

'I don't, Ma,' I say honestly, 'but I'm willing to take that chance.'

'You must love that boy.'

'I do.'

Her eyes brighten into a blue-green shade I recognize, the joy in them I often see when she has her brood fed and content. 'All I want is for you to be happy.'

'I am, Ma. Whatever happens, I've had this time with Jeff. That's all a woman could ever ask for.'

'I see the world changing around me so fast.' Ma wipes the flour off her hands onto her apron. 'Lucy flirting with every soldier who comes through here, Junior getting into fights. Pop coming out of his shell and getting excited about the war news.' She takes my hand in hers and holds it tight. 'Look at my Katie, all grown up. Yes, I understand. You *are* a woman.' Then she stops talking. Like she's coming to terms with this new world she finds herself in. We sit for a long time and don't speak. We don't have to.

We found peace between us in our time.

* * *

Sunday continues to be a strange day after church and my talk with Ma, the air so still not even the sound of a motorcar rumbling down the street grates on my ears. No neighbors chatting, kids playing. Like everyone is nestled in their home, getting ready for another wartime Christmas. Mothers and fathers add a blue star to the flag hanging over the fireplace, meaning their boy or girl is in the service. The only present they want is a letter from them, along with the hope they'll be home for next Christmas.

After a rocky start to the day earlier, Pop asks me to play checkers with him.

'Your move, Kate,' Pop says. Most folks play cards during the war, but my father is a hands-on worker with a fine mechanical mind. He likes to tinker with his tools. So no one is more surprised than I when he sits down and dusts off the checkerboard, though I sense his mind is elsewhere.

'You sure you don't want to change your last move?' I'm curious where this will lead.

'Nope. Some things never change. Like your Ma. She's made my coffee and toast the same way every morning for more than twenty years. Black with a squirt of milk, and two perfect patties of butter on my toast.' He chews on the end of his pipe. 'Since the war started, she still gives me two patties of butter every morning. She gives me her ration. If I say something, it will hurt her feelings. I'd rather swim down-river with a mean possum on my tail than do that.'

'Me, too, Pop.' I jump over three of his pieces. He never blinks.

'Sometimes things got to change.'

'Yes, Pop?'

'Starting tomorrow, I'm having one patty of butter with my toast.'

'Why?'

'Because this war has set me to thinking that by not saying what's giving me an itch up my overalls, I'm hurting the ones I love.'

'Ma would never think that, Pop.'

'It's not your ma I'm talking about, Katie Marie.' He looks straight at me, his pipe in his mouth. 'It's you.'

'Me?'

'I know what you done for me. How you stood up to Mrs Rushbrooke, giving her a taste of her own fancy talk and not letting her run your old pop out of a job. You don't have to worry about me. Your ma explained to me you ain't a little girl no more. You found a good man who loves you. I've been mighty blind not to see it myself. Then again, I ain't your ma. If she says so, then it's right. You go after Mr Jeffrey if he's the man for you.

'He is. Oh, Pop, I love him so much.'

'Your ma told me, and she ain't never said nothing that weren't true. So I'm not keeping quiet no more. I imagine the boy will be called up soon and leaving for training, so you don't have much time. You marry that boy if that's what you're after.'

'It is, Pop,' I say, exhaling. 'It's more complicated than that.'

'I'm not asking you to tell me anything you shouldn't. Your ma and I love you and we'll stand behind you.' His eyes hold me, real concern in them. 'I'll give it an extra prayer next Sunday to keep Mr Jeffrey safe. He's a good man.'

'You're the best, Pop.' I fling my arms around him and hug him. I feel the shift in energy in the air as the hour grows late.

Ma spoke to him after our chat because we never have this talk back then and it warms me through and through. I'm glad we did. It will make it easier for him to help Junior when he comes home from the war.

'Now, where is my pipe tobacco?' he says, wiping the checkerboard clean with his last play, jumping over my remaining pieces. I grin. Pop poured out his heart to me and it closed up an emptiness in him he never come to grips with before. So ends our Sunday talk.

I kiss him on the cheek and put the checkerboard away on the end table next to the radio. As I stack up the red and black chips in two neat piles, I watch my father's expression deepen to a look I saw only once before. On December seventh. A determined look to go forward, accept what he couldn't change on that Sunday afternoon when we gathered around the mahogany box in the front room and found out we were attacked at Pearl Harbor. A day when we bowed our heads and joined hands, each of us saying a prayer that we win the war.

Now he's losing his little girl and he's worried about her losing the man she loves. I want to comfort him, tell him my plan, but I can't. My father opened up to me, but he has a blind spot. Him looking into the future is like looking into the sun... he can't see what's coming, only what's behind him. So I keep quiet. The end of the war seems so far off. I wish I could be here to see his face when they announce the defeat of Nazi Germany, and later the surrender of Japan. At least our talk made him more willing to share his emotions.

I catch Lucy on her way out, smelling of my perfume and wearing the charm bracelet I gave her. She takes a moment to give me a look I can only describe as winsome yet heartfelt. Eyelids flutter, cheeks tint pink. As if she's cognizant beyond a doubt I'm not the same sister she knew, though she doesn't know why. Then she gives me a quick peck on the cheek and is out the door before I say a word. I smile. I'll see her soon. Junior? He's off with his friends after church. I have an uncanny feeling he'll find his way home when I go back to my own time.

I start up the stairs, then stop and look back. Ma is sitting in my place, the two of them whispering and holding hands. She chuckles at something Pop says and all is right in their world. Soon they'll be setting up the artificial tree they got last year, getting out the ornaments, mixing soap flakes with water and then brushing it on the branches to look like snow. Giggling like two teenagers very much in love.

I linger there for a while, breathing them in. I want to remember them like this because I'll never see them again.

* * *

Mildred is waiting for me in her dented old pickup truck when I sneak out of the house early the next morning. I'm running on adrenaline and so nervous my chest hurts, but I can endure anything to save Jeff. She sits in the driver's seat, smiling at something she reads in a letter she's holding, her truck parked not too close to the house to avoid catching Mrs Widget's eye. I have no doubt the post is from the reverend and I make a mental note to reconnect with her when I return to my own time.

My heart skips so fast I don't feel the cold when I race over to her, carrying my overnight case, and jump in. I press my lips together tight to prevent blurting out the madness driving me forward, that I *can* change the past and save Jeff. Nothing has ever made my heart beat faster than knowing what I have to do today, pound so loudly in my ears I barely hear the truck's engine purring. This is my last chance to tell him about the letter. I gave him plenty of hints, but I haven't told him the truth. Where I'm from, why I'm here. My heart is ready to bust open, wanting to tell him. I never expected the forces of time would be so stubborn and take me on a journey with so many twists and turns. Like they're toying with me.

Not today. I know what I have to do. I smooth down my red coat, playing with the buttons. One will soon be missing. Like a piece of my heart. I'll leave it here with the people I love, while I pray my man will escape from the nightmare that awaits him.

To make that happen, I wear the same gray silk suit, stockings, and shoes I wore coming through time along with my blue silk hat. I have to play this scene out step by step so I don't upset anything in the fragile timeline that runs along an invisible track side by side with what already happened. I've yet to understand it or the whimsical power of the Christmas train, but I have the feeling the two tracks will mesh together somewhere to create a different future.

*If* I do this right. No doubt. It has to be magic.

'I never thought doing the Lord's work would have me helping a runaway bride, Kate.' Mildred puts the truck into gear and takes off with the biggest grin on her face. 'So I don't forget, here's your train ticket.' She hands it to me. 'Jeff asked me to give it to you.'

I fidget with my gloves as I take it from her and lay it on my lap so I won't lose it. 'I'm more jittery than any bride.'

*I'll never be a bride if I don't save Jeff.*

'Jeff is a lucky man,' she says. 'Let's get you on that train.'

She races down the road spitting up dirt and gravel, trav-

eling much faster than the thirty-five mile an hour speed
limit set by the government to save gas. I'm grateful the road
is empty and I thank the stars no one is about.

I speak too soon. I lean in, my eyes disbelieving. My God,
Mrs Canton is rambling straight toward us in her big empty
bus. Spewing up debris, the gears grinding. Her head
hanging out the window, blonde curls whipping in the wind.

'What's Mrs Canton doing out on the road so early?' Panic
creeps over my skin like someone dumped a kettle of cold
fish down my back. She's still heading toward us, trying to
force us off the road.

*It's not on the timeline. She'll ruin everything. What am I
going to do?*

Mildred grimaces. 'I bet she overheard me talking to
Mary Sue about going on a mission of mercy at the gas
station yesterday. It didn't help when I started humming
"Here Comes the Bride".' She exhales in a loud whoosh. 'I'm
so sorry, Kate. I can't believe I was that foolish.'

*No. No. No.* Since Mary Sue took over as attendant at the
local gas station to free up the men, it's more of a gossip stop
than a gas stop. I bet Sarah Canton saw Mrs Rushbrooke
chew me out at the dance and put two and two together.
She'll do anything to ruin me.

'We've got to outmaneuver her before she does something
stupid.' The morning chill seeps through me and my skin
tingles. 'I can't miss that train.'

'You won't.' Mildred grunts as she shifts gears. 'As the
reverend says, God is our co-pilot.'

She takes off so fast, I have to hold onto the door handle.
We hit fifty, then sixty miles an hour, the vehicle racing along
the far side of the road, its bulky, metal frame rattling from
side to side as we zoom by the school bus with just inches to

spare. A close call, but Mrs Canton isn't done with us. I spin around and see the bus screech to a stop behind us and do a one hundred and eighty degree turn and keep right on our tail. Is there no stopping her?

'She's behind us,' I sputter, not believing what I'm seeing. I have no one to blame but myself. I wouldn't be in this predicament if I didn't challenge her authority. I was so hungry to see Jeff, I pushed the timeline to the limit and I'm paying the price. Who imagined she'd turn up now?

'I have an idea, Kate.' Mildred slams her foot on the gas and, putting her shoulder into it, she turns the steering wheel hard, making a sharp right onto a dirt road and heads toward the train station over an old horse and wagon trail.

I whisper a prayer and twist my head around to see if Mrs Canton is following us. Yes. Somehow she keeps on our tail, zigzagging along the trail, honking her horn. I get a bad feeling. Why won't she let it go? I'm racked by a scary thought come to visit me. Back then, we rushed to the train station but Mildred got a flat tire. That incident is part of the original timeline. Yes, I've altered some events since I've been back, but what happens today must stay the same. It's the key to my saving Jeff. I'm afraid if anything changes, it will put the whole timeline off and I can't save him. I feel it in my bones. A silly notion, but I can't shake it off.

The truck keeps going, making deep tire marks in the soft dirt, going over rocks and shaking us up. We hit one rock so hard, I bounce up on the seat and hit my head on the windshield. A sharp pain from the impact slices through me, making my eyes blink rapidly, sending me into a controlled panic. No, God, *no*. I can't go back now. *I can't.* I force myself to hold steady, not lose consciousness, keep focused. No way am I going to black out like I did on the train.

I turn around, keeping my eye on the bus following us, my body humming in a fast rhythm. Mrs Canton is gaining on us, driving so recklessly she doesn't see a low hanging oak branch. She swerves around it, but she's not quick enough. The branch slaps down hard over the roof of the bus and covers her windshield, forcing her to screech to a halt.

I let go the breath I've been holding. She won't bother us anymore. Now to get to the train station.

'You did it, Mildred.' I rub my forehead, a headache pinching my brain. Thank God I'm still here. 'Thank you.'

She squeezes my hand. 'You can thank me later, Kate. We're almost there.'

The pickup truck bounces over the road, hitting rocks and brambles and jostling us from side to side. I pray with every bounce we get there before the train leaves. My stomach is churning and I can't help but wonder if I'm fooling myself. There never was a chance to save Jeff, it's all a cruel joke. That makes my heart ache more than my head, praying the love I have for him is strong enough to overcome whatever forces are at play here.

What if he's gone when I get there... No, I can't give up. This is another test and if I have faith in what Ma calls the power of the *unseen hand to guide us through the darkest night*, I'll make it.

Then a familiar note strikes a chord in my brain. The truck's engine sputters and coughs when Mildred zooms over a large mound of dirt in the middle of the road. We don't see what's on the other side until it's too late. A big hole. We stop dead.

'Lord, help us, please,' Mildred prays, grinding the gears, her foot jammed on the gas. When I lean out the window, all I see are the big heavy wheels spinning in the dirt.

I jump out, a strange blip clicking in my brain, like something snaps into place. An urgent chill seeps through my red coat, pushing me to look down, see, believe, *go*. Well, I'll be—. The front end of the truck sank into the hole and leans to one side. We have a flat tire. The first time we ran over nails and debris in the road, but it's a flat tire nonetheless.

I swear I cry from sheer relief. Whatever I changed since my return didn't affect this critical moment. I don't know what forces are at play here, dark or whimsical, and that's what scares me. I'm running out of options. I have no idea how much longer I'll remain in this time. It's not something I can pinpoint.

But I have a feeling whatever brought me here is warning me to get this over with and go. That I'm living in a fairy tale and the clock is getting close to striking midnight.

I'm not leaving until I warn my prince.

Mildred thinks I'm crazy when I hug her and ask her to understand if I don't remember the details. She nods, believing I mean when I hit the windshield, knocking the breath from me. I grab my case. The timeline is intact.

I catch the wind at my back and I take off running, pushing myself to run faster than I ever have. I don't want to give this fickle notion called time any reason to stop me from finding Jeff. I have to get on that train and warn him.

While I still have a chance to save him.

## 23

The long, blaring call of the train engine's whistle slams into my ears as I push through the turnstile, my red coat whipping around me, the tension building in me as I try to keep out the cold. I don't slow my pace but jostle my way through the arriving passengers, who are tired and weary from a trip with each railcar filled to capacity. Soldiers home on furlough wander through the station along with a few civilians who offer to give them a ride into town. I don't see my man anywhere.

*Don't do this to me. Please, Jeff, I must see you. Where are you?*

I run up and down the platform. Waiting for something to happen, like the century old wood to buckle, the wind to smash into the weather vane and spin it round and round. Lightning, thunder. *Something* that propels me into the scene.

I wander aimlessly like an actor who forgot their lines. Do I move stage left, stage right? How do I find him? I don't even know what railcar he's in. Wait. My ticket. I reach into my side pocket, but no, the letter's there. I tucked it away before I went through the tunnel back in my own time, but I don't have time to check it. The other pocket is empty... oh, no, I was in such a hurry, I left it in the truck. Different from before when Jeff had the tickets. This time he gave mine to Mildred to give to me.

I stop. I don't know where to go, can't move, as if I hang suspended, hovering between here and my own time, a dreamlike, pearl-gray steam hissing between the wheels of the big locomotive. Since the hour is so early, only a few local ladies are on hand to give out coffee and donuts to the soldiers hanging out the passenger windows.

Then I hear whistles, catcalls. Seeing me, a soldier jumps off the train, asking to carry my overnight case. *I'm waiting for my fiancé*, I say. *Lucky fellow.* He whistles again, then gets back on the train to tell his unhappy buddies.

A moment later, as if on cue, the final call of the train whistle blows and the locomotive comes to life. Huffing and puffing like a fairy tale dragon in search of a storybook to tell its tale.

*Not without me, you don't.* I head for the end railcar, holding onto my blue silk hat and gripping my case, making my plan. *Start there, keep searching, the sleeper car, dining car, observation car, until you find him—*

'Miss Arden, Miss Kate Arden,' I hear someone paging me.

I spin around, anxious. I heave out a big puff of air. I don't realize I'm breathing so hard. Nerves. 'Yes.' The word comes out a whisper. Barely.

Smiling, the stationmaster tips his hat. 'A gentleman asked me to give you this if he missed you. He said he couldn't wait and had to get aboard the train.' He hands me a letter.

Yes. *That* letter.

I don't open it. I know what it says. That he has to leave without me. He's under orders and can't tell me the details, but he'll get a furlough before he goes overseas and we'll be married as planned. But he didn't come back and we didn't get married.

I put down my case and grit my teeth to keep from shattering into pieces. I never felt so alone, so wrapped up in darkness that it suffocates me. I can't bear to read it, so I crumple up the sealed letter and stuff it into my suit pocket. We *didn't* miss each other back then. After I read the letter, I searched the station until I found him. This time something shifted, pushed him to get on the train earlier, which upset the original timeline. It was intact till now.

I need to find out why that happened. A sudden awareness teases my brain, telling me who's behind his sudden departure. Mrs Rushbrooke.

'Was there a woman with the gentleman who gave you this letter?' I ask the stationmaster. 'Wearing furs and a pillbox hat?'

He looks down. I see his nose twitching. 'You wouldn't mean Mrs Rushbrooke, would you?'

'I would.'

He nods. 'Right pushy she was, if you don't mind me saying so.'

'I don't.'

'The gentleman kept looking over his shoulder, but she'd have none of it. Hustled him aboard quicker than a greased pig on a run, but not before he slipped me the letter to give to you.'

I notice the stationmaster doesn't mention Jeff by name. I suppose he figures he's said too much already.

'Did she get on the train with him?' I have to know.

The stationmaster shakes his head. 'The gentleman insisted she go home. It didn't take too much to convince her. She didn't look none too pleased surrounded by rowdy young soldiers.'

This new development makes my heart stop. I pray her showing up doesn't shift this critical part of the timeline into a new direction I can't fix. She's like an errant queen bee intent on jabbing her stinger into anyone who gets in her way.

Did she know Jeff was waiting for me? She must have. I had a few minutes to say goodbye to him back then. Now I don't. It has to be her doing. I'll never forget her snide remarks and the catty look on her face at the dance, like she knew Jeff would get the urgent call to report to Washington. Then she ruined our elopement plans by making sure he got on that train. Without me. Leaving me standing here without any chance of seeing him, holding him, or telling him about the letter I received back in my own time.

I *have* to get on that train.

The first time I didn't press him when he told me he had to go alone. That I couldn't ride with him till the next stop. I was a lot braver then, believing I'd see him as soon as he got a furlough. I felt proud, determined to start acting like a good officer's wife even if we had to wait to get married.

Now with the unbearable fear of not finding him urging me on, I push such thoughts to the back of my mind. Saving him is the only thing that matters.

I ask the stationmaster where Jeff boarded. With a big smile, he points out the middle car and wishes me luck. I run hard down the long stretch of tracks, my lungs bursting as I race from the back car toward the middle where Jeff is. I swear I hear the fates of time laughing at me when the locomotive starts pulling out of the station before I get there, the big wheels creaking and groaning.

Faster and faster. Steel grinding against steel... the tracks wet and slick from the steam.

My heart breaks. What capricious wind of time would do this to me? Whip me into a frenzy and then leave me here? The train picks up speed, the soldiers hanging out the windows, waving goodbye, eager to be on their way. Somewhere Jeff is among them.

I drop my overnight case and keep going till I'm out of breath, my ribs hurting, my cheeks red. I don't stop. I can't lose him again. A man who filled my heart as a young girl and then tipped it with sadness when he left, leaving me a lopsided mess of vanished dreams. I run faster and faster until I see him through the window. Looking for me, his face etched with a piercing pain.

'*Kate!*' he yells, and then he disappears from the window.

'Jeff, *Jeff!*' I scream. In no way I ever imagined, I get close enough to the train to grab onto the side metal handlebar a split second before Jeff appears. I keep running, how I don't know. I swear my body leaps onto the bottom step of the railcar as he grabs me by the arm and pulls me aboard. I nearly collapse, then take a moment to catch my breath. In doing so, I turn around and watch as the train pulls out of the station disappearing behind me.

Then I see her.

Yes, *her. My other self.* She comes out of the shadows in a flash of red and every fantastical moment of this strange trip is ripped apart in an instant. Flying to the winds like silken fibers on an invisible cloak come undone. I have no doubt in my mind what I see on the platform. The girl in the red coat was waiting on the sidelines for this moment to reappear.

Standing there, shoulders slumped. She's waiting for me to do what she can't before she returns home to Ma and the others waiting for her. Find Jeff. She can't go any farther.

I can.

This is where my journey ends. On the train. The whimsical forces of time bringing down the curtain, but not before giving me a second chance to tell Jeff about the letter. I know now I can't co-exist with my other self so I may look different to him. It's something I feel – my suit fits snugger like before, no doubt my face is more angular – since I left my other self behind. In the dim light and excitement of the moment, I pray he won't notice. I picture the skepticism in his eyes, the swirling questions, and I admit, I'm very upset to realize he may not believe me. That idea sends me into despair, more grief than I experienced after the news came he was killed in the war. Because here, now, I can change that. Make sure it never happens.

I can't stop the tears forming in my eyes. Hot tears, but not bitter. I can't explain it, but it's clear to me no matter what happens, it's time for me to move on. First, I have to change the future. A rumbling beneath my feet makes me shiver and my skin goes cold. A warning not to dawdle. I look down at my coat. The bottom button is missing.

'My God, Kate, you could have been killed.'

*Jeff.*

He scoops me up in his arms and holds me so tight I can't breathe, his lips hot, his embrace making me feel every inch his woman.

'My darling,' I whisper. 'I've found you. I can't let you go, not now, not ever.'

'I can't tell you how miserable I've been, Kate, since that I got that call... my orders came through and I had no choice. When I didn't see you, I thought my mother told you not to come, but you did anyway. Oh, God, I love you, Jelly Girl.'

I silence his lips with my finger. 'Don't say a word. We don't have much time. Listen to me.'

'No, let me look at you. We'll have time to talk when I get a furlough. I'll be gone two weeks, maybe three, then I'll be back home before I'm shipped overseas to train in Scotland.' He's so excited, the words slip out. He's talking about being trained in a special facility in Scotland for operatives dropped into France. 'As much as I want you to come with me to the Capitol, I can't take you. Someone from the War Department is meeting me and there's no telling what he'll do if he sees a beautiful girl like you with me.'

I nod. I understand. They'll label me what the military calls a good-time Jane and send me home with my tail between my legs. His mother will never stop gloating and make my life miserable. He's trying to protect me and I love him for it.

He turns, looking for the conductor. 'I'm stopping this train. Tell the stationmaster to have our company car pick you up—'

I pull on his sleeve so hard, he stares at me, disbelieving. 'I'm not going back, Jeff. At least not back to Posey Creek, not to the time I left.'

Jeff stares at me, his eyes sparking. 'What are you talking about?'

'I've never been so sure of anything, Jeff. Please don't stop me. I know about the special orders you received, the training overseas, the secret mission for the OSS, Office of Strategic Services—'

'Stop right there, Kate. Do you know what you're saying?'

He keeps his voice perfectly calm, though the shocked look in his face says otherwise.

'Yes… there's more.'

'More? What the blazes are you talking about?'

'Your life is in danger.'

\* \* \*

How do you explain to a man about to go into a war zone he won't come back?

I take deep breaths to gather my courage while I note the curious stares from the servicemen milling about the railcar. I wonder how much they heard but I doubt they're listening. Most likely they're replaying in their minds their own departure with that special someone. The loud steam whistle blows as we pick up speed. I hold onto Jeff since we haven't found seats yet, but surprisingly no one is pushing or shoving their way through since this train doesn't appear to be full. A lucky break for me.

God knows I need some luck. I want to tell Jeff about the letter, but I can't. I need to gain his confidence first. Not easy to do. I'm not surprised by his hard stare, the quizzical look in those dark eyes, the curve of his sensual mouth as he mulls over my words. Then he cups my chin and tries to read the truth in my eyes, see if I'm ribbing him and this is a fantastic joke.

That's when I tell him I know the future.

He stops, stares, smiles in that funny way of his, and then stares again. Taking it in, and if I know him as well as I think I do, he won't laugh. He doesn't.

No, this gorgeous man who defies society's mores and walks his own path in life holds me close. He whispers in my

ear he loves me no matter what crazy things I say, giving me
the feeling I'm the luckiest girl ever and I must have a good
reason for making such outlandish statements. I have to tell
him everything. The bond between us will either break or
become stronger. That scares the hell out of me. I settle
down, stop fidgeting with the buttons on my coat, finding
some comfort in seeing the familiar empty buttonhole.
Which reminds me that Lucy needs me back in my own time
to help her save her marriage. I can't let her down, but first I
have to get my own life put back together.

Thinking this has a profound calming effect on me, that I
can deliver the facts in a clear voice about how I got here,
why I'm here, and what Jeff must do to avoid being killed. I
also feel a sense of acceptance that whatever happens, I've
been a player in this drama and done my best.

Not yet. There's some business to deal with first.

'Ticket, miss,' the conductor says in a nonchalant
manner.

'I – uh, lost it.' I look at Jeff with sad eyes. 'Mildred had a
flat and—'

'I'll buy the lady another ticket, conductor.' He whips out
his wallet. I breathe out, relieved. Thank God he changed his
mind about stopping the train. I pray it's because he believes
me.

'Sorry, sir.' The railroad man shakes his head, giving me
the onceover. Disapproving of my disheveled appearance, not
to mention that I have no luggage. 'We're not allowed to sell
tickets on a moving train. War regulations.' Not true, but
there's no arguing with him. He thinks I'm a V-Girl. 'The
young woman can get off at the next stop and buy a ticket
there.'

'I can't do that,' I protest, grabbing Jeff's hand. He gives me a warm squeeze and that gives me courage. 'What if the train leaves without me?'

The conductor shakes his head. 'Sorry, that's the best I can do. There'll be another train.'

Not for me, there won't.

He tips his cap and then moves on down the car, checking tickets. He assumes I'll get off the train. He has no idea what's racing through my mind. That I have no intention of getting off at the next stop.

Even as my nerves twist into tangled knots, I don't show it. I have to appear to have the situation under control if this is going to work. In a low voice I say, 'I'll explain everything as soon as we find a seat.'

He nods. 'You have no idea how much that idea intrigues me.' He tries to smile, but there's an edge to his voice that tells me he isn't on board yet with my wild story. I had better make him believe it pretty damn quick before the train stops.

We find seats in the back next to a snoozing – or should I say snoring – woman with a feather on her hat that dances on a puff of air every time she breathes out. A little girl sits next to her, mumbling to her doll she mustn't complain about being hungry.

Now to settle my news on this dear, unsuspecting man who keeps his arm wrapped around me, his lips brushing my cheek. As if he's afraid I'll disappear. He doesn't know how right he is. I settle in against his chest, allowing myself this moment of contentment. I wish I could stuff it into a bottle and toss it into the sea ruled by the changing tides so it will wash ashore in my own time. I want to stay in his arms till the end of the line. Let his heat fill me up down to my cold toes in my flimsy black pumps. His lips burn my skin, his hands wrap tightly around me.

*I'm not ready to leave you.*

'Do you love me, Jeff?' I say, stalling.

'Love you? You're my world, Kate.' He nuzzles his face in my hair. 'I adore you.'

'Even if what I tell you doesn't make any sense in the scheme of things?'

'Let me guess,' he says, coming back with a quip to break the tension between us. 'You want to marry Santa Claus instead of me.'

'Careful, Jeff.' I nod toward the little girl. 'We're not alone.'

The child perks up. 'Is she really going to marry Santa, mister?'

'Not if I can help it.' Jeff smiles big. 'She's going to marry me when I come home on furlough.'

*Oh, Jeff, if only...*

The little girl heaves out a big sigh of relief. 'Oh, goody. I was so scared.'

'Scared? Why?' I have to ask, putting my own problems aside. Or am I delaying the inevitable?

'Santa doesn't have time to get married. He's too busy getting ready to bring Tillie and me presents.' She hugs her doll tight.

'I'm sure he won't forget you and Tillie.' My heart goes out to the child.

I'm ready to blurt out everything – how I got here, the letter, what it says – when the train stops and the conductor makes his way down the aisle toward me. The skin around his eyes wrinkles up like tight knots when he sees us holding each other. It doesn't change his mind. 'Time to get off, miss.'

'Please, we may not see each other for a long time,' I plead.

'Sorry, the rules say you can't go any farther.'

'One more stop—'

Then Jeff does an amazing thing. He pulls out a telegram from his breast pocket and unfolds it. 'These are my orders from the War Department for special assignment overseas. I have no idea when – or if – I'll return home.'

I'm too startled to speak. *He does believe me.*

I look at him closer and see a thoughtful but shaken young man waiting for me to confirm what he already knows. The assignment is a dangerous one and he wants to hear my story. Wants it badly enough to show his hand.

'Well, sir, I don't know...' the conductor says, debating whether or not to believe him. Before he can make up his mind, the train starts going again, as if another hand guides it.

'We're leaving the station.' I stand up, then look over my shoulder as the train whizzes by the passengers left standing on the platform. Yes, those whimsical forces are at it again.

'That's mighty strange.' The conductor checks his pocket watch. 'We barely stopped here, but we're not behind schedule.' The whistle blows a long, shrill blast. 'You'd best sit down, miss. The engineer is picking up speed, though I don't know why. You can get off at the next stop.'

'Thank you, conductor,' I say without any apology in my voice. 'You'll never know I was here,' I mutter under my breath.

Jeff starts to say something when the floor of the railcar begins to shake, jolting us. He stares at me, holding his breath. I hold onto the seat tight as I sit down and the floor rolls beneath my feet, then it stops as abruptly as it starts.

A warning.

I don't have much time left.

## 24

'I came back to Posey Creek, Jeff, to save you from a mission gone wrong.'

'Save me how?' he asks, his mind working hard to grasp my words.

'It's rather complicated,' I say, going slow.

'I'm listening, Kate.' His voice is gravelly, like he's reaching down into his battered soul to find answers. 'Why, I don't know, but I am.'

I fuss with the buttons on my red coat, choosing my words with care. 'I'm not the same girl you knew.'

'I believe you, Kate.' Jeff's sincerity comes through in the touch of his fingers entwining with mine. 'There's something different about you... the way you walk, look at me...'

'The way I kiss you?' I whisper.

Coal-black eyes lock with mine, the passion of that kiss not forgotten. 'Damn it, Kate, if you only knew the terrible guilt I carry around about keeping you out all night. I swear, I had no idea I'd be called up to Washington today.'

'I know.'

He looks away, his mind spinning. 'What's going on? Why have you changed?'

'You said I've been acting different. Well, it's because I *am* different, Jeff. I'm still me, but I come from another time – years into the future.'

'Okay, I'll bite,' he says, going along with me. For now. 'How far into the future?'

'Twelve years.'

'Is the war over?'

'Yes.'

For the first time, I see a smirk on his face. 'Then we won. We beat the Nazis.'

'Yes, my darling, we won, but you...'

I waited for days for this moment, to finally tell him what haunted me for twelve long years and I can't say the words. My face feels warm and my lips dry as I watch his reaction to a slew of words that hit him hard. He faces me head-on, shoulders strong and straight, fists clenched, as if I confirmed what he already knows.

'I didn't come back,' he says slowly. 'That's why you're here.'

'Then you do believe me.' *Thank God.* 'Oh, Jeff, I was so afraid you'd think I lost my mind.'

'I should think that, Kate. Any man in his right senses would. I suspected something ever since that day you found me cutting down the big fir tree. There was a different look about you, especially your eyes. A deep sadness I never saw before. My young bride-to-be was replaced by a different woman. A woman who knew deep sorrow.' He ruffles his hand through his hair in that familiar way I love so well. 'I couldn't shake the feeling it had something to do with me.'

'Yes, that was the day after I got here.' I explain to him

how I was on a train heading back to Posey Creek in 1955, reading a letter, when the train nearly clipped a stopped railcar, and how I slipped and hit my head.

'So that's why you came with me to the house on the river, let me hold you in my arms and caress your beautiful body. I wanted to stop a thousand times, but I sensed this would be the only time we'd be alone together for a long time. I acted selfish and kept you with me all night.' Jeff groans. 'I'm sorry, Kate. I never meant to hurt you.'

'Hurt me?' Wanting so to make him understand that he made me whole again, I blurt out, 'Whatever happens, I'll always have that night with you holding me, loving me, my darling. Never forget that.'

He nods. I read in his eyes that he has questions. 'There's more, Kate, isn't there?'

'Yes. A letter I received from an old Army buddy of yours.'

'A buddy? When?'

'He wrote it after the war with instructions to send it to me after his death. That's why I didn't receive it until twelve years later. What you must know is that after you parachute into France and meet up with the underground, there's a traitor among them. A Frenchman you call *Leftie*.'

He lets out a low whistle, shocked at what he hears. 'How the hell do you know I'm going to France?'

I bite my lip. 'It's in the letter the sergeant sent to me.'

'I don't know any sergeant.'

'You will.' I hold back a beat, no more. 'His name is Sergeant Herbert Drew Peterson. Herbie. According to him, you mustn't trust this man Leftie. He'll sell you out to the Gestapo—'

Jeff flinches. 'The Gestapo?'

'Yes. They'll be waiting for you at the rendezvous point.

That's when...' Another beat, because my heart stops. I can't break down, go soft on him. Somehow I have to weave a story with each thread so perfect, so strong he'll *have* to believe me. That he won't push me away. No, instead he'll take me in his arms and hold me, the fine wool of his suit jacket scratching my cheek when I bury my face into his chest. I swear I won't cry, that he won't see even the tiniest tear when he smooths my hair away from my face.

He grabs me, holds me, and this time I glimpse the innate fear every man has going into combat, even if he won't admit it. 'Tell me, Kate. I can take it.'

'The sergeant said you were killed or captured by the Gestapo and most likely, tortured to death. No one ever heard from you again.' I stop to suck in a breath. 'Months later, you were declared Killed in Action.'

There, I said it. I don't feel relieved. If anything, I wonder if this is a big mistake coming back here. That I planted information in his mind that will make things worse. A moment, then two. He doesn't say a word, as if the truth hovers in the background and he can't decide whether or not to grasp it. Then a funny smile comes over his face. 'I get it. There is no letter. This is your way of trying to keep me safe. Looking out for me, like you did when we were kids.'

I panic, hardening my resolve not to be so easy on him, to tell him *everything* so he'll have to believe me. 'It's true, Jeff, please listen to me.'

'No, *you* listen,' he says, butting heads with me, his male pride showing in his assessment of my story. 'You're guessing I'm going to France because I speak French. You know about the trips my father and I took to Europe. How you figured out I'm joining up with the OSS, I don't know, unless you're listening at keyholes. Not that I blame you. I'd do the same if

I thought I was losing you.' He kisses the tip of my nose. 'I love you for it. To think you almost had me fooled.'

I blink. This is *not* the reaction I expected.

'The letter exists, Jeff. I swear. Here, I'll show it to you.' I dig into my pocket, afraid if I look at the letter, I'll be swept away in a time vacuum. I have to prove it to him. 'Take a look for yourself.' I pull out the crackly paper and unfold it. '*Oh, no.*'

The letter is gone. Instead, I hold the drawing he made of me. Somehow it got into my pocket. I remember now. My younger self put it there back in 1943. I carried the drawing with me for good luck that day and gave it to him before he left.

I want to cry. It's a terrible blow to my heart to know I failed. The letter didn't travel back with me. How can it? It isn't written yet. I'm a fool. How am I going to make him believe me? I don't have much time. The conductor will escort me off the train at the next stop.

'I understand you don't want to accept the fact you're betrayed by someone you trust,' I argue, feeling uneasy with his admission that he doubts my story, 'but it can't hurt to be on the lookout for a traitor.'

'Why are you doing this, Kate?' He holds me by the shoulders. 'I want to believe you, but I can't.'

'Because I love you with all my heart, darling. If there's the slightest chance I can save you, I have to try.'

I grab his hand, while keeping my eyes fixed on his face, his mouth drawn tight and his eyes filled with so much anguish, his pupils shrink to pinpoints. I can't look away. His hand is cold and we're both trembling. Oh, God, the train is vibrating. I stand up then stumble, the shift in the car signaling a change in the time and space I occupy. Not anyone else, just me. I don't know what other way to describe it, that every moment counts.

*Is my time here done? Give me a sign... please.*

I glance out the window at the woods with their trees in winter undress, gray and white and thick with frost. A heavy fog lies over everything. The engine whistle blows again, startling me. I pull down the window and stick my head out. I ignore the cold air blast stinging my cheeks. A tunnel lies ahead, waiting to devour the mighty train entering its depths, the thunder of the metal beast loud in my ears. I swear the tunnel opens its deep jaws wider, waiting to swallow me up.

A chilling fear sucks the breath out of me.

I feel my body going completely still, the blood draining from my face, as if I'm standing at the precipice of a hole so deep and black, one wrong step and I'll never stop falling. Hot then cold, and a kind of unholy premonition sweeps through my body. Somehow in my bones, I know these are my last moments with Jeff. That when the train comes out of the tunnel on the other side, I won't be here. I'll be back in my own time.

*How? Why?*

The answer is clear. When I got on that train in 1955, I wanted to see him again so badly, the will of my mind opened up a door for me to jump through into my old self. Like going to sleep and experiencing the most fantastic dream. This dream is real. I set the stage by wearing my red coat and then reading the letter. It caught me at a moment when my mind was open to anything. Especially during the holiday season. It's as if the portals of time open all at once, allowing us to slip back to a certain moment and relive special Christmas memories as real to us today as they were then.

I went one step further. I embraced the magic of Christmas to change the past.

My heart races, my arms ache as I look at my love. I want to press my mouth against his and never let him go, surrender to him when he blows his hot breath into me, but I have to sacrifice his warm lips and deep kisses to make him believe the truth.

On this frosty December morning, nervous and hopeful, I make my plea, leaving my fate in the hands of whatever supernatural crack in the universe allowed me to slip through and make my peace with the past. I tell him things that make his heart pound. Blood rushing through him, his face hot and perspiring as he tries to control himself when I speak of the horrors to come on the beaches of Normandy and the bombing of Dresden. He's trembling inside. So much so the tiny jagged scar above his right brow looks like a streak of lightning slashed white across his forehead. Then he exhales, his heart slowing, as if he arrives at a safe place when I tell him about France being liberated and Japan surrendering and...

'What else, Kate, for God's sake?' he wants to know, his mind absorbing too much at once.

I'm faced with a moral obligation about how much information I can – or should, tell him. I can make things worse with my meddling, something I've thought about many times. Yes, I nudged history a bit by helping folks back here at home. Somehow this is different. This means telling Jeff about events that involve so many soldiers I can't conceive of the effect it could have. Like changing the course of one life may domino to losing others.

Does that make me selfish because I want to save him?

Guilt weighs upon my shoulders for saying it. I have to

believe that saving him is the reason I'm here. That I'm doing the right thing, not only for myself – who knows if he'll marry me after the war? – but for his family and our town. For Posey Creek. Jeff could pull the mill out of its problems after his brother Timothy let it go and so many men, including Pop, wouldn't lose their jobs.

A minute, maybe two left before we race through the tunnel.

'Listen, Jeff, please. You don't believe I come from the future. What if I prove it to you? Will you believe me then? That there's a traitor among you on your mission in France?'

'I'm worried about you, Kate.' He frowns. 'I'll call the conductor. Make sure you get on a train back to Posey Creek.'

'Jeff, listen to me, *please*! When we go through that tunnel, I don't know why or how, but when the train comes out on the other side, *I won't be here*. I'll be back in my own time. Will you believe me then, *will you*?'

He stares at me, his eyes clear and sharp, his breathing calm. 'Yes, Kate, I'll believe you.'

Does he mean it?

'Take the drawing with you, Jeff.' I fold it into his hand, my heart beating so fast a lightheadedness comes over me. 'That way I'll be with you when you lay your head down at night wherever you are until you come back to me.'

Without a word, he puts the drawing into his pocket and takes my hands in his. His eyes are serious and I swear he believes me. Then he says a strange thing. 'It's best if you never speak of this to anyone nor will I. My mission is of utmost secrecy. Many lives depend on it. Promise?'

'I promise.'

He smiles at me and looks at me with such love in his

eyes. 'I love you, Jelly Girl, and when I get back we'll be married right away—'

His words fade in my ears. I feel a rumbling beneath my feet. Sharp, constant. It's time. I stand up. Waiting.

There it is. The tunnel.

I wince at the idea of leaving him, begging for one last moment with him. I turn to look at him, his eyes searching mine, a burning to know the truth when—

*Whoosh.*

The train races through the black tunnel and I brace myself for the moment I know is coming. The wild sensation of being whirled around like a dervish, my bones pulling apart, teeth clenched, my heart pumping so hard to keep up with the wild ride. The erratic shaking hits me first. I'm not frightened this time. Because when I see light again, I'll know whether or not my coming back here changed the future.

Do I save Jeff? Or is it a dream?

What if I can't get back to my own time?

The thought hits me so quickly, if Jeff is alive I'll never see him. I'll be trapped here between two worlds. Forever. I wanted so desperately to save him, I never entertained the idea I'm putting myself in danger. I assumed... assumed what?

There's no price to pay for my folly?

Yes, I went back in time. Maybe, just *maybe* I saved Jeff's life. At what cost?

That terrifying thought crushes me. I'm alone in my pain, but I wouldn't change anything. I've known the love of this man as a woman, not a girl, and that's worth everything. I push aside the anger pulsing through me, making my head ache, my bones crunch like I'm disintegrating. I refuse to regret a moment over the past week because I love him that much.

How can I ever replace those moments with Jeff? With my family?

Sitting around the kitchen table with Ma fretting over her ration book with red and blue stamps. How she'll get what she needs to make spice cake for the boys. Pop enjoying his pipe and never saying a word, but looking pleased at having us all safe under his roof. Lucy arguing with Frank Junior over him telling her latest admirer she's in high school and not to kiss her again or he'll let him have it. I smile. They're a trying, crazy family, but they're my family and I'm grateful I had this time with them.

Most of all, I relive over and over that night with Jeff in the house on the river that would have been our home. We held each other and I fell asleep with my head against his broad shoulder, his hand holding mine. When I woke up, I was alone. His scent still on me. When I found him standing by the riverbank, he told me the story of his boyhood and the woman who forged his interest in art. Aline. She'd be so proud of him.

A bright light in the distance calms me, telling me I'm not lost forever.

I have a chance.

I land with a thump, hard and painful. I don't know where, it could be on a rock on the shore because I hear whooshing in my ears like the sound of crashing surf, or a street... or God help me, the floor of a railway car. The wheels of a speeding train vibrate in my ears. I press my hand to my cheeks but I don't open my eyes. Not yet. My face is hot, perspiring. I check my hands, arms. Legs. Nothing broken.

*Am I back?*

A low, husky whisper tickles my ear with soft words, then it gets louder as my hearing becomes more acute. A man's voice. Comforting me as I come to. I lie on the floor of the railcar where I fell. I can't understand what he's saying.

Then a streak of light falls across my face, tapping on my eyelids with a healing warmth and after what seems like a long, long journey, I open my eyes.

Then I see him.

A tall, broad shouldered man leans over me, holding my hand, patting my forehead with a damp handkerchief. My vision is blurry and I can't see his face. He wears his hat at a low angle hiding his eyes, but I'm aware of his strong jaw, big hands, and pure masculinity as he raises me up into a sitting position.

It's Jeff; it has to be.

# 25

'You're alive, you *did* believe me!' I mutter, gliding back into this time and into his arms, my heart in my throat, my emotions cascading through one crazy feeling to another. I'm so sure of myself, I don't hold back. He couldn't be more shocked when I pull him close and plant a hot, wet kiss on his lips. I lean into him, passion surging within me. I want to go on kissing him forever, but he doesn't kiss me back. I'm hurt. Why? Doesn't he want to? I sense a quickening of his breath, an impulse to press his lips against mine, but he stops. The Jeff I know wouldn't do that. He'd capture my lips with a burning touch I'd never forget. *Is* it him?

No, something is different. He seems distant, puzzled. Jeff is warm, combustive, bursting with love and affection. Not this man. Instead, he scoops me up in his arms and says something to the conductor behind him I can't hear. I *know* it's Jeff, but he isn't the man I expect to find back in my own time. I admit, his nonchalant kiss shakes me up. I swear my mouth melted into his in the most familiar manner. Now I have my doubts. He's a big man like Jeff, but he isn't clean-shaven and he has several days' stubble that enhance his square jaw, fitting somehow to this irresistibly sexy man. He wears a black Fedora pulled down low over his eyes and his clothes look like something you see in a black and white foreign film.

Why do I say that? Because I'm looking for excuses as to why he doesn't know me, like he's not from here. Besides, I detect an aloofness about him that makes me wonder if I'm wrong and it's not Jeff.

I saw what I wanted to see. Even though my heart is breaking, I have to accept the truth. This man acts like he doesn't know me.

I let my body go limp in his arms as he carries me back to my empty seat and gently lays me down. I turn my head away, embarrassed at my outrageous behavior. I made a fool out of myself. I wished so long for Jeff to be alive, dreaming of this moment, I did what my heart yearned for so I make myself believe it happened.

I kissed a man who wants nothing to do with me.

* * *

'You had a bad fall, ma'am,' he says, his voice deep and husky and somewhat amused by my amorous embrace. As are the other passengers, the men snickering, the ladies swooning. He called me *ma'am*?

My head clears, my vision coming into focus. That doesn't change anything. I *swear* it's Jeff. I can't convince myself otherwise. I don't understand why I feel this way, but I can't shake it. He's big and strong, his expensive suit fitting snugly over his muscular body. He doesn't go back to his seat. Hovering over me, looking me up and down from head to toe.

Not in an off-putting way. More like he's assessing the situation.

'Yes... I made it. *I'm back*,' I mumble to myself because I don't want to face the truth. Nothing changed the way I expected. Jeff doesn't know me.

'Allow me to be of assistance,' he says, flashing me a curious look. 'Though I'm intrigued why a beautiful woman is traveling alone without a man to protect her.'

'I'm going home for the holidays. To Posey Creek.' I peek over my shoulder and see him watching me as I gather up my handbag and my hatbox, sitting where I left them, and smooth down my red coat. He loved that coat on me. Will that jog his memory?

'Alone?'

'I could ask you the same thing. A debonair man like yourself without a woman on your arm?' I say, smiling. Brazen, but I'm desperate to know why he's traveling alone. No wife, family. 'How bourgeois.'

He throws his head back and laughs. Again, that eerie sensation tickles my spine.

'I'm also going to Posey Creek... on business.' He makes no attempt to return to his seat, though he keeps a respectable distance between us. My heart thunders in my ears. This conversation is going nowhere with the two of us volleying back and forth with small talk. What choice do we have? We're an item, with the interested passengers leaning forward in their seats, eager to see what happens next. I never dreamed our reunion would be so public. There must be another way.

First, I have to think this out. If I *did* traverse the tracks of time and hopped aboard the train going back to 1943 and changed the future – like one train passing another in the thick of night – I'd be snug and warm with Jeff at home in Posey Creek in the house on the river. Children playing. A dog nipping at their heels. A lovely dream that makes me feel warm all over.

*Why didn't things turn out like that?* my brain screams. I have no answer. Nothing changed. I smell the pine, see the festive, twinkling lights framing the passenger windows, the soft red velvet seats. The late afternoon sun glows distinctly bright on a clear December day, but there is no warmth shining through. It's cold outside, in the twenties and windy from the trees blowing as the train speeds along the tracks.

I'm the same woman I was when I got on the train. The *Mistletoe Flyer*. A lonely, thirty-one year old food editor who traveled through time and still loves the man she lost. I'm wearing my red coat and I'm certain if I put my gloved hand into my pocket, I'll find the letter nestled there. I hear the crackle of the paper between my fingers as I fumble for it, certain it isn't the drawing Jeff did of me.

*You gave it to him before you came back, remember?*

What's more disturbing, I'm aware I've returned to a very different world than the one I left in 1943. I haven't been gone so long to forget that here women no longer wear the awful foxtails Mrs Rushbrooke favored. People look for flying saucers in the sky instead of enemy planes, and coming-out parties for young debs are all the rage instead of girls taking war jobs. And me? I'm on my way home for the Christmas holidays with a heavy heart.

No. I take that back. My heart may be heavy, but I tasted the sweetest honey, sucked it dry, and then I found myself back where I started, wanting more. Wanting Jeff. I can't have him. Dry-mouthed, exhausted, I keep telling myself it was all a dream. I never left this train, but I don't believe it.

As I hold my throbbing head, I still feel the warmth of Jeff's arms around me during those last moments back in time, holding me, kissing me.

Now he's here. Close to me. I'm sure of it, but I don't know what to do about it.

First, I have to get myself together so Lucy doesn't panic when she sees me disheveled and disoriented. I'm not hurt. No bruise on my forehead, no bleeding. I never felt better. *You don't really get pulled apart when you time travel*, I tell myself with expert authority since I've done it. It just feels like it. God knows I experienced an electrifying sensation when the man I want so much to be Jeff scooped me up in his arms and carried me back to my seat. The one across from me is empty, giving me a chance to gather my wits. It's important I throw myself into the holiday spirit, make sure Lucy gets back on the marriage track.

I open my handbag – everything is there, wallet, train ticket, the usual – and then slide on a fresh coat of lipstick. Not the dark red we wore during the war. Brighter, reflecting the times. I smack my lips and I peek at the man I swear is Jeff in my compact mirror. I pretend to check for lipstick on my teeth, but I'm staring at him. He takes a seat across the aisle from me and looks out the train window. I can't get a clear view of his face, frustrating me. I begin to sweat, my pageboy drooping, and in that moment I see myself in the mirror. A woman. Not the nineteen year old girl I was for the past week.

No wonder he doesn't recognize me, but I have an idea what he'll look like in this time, a tall, sexy man in his mid-thirties. His body still muscular but filled out in broad strokes, his walk that defines his masculinity like a mature lion ruling over his pride. Like the man in the Fedora.

*Calm down, don't say anything. It has to be Jeff. Why won't he say something? What's wrong?*

My heart breaks when he keeps his distance and doesn't make a move to check on me, even if I'm merely a curiosity to him. I see now how fragile time is, like a kaleidoscope – the reflection of what we think is true can change in an instant when seen from a different angle. I can't stop the memories of him flooding into my head. Remembering the anticipation of seeing him... then the smell of ripe tart cherries carried on a night breeze, that moment of skin against skin... whispered words, his hot, burning kisses that go on and on.

He turns and stares at me, as if he wants to say something but doesn't. Instead he does his duty. *Keep the damsel in distress under your wing till the castle is in sight.* Or in this case, the train station. Which isn't far according to the conductor's hearty call, 'Ten minutes from Posey Creek, next stop Posey Creek.'

That encourages my knight in a pinstripe suit to make his play. He gets up from his seat and approaches me with a boldness he didn't display before. As if he's made up his mind about something and he's acting on it.

'Is your husband meeting you at the station?' he asks, concern deepening his voice. I thrill to his familiar tone, my toes curling. I ache for him to touch me, but he's careful to keep his hands off me, though I sense he doesn't want to. Did he finally recognize me?

'My husband?' *Oh, no, what did I do?* Did I marry someone else? It never occurred to me that that would happen. My heart breaks. No wonder he called me *ma'am*. He thinks I'm married.

I rip off my glove, check the ring finger on my left hand. *Bare*, thank God. I look up at him as if to say, *now what?*

A change comes over him then, as if he's been waiting for me to say something. I see his face light up with a big grin and a shiver of anticipation slithers down my spine. Is this the moment I'll have him back? Is it? I keep quiet, watching him, waiting, then—

He seems reluctant to let go of a deep emotion ripping him apart inside. Instead, he says in an amused voice. 'You look as beautiful as a red rose in the *Marché aux Fleurs,* flower market, in Paris, and as flighty as a bird flitting around the stalls in search of a few crumbs.'

'I'm not flighty,' I insist, adjusting my clothing. 'I'm confused.' I can't go on until I understand why he's acting so strange. 'Don't you know me, Jeff?'

'I'd know you anywhere, Jelly Girl.' he says, his words tender, and my heart pounds in my ears when he sits down next to me. I want to grab him, but I don't. I have the feeling he's as confused as I am. His jaw tightens. Did he also feel the shift in time when I returned?

'Then why didn't you kiss me back?'

'I didn't think your husband would approve... especially with an audience watching us.'

It's true. I can't help but be aware of the sly looks from the passengers, whispering, waiting to see what I'll do next, what Jeff will do.

'I waited for you all these years, Jeff. The last time I saw you, we were on the train back in 1943.' I attempt a smile, while trying to shake off the profound and eerie sensation he's trying to process seeing me again, put the pieces together.

'I heard you were engaged, so when I saw you I assumed—'

'I was,' I cut him off. 'It didn't work out.'

His eyes take on a distant look, as if he's seeing back into the past and it's painful. Which makes me wonder, where was he all these years?

'Oh, Jeff, where have you been?'

'Living in France.'

'France? Why?'

'After the war, I wasn't the same man.'

'What happened to you?' I have to know.

'After I was captured by the Gestapo, I was sent to a concentration camp in Germany, then a displaced persons camp after the war because I had battle shock. I lost my memory for a time. I wasn't sure who I was since I carried French identity papers on me when I was caught.'

'Then you don't remember our last meeting on the train? The letter I told you about?' My world crumbles.

'For a long time, I thought it was a dream, that you were a dream. Then everything you said came true. The mission was crucial – set explosives on the tracks with incendiary fuses to derail the supply train and stop more trains from coming through. For two days I watched the man you called Leftie sneaking off and when he came back, his face was flushed, his nose twitching. I swear, his pocket bulged with rolled up franc notes he no doubt intended to trade for *Reichsmarks.*'

'Money he made on the black market?'

'I thought so at first. Then I found him going through the British officer's bedroll at the church where we were hiding out. I stayed out of sight when I saw him unscrew the man's pipe, take it apart and look inside, as if he was searching for something. It was empty. He looked around, saw no one, and replaced it.'

'What was he looking for?'

He smirks. 'I'm not sure, but I kept hearing your voice

telling me not to trust him.' He pauses, wipes the sweat off his face with the back of his hand. 'I would have been killed if I hadn't heeded your warning echoing in my head and made that split-second decision to go after him before the Nazis attacked. The mission was a success, but it took me a long time to find my way back.'

'You never came home to Posey Creek?'

'I couldn't talk about my experiences in the OSS because of military reasons – my participation wasn't declassified until recently. After I recovered from my injuries, I stayed away because of the nightmares plaguing me. Men dying, men I couldn't save. The sweats. I had anger issues that took me years to control. I wasn't the Jeff you knew, Kate. You deserved better.'

I understand. Doors closed years ago in a fury. Against the backdrop of war. Pushing out everything else except survival. I can only imagine the torment he suffered losing so many days, weeks, months he can't account for. Worse yet, not being able to feel the emotions of those times. Moments big and small, even if they're painful, not feeling them because he can't remember them is akin to losing his soul.

Unthinkable.

I don't ask him any more questions. An incurable insanity is brewing in my mind, pushing me someplace so extraordinary, I'm more scared than I've ever been. Scared if I'm wrong, I don't know if I'll ever recover.

Does Jeff still love me?

I have to deal with the most explosive thing my heart has had to cope with in a long time. Coming back to Posey Creek. Seeing Jeff. It's like squeezing every emotion I ever felt into a tiny, red velvet box and sealing it up with a green satin ribbon and praying it won't explode. When I know very well it can.

'Do you have the drawing you made of me?' I ask, treading carefully.

'Yes. It sustained me through it all, gave me courage. I couldn't go back to my pampered life, not after what I saw over there. So I became an architect and rebuilt France. Better I stay dead to everyone, including my family, and especially when I heard you were to be married. I didn't want to ruin your life. I saw no reason to come back to Posey Creek.'

'Then why now?'

'When I found out the house on the river we were going to live in was scheduled to be torn down, I had to come back. After I rebuilt so much after the war, to have that last link to you, to us, torn down hurt me more than I can bear. I intended to have it declared a historical structure, now I want to remodel the house and return it to its former glory.'

'Oh, Jeff, that's wonderful!'

He heaves out a deep breath. 'I had no idea you were on this train, Kate. It's quite a shock, but it doesn't change anything between us. Nothing could. You know how I feel about you.'

'Oh, Jeff,' I say, more under his spell than ever. 'Thank God, you came back to me.'

A knot of fear and anticipation make me nearly burst when I see him reach for me, a pure joy coming into his eyes. He picks me up and swings me around, kissing me and holding me tight. A fever in that kiss makes me ache to be alone with him.

'I'm never leaving you again, my darling,' he says in a low, husky voice.

'Then you do love me?' I beg him, drawing his face to mine, wanting with all my heart to kiss him again. I wait, because I can't bear to spend another second not knowing. I pay no attention to the crowd in the railcar clapping, the heavy sighs. My body hums in a hot, steady rhythm as he wraps his arms around me so tight, I can't breathe. Then he whispers in my ear what I waited so long to hear.

'*Will you marry me, Jelly Girl?*'

'Yes, Jeff, *yes!*' I can't hold back the hot tears forming in my eyes. I'm home for Christmas.

With Jeff.

## 26

Christmas Day is cold and snowless but as Jeff and I sit on the old sofa dotted with Ma's lacy doilies before a roaring fire, it's fitting somehow for the lack of snowflakes mirrors that day back in 1943. As if the two timelines run parallel in harmony. When I kissed him on the train, I pulled them together into one glorious moment that set my world right again.

A melody of holiday favorites playing on the radio lends a timeless lift to our spirits and a big Christmas tree smelling of pine and decorated with silver and blue and red balls sets the mood. Multi-colored lights tied with string to the tree branches twinkle at us as we sort out the amazing series of events that brought us back together. I can't tell you the pangs that went through me when I saw the fresh-cut tree and remembered that day with Jeff swinging the axe. His tall, muscular body making me ache for him, crave his warm touch. I never dreamed when I returned to the white clapboard house where I grew up, I'd be holding Jeff's hand in mine. It seemed like I'd been here hours ago, not years.

I had, in a way.

And I embraced those warm memories with Ma and Pop like snippets of a song that linger in your head long after the tune ends. I wonder what Ma would think if she was here with us. I can see her fluttering around like a busy mama bee, making the stuffing for the turkey and don't forget the sausage, she'd remind me, then measuring the spices for the mince pie. Smiling with glee when the twins make their first ever sugar cookies and don't burn them. I can't help but wish she were here. Pop, too, chewing on his pipe and conning us one by one into playing a game of checkers with him.

Every Christmas has its own unique footprint evoked by the smell of fresh pine or the sound of boots crunching in the snow. This one is no different. First, I need to take a moment to tend the fires of the past. A special memory sparking to life, if only for a few moments before it's gone. My journey back to Christmastime 1943 remains so vivid in my mind, I let the flame burn longer, going over every detail of how I got there, every life I touched. Mildred, Mr Clayborn, Helen, Freddie, the ladies at the mill, and my family.

God, I love them.

I can't say for sure why it happened, what forces of time were in harmony that day on the train to send me back, but I've never been so filled with a sense of completeness. Perhaps I don't have a right to be so happy, considering the years I spent feeling sorry for myself. No woman who lost her man in wartime is immune to the allure of wanting him back, if only in her dreams.

I remember every moment I spent with Jeff, trying to understand his elusive past, while falling in love with him all over again. Then when everything seemed so bleak, gone so terribly wrong, somehow I found the strength to keep going. Push through, break down the closed doors in my mind, my broken heart keeping me in a cage all these years. The hunger in me to dig up the past so strong, I wouldn't give up. A desperate woman who traversed the slender tightrope between the spaces of time to find him.

Then Jeff came home to me and no way, not ever, will I let him go.

His dark eyes filled with the clear recognition of who I am when he saw me stand up on the train, then fall. He didn't know what to think, what to do. He never expected to see me again. Then it hit him with such force, the distant but profound memory of him leaving that day, he couldn't deny his heart any longer. He had a life with me once and he sacrificed it to help win the war. When he found out I waited for him, it was time for him to get it back.

I felt the change in him when he called me his Jelly Girl. It wasn't a blast of cold wind from the past that struck him, he says, more like it burst into a flame from the embers smoldering in him, never gone, surviving in spite of the violence of war. He couldn't believe I was here in his arms. He vowed not to lose me a second time.

In my dreamy state now, cuddled up next to him, I smell the woodsy scent he never abandoned, a steady compass he clung to, even when he struggled to find himself after the war. Resting my head on his shoulder, I finally close my eyes, knowing in my heart he'll be there when I open them. I paid the price time demanded of me, endured those long, lonely years without him and in a strange way, my refusal to give up his memory is what brought us back together. We never would have met on that train if I hadn't, however you want to see it – either gone a little crazy after I read the letter from the sergeant, or traveled back through time.

Jeff would have gotten off the train at our small town

railway station, maybe brushed by me, our shoulders touching, my eyes catching a quick glance of him but not seeing his face under his Fedora. We wouldn't have stopped to acknowledge one another in the holiday rush. Or in my case, the heartrending homecoming. We wouldn't have taken the time to see the loneliness etched on our faces, the despair of two people who never allowed themselves to fall out of love with each other.

In the end, it's that despair that brought us here. Two single people with nowhere to go, no one to spend Christmas with. Fate was laughing at us, I'm certain, watching us pass each other in the night. Instead or maybe because of our deep love, the muses who rule time gave us a second chance and we took it. Otherwise, Jeff would have checked out the house on the river, filed his historical claim, and then left on the next train. Never knowing I'm here, waiting for him. That I came back to Posey Creek to find him.

I broke the news to the family. I can't tell you the craziness that ensued when I brought him home. Lucy couldn't stop the tears and nearly collapsed. Whatever fight she'd had with Jimmie fixed itself. She wanted me to come home, she said, because she's having another child and needs my help for the holiday.

Jimmie is at her side, giving her his special smile and strong arms to hold her. Frankie can't stop shaking Jeff's hand. Yes, he came home as I hoped. I believe he recognizes a fellow soldier who's known the horrors of combat and came out on the other side. When we went to church services early this morning, I told Mildred and the reverend that Jeff is back and they both wept with joy. We decided to break the news about Jeff publicly at a later time when the whole town can welcome him home.

Today is Christmas and there's nothing we want more than for him to spend the day with us. He has some healing to do. No one knows yet the whole story of where he's been, what he did in the service of the OSS over in France during the war.

Earlier this afternoon, I showed Jeff the letter from the sergeant as we stood under the cherry tree. He feels rooted to his past here, our past. It's the only time I've seen him break down and bury his head in his hands. Nothing I say can compare to the heartfelt, wrenching words written by a brother-in-arms. What happened to him is more real with the letter. Making it easier for him to accept the truth.

He has to look forward, but first confront the past and let it slowly turn in his mind. Face the reality learning his father is gone, the mill closed, and his brother left town. More worrisome is how Jeff feels about his mother leaving Posey Creek and never looking back. He doesn't mention going to see her. I have the feeling he will when the time is right. We'll make peace with her as a married couple and I hope she'll accept me.

Then it's his turn to talk and mine to listen.

'The whole thing with the War Department was my mother's doing,' Jeff said, looking over the horizon toward Wrightwood House. 'She received a phone call from the Washington hotel asking if Mr Rushbrooke and his guest would be staying longer than two days since rooms were impossible to get during the war and they needed it for a visiting dignitary.'

'Our honeymoon.' I never tire of hearing his sexy, hypnotic voice, deeper and richer now.

'Yes, and when she found out the reservation was in my name, it didn't take her long to unravel the cord and wrap it around my neck. She'd planned to have me called up to Washington after her big New Year's Eve party. After that, she pulled some strings to get me away from you sooner.'

'Didn't she know she was sending you into danger?'

He shook his head. 'No, she assumed I'd spend the rest of the war behind a desk, but the President's office called late Sunday afternoon with a change of plans. I was to speak to no one, but leave the next morning by train for Washington.'

'The President?'

He nodded. 'I intended to do my part, wherever they needed me, so when the sudden need for a French speaking agent came up, I jumped at the chance to join a special operations team working in France.' He took a moment to reflect. 'I never dreamed my years in military school learning how to use a weapon, making maps, and combat training would save my life more than once. The mission was very hush hush, so they sent a special car to pick me up that morning. My mother kept peering over my shoulder all the way to the railroad station as I wrote you that letter. I told her I was making notes for my meeting with the President and his staff overseeing clandestine operations.'

'I was devastated when the stationmaster gave me your letter.'

'I can't tell you what great pain pierced my heart when I had to tell you I couldn't take you with me, Kate.' He held me tight under the cherry tree. 'But I had every reason to believe I'd get a furlough before I went overseas so we could be married.'

I nodded. 'We were at war, Jeff, you did what needed to be done.'

'So did you, Jelly Girl,' he loved to tease me about traveling through time. I'm not sure he's convinced, but he has a recollection of me disappearing that day in 1943 after the train came out of the tunnel. He thought he dreamed the whole thing when the conductor claimed not to remember me. I imagine he didn't want to lose his job for allowing me on board without a ticket.

We continued talking when we went back to the house, filling in our lives right up until the moment we collapsed on the couch in the parlor next to the fireplace. His hands wrapped tight around my waist, his face nuzzling in my hair. We haven't spoken for a while, sitting here, wrapped up in each other. I can't tell you how much I love resting my head on his shoulder and holding him. The lovely smells of turkey roasting and pies baking is enough to keep us happy until eating time. We're both exhausted with little sleep and so many years to catch up on.

We hear the chatter around us, the family doing what folks do on Christmas Day. Opening presents, grabbing cookies and coffee, calling friends on the phone, thanking God for this blessed day and stealing kisses under the mistletoe.

Lucy smothers her husband with hugs and kisses under its tiny white flowers and green leaves. Next, Frankie and his girl, Anne. Lucy was right. She's real nice, a social worker he met when he was hard up last Christmas. He found himself down to his last dollar and standing in line in downtown LA at the mission for a turkey dinner with mashed potatoes. Frankie loves Ma's mashed spuds and started talking to the pretty girl serving them up about how his ma added garlic and onions. Anne was a volunteer intrigued by the handsome young man who never said a word until he tasted those potatoes. Then he talked and talked and she listened. I won't be surprised if they head up to the city after the holiday to tie the knot.

Mildred and the reverend are also here with us – they're like family – and take their turn under the mistletoe when they think no one is looking. Such a deep love between two people I've never seen. I'm sure God is proud of His pastor and the good work he does here in Posey Creek. Earlier, at the church services this Sunday, the reverend spoke of how we can never give up, how faith is like so many of God's creatures who return each year to a certain place to nest, never failing to find their way. Sometimes a violent storm sends them off track – he looked directly at the two of us keeping a low profile in the last row, Jeff holding my hand tight – but when the storm clears, all is well.

As for Jeff and me, we haven't tried out that mistletoe yet. We're of the same mind, once we get started, we won't stop.

'Kate's quite a girl, isn't she, sir?' Frankie joins us on the couch while Anne volunteers to help Lucy in the kitchen mashing the potatoes. She wants to get Ma's recipe so she can keep her man content. A perfect couple, and I'm so happy for my brother.

'Your sister is the best, and please call me Jeff,' he says, holding me tight. I can't get enough of him and I can see he revels in the comfort and coziness of finding a family again.

'Enough, you two,' I break in, embarrassed by the attention. 'Or I'll hang up my Miss Christmas Wrap poster,' I tease Jeff, grabbing the rolled up poster from under the tree. Lucy's brood, Billie and the twins, opened their presents after church, but we have a few left for the adults. 'It'll jog your memory.'

'Where'd you find it?' Jeff asks, curious.

'You have me to thank for that,' Mildred chimes in, laughing. 'I came across it in the church basement and thought it was a fun welcome home present for Kate.'

'Did I really look like that?' I say, wondering *Who is that girl with the not-so-innocent smile*? Only I see the depth of that smile and the secret she's hiding. I was so sure I could bend time to my will. I like to think I taught the forces that brought me there a thing or two, though I'll not try it again. I've got my man and, like Ma's thick turkey gravy for Christmas dinner, it makes everything perfect.

'As my Marines in the Pacific would say, she's what they were fighting for,' says the reverend with a lump in his throat. 'The girl next door.'

'My girl next door.' Jeff pulls me up on my feet and guides me over to the mistletoe with a quick whisper in my ear that he's waited years to have me in his arms at Christmas and kiss me. It's going to be a good one. My feet can't get there fast enough. The twins giggle when he takes me in his arms and his lips brush mine. I let go with an embarrassed sigh. I soon forget I have a parlor filled with family when he kisses me with a hunger that matches my own.

It's a kiss I'll never forget. Filled with tenderness, but also the mature kiss of a man who wants to devour me. Claim me as his own after losing me in the most horrible way possible, during a war when so many men gave their lives and never saw their sweethearts again. The desire to give him back what he lost thrums in my blood like a wildfire I can't put out, nor do I want to. We've been starved of love for so long, not only the physical need that burns beneath the skin, but the emotional depth that fills the heart with hope and delight, we keep kissing until we're out of breath. Then he holds me close to him, my cheek rubbing against his chest. It feels so right, I let a tear fall.

'I knew in my heart I'd never love anyone but that girl in the drawing,' he says, fisting my hair with his hand. 'I never thought I'd find her again.'

'You have now,' I say in a husky whisper, letting go of all those lonely years, wanting him so bad I woke up at night drenched in sweat, exhausted from looking for him in my dreams.

'I'm so glad you never stopped loving me.'

'Never.'

He kisses me again and I'm lost in the moment, so lost I don't realize everyone has scattered and we're alone in the parlor until—

'Soup's on!' Lucy yells from the dining room, then pokes her head through the doorway, her eyes shining. 'Time to eat, you two lovebirds.'

'We'll continue this later.' Jeff breaks the kiss, but he doesn't let me go. I nod, loving that he keeps my body pressed closely to his, but neither of us can resist the heavenly smells of creamy corn and roasted turkey along with homemade buttery biscuits.

We hustle into the dining room and my heart swells, remembering the grand times I had here. Ma and her lady friends planning the war. Pop and I playing checkers. Making the bet with Lucy about me getting married by Christmas. Helping Frankie get through his teenage years. Most of all, scooping cherry jam into glass jars when I was a young girl and dreaming of the boy who slid down the bannister and told me some day he'd marry me.

All these thoughts cascade through my mind in a lovely rainbow of memories as I sit down with the man who will be my husband as soon as we can arrange it. Mildred offered to help me with the church wedding preparations and the reverend will marry us. We intend to keep it private and then announce to the press Jeff has returned. How much of his story we can reveal will come later when he contacts the War Department. I can imagine the clerk in the archives section trying to dig up his Army records, especially when he was declared 'died in enemy hands' after his initial identity was compromised. Only the higher ups ever knew he assumed the persona of a lost partisan to continue his work during the war. The Army will issue an official statement and we'll stick with that.

I put that out of my mind for now. Time to enjoy the bounty of our holiday dinner. I'm honored when the reverend says grace for us, his words so special and perfect.

'We thank you, Lord, for bringing our boys home in both mind and spirit,' he says, 'through a terrible war hard fought by everyone, both on the battlefield and here on the home front.'

We bow our heads as he finishes the prayer and I hold hands with Jeff under the table, then Lucy grabs my other hand. Nothing could be better except if Ma and Pop were here. I fight back the tears. The gods of time must be in a benevolent mood this holiday because I swear I hear Pop whispering something in Ma's ear followed by her sweet laughter.

Then they're gone.

I revel in the fun of having a bunch of happy females bustling about in Ma's kitchen. My love for Lucy deepens, not only because she's the best sister ever, but because she never gave up on me. Never stopped believing I could regain my Christmas spirit. I look forward to spending a lot of time here, helping her out with the house and the kids, making sure she doesn't overdo things. And when the time is right, we'll have a long talk about nylons and trains.

The funny thing is, I have to ask her for a few pointers on keeping house. On keeping a husband happy? I've got that down pat. Advice from Ma.

Always give him the biggest piece of apple pie.

And never stop telling him how much you love him.

The next morning, Jeff and I drive over to the house on the river. We want to be alone, talk about the future *and* the past. He has gaps in his mind to fill in that will take months, but I cherish every moment I spend with him.

Some folks will say I dreamed my trip to the past and the rest is a matter of happy coincidences. Jeff keeping the drawing of me during the war, his instincts alerting him to the traitor. Then he became curious about the old house where he spent his youth, made inquiries, and discovered its fate was in his hands. So he made the trip home and our paths crossed on the train. As sure as the Christmas star shines bright, it *did* happen and our love will endure.

As for me, my time traveling days are over. I'm home.

We cuddle up together on the comfy old divan in the front room looking out the window, sunlight dancing over the ripples in the river like sugar plum fairies. All that matters is that Jeff is here with me.

'Merry Christmas, darling,' I say, praying by next year we'll have a child of our own to share our happiness.

'Merry Christmas, Jelly Girl.'

I let out a soft moan when I feel his hand slowly rubbing my back. A comforting touch that a husband gives his wife, showing his love. I can't wait for us to get married. Stretching lazily, I find that special place in the curve of his shoulder and lay down my head. I yearn for his kiss that transcends the past forever, for the moment when time comes full circle and wraps us up in its embrace. I know without a doubt my heart, my soul, belong to him.

Jeff senses what I'm feeling and leans down and presses his lips against mine in a hot, lingering kiss, enfolding me in a love that will last a lifetime.

I let out a deep sigh when the kiss ends. 'Can we do that again?'

'How much time have you got?' He kisses the tip of my nose.

I wrap my arms around his neck and lift my face for his kiss. Tender and warm and so filled with love, it makes me wiggle my toes. I never dreamed when I got on board the Christmas train on that cold December day, I'd find my man. Which gives me an idea I can't wait to share with him.

'I've been working on a book about us.'

'Us?'

'Why not? You and me before the war, then how I went back through time to save you from the Nazis, and how you spent years gallivanting around Europe and rebuilding France.' I stop to take a breath, wishing I had my typewriter, my fingers already tapping out the first chapter. 'It has everything you could want in a memoir. Excitement, intrigue, a wartime romance.'

'A beautiful heroine.'

'A handsome war hero with a sexy scar.' I trace the outline of his brow with my finger, thinking the plot doesn't sound anything like a memoir. 'I'll have to write it as fiction. No one will believe it.'

'I do.'

With those sincere words and a smile from him, I have the answer to a question on my mind all day. Whether or not Jeff believes me when I tell him about my journey back through time. My heart lifts with his simple admission. I'll never have to ask him again.

Did I change history?

I like to think I did.

## ACKNOWLEDGMENTS

I am so grateful to everyone on Team Boldwood in making my Christmas story the best it can be. A special thank you to my editor, Nia Beynon, for her support and expertise and her wonderful enthusiasm for my journey back to an era of red lipstick and wartime romance.

And a big thank you to all my readers who, like me, enjoy stepping back in time.

# MORE FROM JINA BACARR

We hope you enjoyed reading *Christmas Once Again*. If you did, please leave a review.

If you'd like to gift a copy, this book is also available as a ebook, digital audio download and audiobook CD.

Sign up to Jina Bacarr's mailing list for news, competitions and updates on future books.

http://bit.ly/JinaBacarrNewsletter

# ABOUT THE AUTHOR

**Jina Bacarr** is a US-based historical romance author of over 10 previous books. She has been a screenwriter, journalist and news reporter, but now writes full-time and lives in LA. Jina's novels have been sold in 9 territories.

Visit Jina's website: https://jinabacarr.wordpress.com/

Follow Jina on social media:

facebook.com/JinaBacarr.author

twitter.com/JinaBacarr

instagram.com/jinabacarr

# ABOUT BOLDWOOD BOOKS

Boldwood Books is a fiction publishing company seeking out the best stories from around the world.

Find out more at www.boldwoodbooks.com

Sign up to the Book and Tonic newsletter for news, offers and competitions from Boldwood Books!

http://www.bit.ly/bookandtonic

We'd love to hear from you, follow us on social media:

 facebook.com/BookandTonic

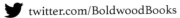 twitter.com/BoldwoodBooks

 instagram.com/BookandTonic

Made in the USA
Lexington, KY
23 October 2019

55974053R00166